MOVING ON

MOVING ON

Stories of the West

by

Jane Candia Coleman

Five Star
Unity, Maine

The stories "Apache," "Lou," "Old Pete," "Good Medicine," "Runs-With-the-Wind," and "Are You Coming Back, Phin Montana?" first appeared in *Louis L'Amour Western Magazine.* "Sand Dollar" first appeared in *The Critic.* "*Corrido* for Billy" first appeared in *Cafe.* "The Bird, The Ashes, and The Flame" first appeared in *The Pennsylvania Review.* "Home" first appeared in *The Voices of Doves* (Ocotillo Press, 1988). "Moving On" first appeared in *The Morrow Treasury of Great Western Stories* edited by Jon Tuska and Vicki Piekarski copyright © 1996 by Golden West Literary Agency. Copyright © 1988, 1992, 1993, 1994, 1995, 1996 by Jane Candia Coleman.

Five Star Western
Published in conjunction with Golden West Literary Agency.

February 1997, Second Printing

Five Star Standard Print Western Series.

The text of this edition is unabridged.

Set in 11 pt. Times by Minnie B. Raven.

Printed in the United States on permanent paper.

Library of Congress Cataloging in Publication Data

Coleman, Jane Candia.
    Moving on : stories of the West / by Jane Candia Coleman.
      p.   cm.
    ISBN 0-7862-0732-9 (hc)
    I. Title.
    PS3553.O47427M6   1997
    813'.54—dc20   96-43960

TABLE OF CONTENTS

Foreword

One of the most striking aspects of the American West, aside from the natural beauty of the landscape, is the variety of ethnic groups and cultures, the *dissimilarity* of those who settled here. Although I was not consciously aware of this when writing the stories in this collection (which were done over a period of ten years), I see now that they are linked by the thread of cultural diversity, much as are those who now live in the West.

Thus we have the Indian in "Apache," clinging to the old ways but fascinated by the new; a trio of stories — "A Small War in Lincoln County," "*Corrido* For Billy," and "Miracles," — which deal with the history, the customs, and the traditions of the early Spanish and Mexican settlers, a way of life which I, as many writers, have found both fascinating and possessed of a grace and charm that have never vanished in spite of what is called "progress."

Whether Levi Solomon, the Jewish peddler in "Moving On," is typical of early Jews in America, I don't know, but his is a character that came to me as a "gift," a character that, as I wrote, made me stop and reflect on what a peddler's life must have been, and what men like Levi, intelligent and scholarly, did with years of solitude.

"Lady Flo," is based on fact. James Delaval, Lord Beresford, did indeed come West to buy and run a cattle ranch and ended up with several in Mexico, New Mexico, and Canada and with a black woman, Florida Wolfe, his "Lady Flo," who lived with him as his wife for many years in spite of U. S. laws concerning miscegenation.

Closer to our own times the West has become home to artists and writers who are inspired by mountains, space, light, and colors, and by those very differences that belong solely to this land west of the hundredth meridian. Mabel Dodge Luhan, millionaire and mystic, is responsible for, among others, the arrival of D. H. Lawrence in America. He was to write a novel for and about her, but to her dismay he portrayed her — factually — in "The Lady Who Rode Away." My story, "The Bird, The Ashes, and The Flame," is based on a true incident — the clash of two vital women, Frieda Lawrence and Mabel Luhan, who desired to possess in death what they couldn't during life — the intangible genius of Lawrence.

In our times we also have the would-be historians, the fanatical "collectors" of our past who, shamelessly and without guilt, rifle historical repositories for memorabilia and documents as in "Charley Tuna and the Junkyard Dogs." And in every generation we have the adolescents, concerned only with self and unaware of past, present, and future, as the protagonist in "Paradise."

"Are You Coming Back, Phin Montana?" is a story of both endings and beginnings, the old ways and the new. Like the unnamed bodies in Lick Log cemetery, Reason Sunderland buries herself in the not-so-distant past, in those days when the railroad opened up the West and made it accessible to all and when the sound of the whistle gave everyone who heard it wanderlust. *The Way of the Chiefs, The Way of the Zephyrs*, and *The Route of the Phoebe Snow* are gone, replaced by unimaginative words painted on freight cars. The old cowboys are almost gone, and the horses they loved and rode, but the land and its diverse people are still here, as is the optimism and courage that brought the pioneers in wagons, on horseback, and on foot, pushing handcarts.

It is this very optimism that I have portrayed in these stories. Those who survived and triumphed in the West had strength, courage, hope. It is their stories that need to be told, not tales of weaklings or failures, cry babies or revisionist anti-heroes. Then, as now, the American West stands as a symbol of possibilities. It may be, indeed, what

Lincoln meant when he spoke of "the last best hope of earth." It is up to all of us — writers, editors, readers, rich and poor, male and female, white, red, black, yellow — to see that hope and ultimately to see both ourselves and the human race survive.

Apache

We never knew where the old Apache came from, or even what his name was. He just came down out of the hills one day, driving a buckboard pulled by an old dun gelding. He unhitched the horse, hobbled him, and turned him out to graze. Then he came in the shed where my dad did his blacksmithing, sat down with his back against a post, and watched like he was plain fascinated with the whole business — how my dad could make anything out of a piece of hot iron, tapping away on it, shaping it, then dunking it in the big trough to cool before heating and shaping it again.

From then on the Indian came every day, usually about mid-morning. He'd turn the dun out and then sit without moving until the sun touched the tops of the Dragoons, when he'd get up, catch the horse, and drive off up the cañon that twisted through the mountains like a thread nobody had ever followed to the end — a maze of washes and side cañons a thousand Indians could have lived or hidden in.

It's been fifty years, but I can remember that time like it was yesterday — the sound of iron hissing as it hit water, the tap-tap of Dad's hammer like one of those pesky woodpeckers that tries to hide acorns in a tin roof, the horses stomping flies and swishing their tails, and how the wind sang around the corners of the shed and in the wire fence around the corral. In my mind it seems it was always summer, and the shade of the shed welcome after the glare of sun on scrub and sand. Summer, and the thunderheads building on top of the mountains till they got so full up they just burst open and rained on us, and my ma's chickens running for cover, and the barn cats holed up nice and dry, and the horses snorty because they love a good soaking. Out here, after a rain, the air's as sweet as woodsmoke, a scent that always stops me in my tracks, makes me sniff the wind like an old hound. There's that sweetness, and the tang of creosote, and something like flowers blooming far off, flowers that got no name, or at least none I ever heard.

Anyway, that's how I remember that time — the old Apache, and me helping my dad when I wasn't out hoeing the corn that ripened fast in that weather and rustled in the wind like corn does. A good sound, meaning food on the table, fat hogs and horses, and hard times licked for another year. The funny thing was that old Apache never talked. Not one word. He'd grunt sometimes, but that was all we ever got out of him.

"Maybe he can't talk," I said to my dad once.

And he said: "More likely he just don't want to."

"What's he come for then?" I wondered.

My dad shrugged. "Maybe he's lonesome. Wants company. We'll prob'ly never find out. Or we'll find out if he ever feels like talking. So we'll let him be. He don't do no harm that I can see."

After a while we got so used to him being there we only noticed him on the days he didn't come, when it was like something was missing or out of order. My dad formed the habit of talking to that old man while he worked, figuring he could understand even if he didn't speak, and I got used to the sound of his voice explaining things I already knew from being there since I was old enough to be trusted around the fire and the forge and the big ranch horses.

"See, Chief, it's this way." My dad always called the old guy Chief, and he'd be talking around a mouthful of nails he was using to shoe. "This critter's got feet the size of pie pans. Uses as much iron as two reg'lar horses. And one front hoof's crooked. Got to allow for that. You saw how I did it, I reckon. Hammered till it fits like he was born with it."

And the Indian would sit there listening, watching, enjoying being around people who accepted him, took him for granted. After a time my ma took to bringing his lunch along with ours, and he liked that.

12

He'd sit there and chew and smack his lips, and nod his thanks to ma who said he was the politest and the cleanest Indian she knew. And that was true. His shirts always looked like they'd been boiled and then bleached in the sun, and his hair was in two neat braids tied at the ends with leather thongs. All in all, he was a dignified old man, even with that black stovepipe hat he never took off and that would've looked plain foolish on anybody else.

Now, it's a funny thing how, soon as you get used to something, it changes, and you got to change with it, else life passes you by, and you're lost in a world that don't exist any more. Writing that makes me wonder if the chief wasn't trying to make sense out of *his* world that had changed right under his nose — that whole way of life gone with the white men, the Army, the long drawn-out war that ended when Geronimo was captured.

I guess the old man knew my family had always been friendly with the Indians. We gave them food when we could spare it, and we left them alone, and they left us alone as a result. So he figured he could trust us when he started coming, and for a while we shared that trust and those long summer days.

But three cowboys gone bad — or maybe no good to begin with — changed everybody's life. Hardcases run out of Texas they were, small-minded, greedy, mean as two buckets of rattlesnakes. They were good hands, though. Had themselves jobs with the Rafter O, and if they were stealing dogies on the side, nobody could prove it, though there was a lot of talk about the number of cows without calves that year. The three of them — Ty Beaudry, Luke Pierce, and Jim Hightower — had a nice string of horses they kept fed up and in good traveling shape.

"Bet they don't have papers on a one of them horses," my dad said after he'd shod a couple and listened to the boys' boasting.

"You mean they stole them?" I asked.

"That's just what I mean. Those three are trouble, plain and simple. You wait and see."

I didn't have to wait long. The doings of those cowboys were the talk of the county. Nothing too bad at first, just high spirits like a lot of hands had. They shot out the windows of the saloon on their day off and spent a night in jail. Then Ty Beaudry won a bunch of money at poker so it almost seemed he was cheating, except nobody had the guts to call him on it, him packing a big .45 pistol and able to use it. And then Jim Hightower run off with the daughter of a traveling preacher, but she got scared before they'd gone a mile and went running back to her daddy. Folks thought Jim should get a good whopping for that one, but he talked his way out of it, saying he'd seen the light and got saved, and the preacher believed him and baptized him then and there in Cottonwood Wash which was running bankful on account of the rain. Jim come up cussing and got a sermon on sinful language from the preacher, but he was still hopping mad because his new boots had got ruined. Personally, I didn't think getting baptized had done much for him or for his disposition.

Those boys, every one of 'em, was a dandy. They dressed fit to kill, hoping to get the attention of the ladies. Old Ty always wore a red silk scarf and a pair of fringed and studded gauntlets. Had him a pair of fancy chaps, too, the kind with conchos on 'em, and he used big, Mexican-style spurs that jangled every time he took a step.

"Mean," my dad said about those spurs. "Anybody'd use them on a horse ought to get a taste of their own medicine."

I remember all this because it seems Ty was always coming to the shop to get my dad to fix something — a busted bit or bridle, or shoes for one of his critters, a job he should have done himself. Any cowboy knows how to shoe.

Anyhow, he'd show up like a bad penny and stand around, saying smart aleck things to me and the Indian who never moved a muscle, even when Ty got to showing his mean streak, like the day that started it all.

"Hey, old man! Cat got your tongue?" He walked over to the chief and stood over him, slapping those fancy gauntlets in the palm of one big hand. "Maybe you're dead. Stuffed. One of them statues outside a cigar store."

When the old man didn't answer, Ty called over his shoulder to my dad. "He your mascot or something? Ain't you scared he'll get your scalp someday?"

"Leave him be," my dad said. "He's not bothering you. Nor nobody else, either."

"That's just it. Settin' here like an old toad. I want to see him hop. Can you hop, old man? Can you do a war dance?"

He prodded the chief's moccasins with the toe of his boot, then said: "I swear, he's up and died on us. Well, good riddance. Only good Injun's a dead one."

"I told you. Leave him be." My dad was long on patience, but he was getting riled. I could tell by the way his eyes had turned the color of gun metal. He had his hands full right then, working on the horse's hind leg, the shoe half nailed on, or he might've taken Ty and thrown him out.

He had a bucket filled with some chemical, I don't recall what, maybe never knew the name, but he could dip his hand in that stuff and then carry a hot piece of metal a ways without getting burned. I knew it. So did the chief. We'd seen my dad do it near every day and never thought nothing about it. But Ty, he saw my dad carrying a hot shoe, and he started in laughing.

"You see that?" he said to the Indian. "You see that? I bet you can't do it. Carry that hot iron. I bet that'd wake you up quick. I bet you five dollars."

Something dangerous flickered in the chief's dark eyes. I saw it, and I got scared. I mean, I thought back to all the stories about Indians and how they tortured people — burying them in ant hills and stuff — and I backed off in a corner and stayed there, watching while the old man got up, not saying anything, with that look on his face that spelled trouble. He looked ten feet tall when he walked over to the forge where my dad had just laid out a piece of iron to get shaped,

15

ten feet tall, and quiet on his feet, and mad, like he'd swallowed all the insults he was going to take.

I wouldn't have been surprised to see him smash Ty in the face with that hot shoe. In fact, I'd have been glad. But that's not what he did. No sir. What he did was to pick up that metal in his bare hand and walk back to Ty, carrying it. I could smell his skin burning. Seems like I even heard it — sizzling like pork fat — and I clamped my jaws shut so's I wouldn't get sick or cry. I wanted to punch Ty Beaudry till he yelled for mercy, brand him with a poker heated red hot, but something in the look on the Indian's face kept me sitting. Waiting.

The look he gave Ty when he dropped that iron on one of them fancy boots and then held out his hand — burnt black and blistered — would've killed any decent person. I never saw hate on anybody's face before that, and never again as far as I know, but I sure recognized it. And I got a chill that ran right down my back. Ty was through. I knew it. The chief knew it. Only Ty was dumb enough to think he'd gotten away with something.

He was staring at the chief's hand like he wished he didn't have to, and I didn't blame him. Finally he dug in his pocket and pulled out five dollars and tucked it in the old man's belt.

"Reckon I lost," was all he said.

My dad turned to me. "Go get your ma. Tell her to bring down some of that salve of hers, and hurry."

He didn't have to tell me twice.

Ma came down running. She was as good a doctor as if she'd studied for it, always helping neighbors with broken bones and babies and stuff. She also had a sharp tongue in her head, and she used it to scold us while she worked.

"Men!" she said. "Bunch of babies if you ask me. Egging each other on. Doin' damn' fool things. You all ought to be ashamed. You, too, Chief. It's pride is what it is. And pride cometh before a fall. Next thing, you'll be darin' each other to jump off that mountain

16

out there." Then she turned on Ty who was standing stock still and looking kind of dazed. "And you! Pickin' on a harmless old man. Your ma should've taken a stick to you when you were little. Too late now, I reckon. The harm's done. But if I ever hear about you bullyin' somebody again, I'll whup you myself, fancy duds and all. And you can count on it."

I had to turn around so's nobody could see me laughing. I'd been on the wrong end of Ma's tongue myself and to see Ty there, meek as a lamb and taking it, seemed like justice to me.

We sent the chief off home, me hitching up his horse, and Ma giving him orders to keep his hand salved and bandaged. Ty took his horse and rode off without saying anything. I figured it was over and done with. I figured wrong, of course. The old man was Apache. He never forgot. Or forgave, either.

He didn't show up at our place for so long I got worried. I missed him — silence and all. "You think he's all right?" I asked Dad. "You think he got better?"

"I bet he's fine," my dad said. "He's tough, and he's prob'ly got herbs and stuff we don't know about. He'll show up one day. Wait and see."

We got in the harvest, gathered our cattle, and then it was time for me to go back to school which I sure hated. What good was school after a summer of freedom and excitement? I spent a lot of days looking out the window and dreaming, wishing for something to happen, but when it did, I never figured I'd play a big part in the action.

A man named Macaddam had a general store down on the main north-south road. He did a good business, too, since he stocked everything anybody needed from nails to needles. After the fall roundup he was flush because folks had money to spend and bought what they'd done without the rest of the year. Macaddam had a daughter named Leila, cute as a kitten, yellow headed and lots of fun. Every boy for fifty miles was courting her, or trying to, but she

17

refused to make up her mind, paying attention first to one and then another, and driving them all loco, even the Texas cowboys who had to stand in line with the rest.

One morning, after a hen-drowning fall rain, Leila showed up hysterical at the sheriff's office. She was soaking wet, mud covered, and had bruises on her arms, and the story she told, when they'd calmed her down enough to tell it, was a strange one.

Someone had broken into her father's store late the night before. They'd busted open the safe and taken the money, but while they were at it, they made so much noise that her father had gone downstairs to check. She heard voices then shots and, taking a pistol, she went down to see for herself what was happening. At the door to the store a man grabbed her from behind. She fought but wasn't strong enough to do much except struggle. In the end he knocked her out and left her lying on the floor. She hadn't seen his face in the dark hall, but she thought he sounded like Jim Hightower. When she came to, she lit a lamp and went into the store. All she found was the empty safe and blood on the floor. Of her father there wasn't a sign.

The sheriff turned Leila over to his wife and organized a posse that came dragging back empty handed two days later. The rain on the night of the break-in had washed away any tracks, and a search hadn't turned up Macaddam, dead *or* alive. They'd questioned the cowboys, Hightower especially, and they all swore up and down they'd been snug in the bunkhouse that night playing cards.

The sheriff stopped by our place on his way back to town. "Keep your eyes open," he told us. "Macaddam could be any place out here, dead or alive. But till we know, there's not much we can do. All we've got is Leila's story and that busted safe. That and the blood. But no body. Hell, maybe the old boy robbed himself and took off for Frisco! If she was my daughter, I'd be tempted to do the same."

My dad shook his head. "Leila's a flighty gal and no mistake, but she's not lyin'. Somebody got the old man and his money. But don't

18

worry. We'll keep an ear out."

"Who do you think did it?" I asked.

"I got my suspicions, is all," he said, frowning. "Can't prove a thing. Now go get your chores done."

Nothing I hated more than chores, the same ones every day. I could've done them in my sleep. What I really wanted to do was take my pony and go out and look for evidence. It riled me that Ma kept me chopping wood that day and the next so I couldn't get away. Grown-ups sure had the knack of spoiling a boy's fun.

A few days later we all got woke up by a pounding at the door and a little voice yelling for Ma. A neighbor woman's time had come and, like I said, Ma was always called to help with birthing. When the chips were down, she could move faster than anybody I ever saw, and I remember how she got the rest of us moving, too. "Dan! Hitch the wagon!" To my dad. And to me: "Will! See your sister eats all her breakfast. The biscuits are in the oven and don't you leave the place till we get back. You hear?"

I wouldn't have dared to go off and have her come home and find my sister alone. I was more scared of Ma than I'd ever been of Indians or outlaws, and she knew it. So after she and Dad left, I made sure little Sara cleaned her plate and then the kitchen, too. That was girl's work for sure. I forked some hay into the horse yard and then walked up the hill to the shed, figuring maybe the chief would pick that morning to come back and be sorry to find nobody there.

It was still early. In the west the Dragoons were colored pink and tawny, and I stopped a minute to look at them and wonder at how they were never the same from one minute to the next, changing shape and color so it seemed they were alive, like animals or even people. I stood and watched and listened to the quiet. Seems even the birds weren't singing, and the wind was calm. Then from the south came the sound of a horse trotting — a good, no-nonsense trot, the gait you use when you want to cover ground without wearing out your horse.

19

A few minutes later Ty Beaudry rode in, and one look told me he was leaving the country. Everything he owned was packed on that horse. "Where's your dad?" he asked, swinging down.

"He's not here."

"Where in hell is he?"

"Took Ma down to Wrights' for a birthing."

Ty was as jumpy as a drop of water in a hot frying pan, and I watched him, wondering where he'd jump next. "How long'll that take?" he wanted to know.

I kind of laughed at that one. The way I saw it, babies took anywhere from an hour to two days coming into the world. I shrugged.

"Reb's front shoe's come loose," he said then. "Reckon I'll have to borrow some tools."

"Go ahead," I said, kind of hoping he'd botch the job and make a fool out of himself.

He didn't, though. He found the hammer and the nails, cross-tied the horse, and set to work.

"Where you headed?" I asked him.

"None of your business," he said around the nails in his mouth. "You're a nosy brat, and no mistake."

"I was just being polite," I said.

"Shut up then. Kids're supposed to be seen and not heard. That ma of yours ever tell you that?"

I nodded. She had for a fact.

He finished the shoe, checked the others, then straightened up, and threw the hammer at me without warning. "Catch!" he yelled.

I ducked just in time.

"Gotta be fast, kid," he advised. "Gotta be a step ahead of the rest or you'll get nailed. Take it from me."

I didn't say anything. I was too mad, and he knew it.

He untied the horse and led him outside, grinning as he went. When he stepped into the saddle, he laughed, a dry kind of sound like he'd forgot how to do it. "Tell you somethin' else, kid," he said. "If I was you, and nosy, I'd go look in my old man's dry well. Yessiree, that's what I'd do." Then he spurred his horse, and they took off, kicking dust and stones back in my face.

He headed up the cañon. If he'd been nicer, I might have told him that the trail led to nowhere, or at least not to any place he wanted to go, but as it was, I just stood there, quiet and thinking about what he'd said.

That old well had been dry for years. It was covered up, and we never gave it a thought from one year to the next, so it was funny, him bringing it to my attention. I ran back to the house and grabbed Sara who, being little and a girl, didn't take kindly to being hauled off by me. She squealed like a calf.

"Hush up!" I told her. "We're goin' hunting."

"I'll tell!" she yelled and screwed up her face like she was going to bawl.

Her telling wasn't going to make any difference if what I figured was true, so I just dragged her across the yard and down into the south pasture where the old well was. We found Macaddam shoved head first into that hole, and he was stone cold dead — had been for a while, and he wasn't a pretty sight. Sara had nightmares for a month over it but not me. I was a hero for all of a week.

A posse took out after Ty — and after Hightower and Pierce, too. Seems like they'd split the money and gone their separate ways. They found Hightower headed for Mexico and picked up Pierce at the railroad station in Benson. But they never found Ty Beaudry. His horse come in to our place a few days later minus his gear, but we never found hide nor hair of Ty.

Hightower and Pierce confessed to the robbery but blamed Beaudry for the killing which didn't do them much good as they got hanged as accomplices anyhow. The sheriff gave the money back to Leila who, without saying a word, sold the store and took off on the train for Frisco, leaving a string of broken hearts behind. Folks said

21

she'd come to no good in the city, but I always believed she found what she'd been looking for.

After a while the excitement died down, and the talk stopped, and winter came, and then spring with a big calf crop.

"Reckon by now folks have figured out what them boys was up to," my dad said. "Stealin' us blind."

"You think Ty's alive some place?" I wondered. "You think he got away?"

"Nope," he said. "I don't."

"How come?"

"I just got a feelin'. Let's wait and see."

Seems like he was always saying that — and with some reason all his own. Well, it was on one of those warm spring days when you look out and see that the buzzards have come back from wherever they go in winter when I saw the chief driving down out of the hills, still with the same rickety wagon and the ganted dun horse.

"He's back!" I yelled and ran out to meet him, feeling like the world had come right again.

"Hey!" I said to him. "Hey."

And that old man looked straight at me, and I swear his eyes were twinkling when he raised up his right hand, the one he'd burned and on it, fancy as ever, was one of Ty's gauntlets, fringe and all. Right then I knew what had happened, knew it as sure as I was standing there on two legs. Somewhere up in those mountains was a grave, and Ty was in it. Now, those hills are big, with places in them most folks never even seen, and they don't talk any more than the old Apache ever did but keep their secrets locked up tight.

It was like Dad said. The chief was an Indian, and he never forgot. When his chance for revenge came, some place empty and far away, in one of those side cañons going nowhere, he took it. I looked square into that old face, those dark eyes that had a glint in them, and I smiled.

"We sure been missing you, Chief," was all I said.

BELLE STARR'S RACE MARE

The world's full of fools, and most of 'em own horses. That's good luck for me because I was born with an eye for a horse, and what I haven't learned about horse trading isn't worth knowing. Like that damn' fool dude that came into Dallas leading the nicest mare I've seen in years of Sundays — leading her, mind you, and her walking alongside nice as you please. She looked like honey in a jar, dark honey, the kind that pours smooth and easy, and that's how she moved. Like she didn't even have to think about it.

So here he comes up to the corrals, and he's wearing a hat so big he couldn't step out of the shade it made. I figured some cowboy had sold it to him as "the real thing" soon as he stepped off the train from wherever.

"Good morning," he says to me, and I've heard birds chirp louder.

" 'Morning," I said back and then was quiet, knowing I was going to end up with that mare if I had to hog-tie the dude to do it.

He scuffed his fancy boots in the dirt a bit, waiting for me to say something else, but I know when to keep my mouth shut, especially trading horses.

"Nice day," he said after a while.

I nodded. I was watching that mare and itching to try her.

"Warm," he said. He was getting desperate.

"Not as warm as it gets."

"Oh." He looked around at the horses, all of 'em busy chomping hay.

"I was wondering . . . ?"

"What?" I asked him finally. "What was you wondering?"

"I need a horse!" The words came out all together.

"You got a horse," I said. "Least, that sure looks like a horse to me."

He shook his head and nearly fell over with the weight of that damn' hat. "Another one," he said. "A pretty one."

Now, I been in the business a long time, and I never saw a prettier horse than the one he had, but that wasn't for me to say. What I said was: "Oh, I've got some real lookers here. You trading the mare?"

He nodded.

I nodded back. "Good thing," I said.

That got him. "What do you mean?"

I walked over and put a hand on the mare's neck, and she turned and looked at me out of the smartest eyes I ever saw.

"She's got a temper," I said, lying through my teeth. "Anybody can tell that just by looking. She'll dump you on the road, if she hasn't already, and besides I got prettier ones than her any day. Like old Joker there."

I pointed to the rawboned, Roman-nosed Joker who nobody ever said was pretty since the day he was foaled. The dude swallowed so hard I could see his Adam's apple going up and down, and I tried hard not to laugh.

He said: "I had . . . I had something else in mind."

'Course he did. Like I said, I'm no fool when it comes to horse trading. "Like what?"

"Well . . . ," he let his eyes go on down the string. They stopped right where I knew they would. On the horse I'd been trying to get rid of seemed like forever. Kiowa. Oh, he was pretty all right — white splashed with red and all curves. But he sucked wind. He sucked so long and so loud you could hear him half a mile away, and those old jaws clamped onto a stump or a fence rail tight as a wolf trap. Truth is, he sounded like a fat man belching, and I purely couldn't stand him, pretty or not.

I said: "You don't want him."

"Why not?"

"Because he's like one of the family. Been here so long I'd miss him something awful." I walked down the line and grabbed that horse's nose just in time to keep him from chomping the rail. He nuzzled me instead.

"See?" I said. "He's like my brother. Almost. Maybe better looking."

"How much?" The little fella had a one-track mind. It made my job easier.

"I don't know. I'm not sure I want to part with him."

"The mare," he said. "The mare and ten dollars."

I scratched Kiowa's ears.

"Twenty!" He sounded like he was going to cry.

"Make it the mare and thirty," I said, hoping I'd not end up in hell for cheating so bad, especially since there were other ways you could end up there that were more fun.

But that's how I got Honeycomb, the running fool, the fastest horse in the territory and probably in Kansas. And that's how come I'm here today, saddling her for a race she's not going to win because I've got plans. Oh my, I've got plans.

John Hargrove's another fool and nasty to boot. He's been running around the racing circuit all summer saying as how his big black horse can beat Honeycomb, and that I can't tell a good horse from a donkey. He's been saying I'm yellow because I haven't agreed to a match. Well, I'll tell you, I've been minding my own business, trading, racing, and not looking for trouble, but *nobody* calls me yellow, and *nobody* calls Honeycomb a donkey. She doesn't need papers to prove she can run. My *eyes* are her papers, and her own four legs, and that fire in her heart that reminds me of myself. We both hate to lose, and that's a fact. And me, I hate Hargrove with that fat belly stickin' out over his belt, his hardware stores, his horse that has better manners than him that owns him.

Some folks think just because they got a horse they're better than other folks. Like Hargrove. All swelled head and mouth. And he

25

ruins his animals. Runs 'em till their legs quit on them then sells 'em for dog meat. I got no respect for a man that does that. More to the point I detest him, and that's another reason I'm here — to fix him good.

I take the mare's head in my hands, and she leans against me. I can feel her pulse in her throat. That big heart of hers is beginning to beat fast. She's ready to run, and I hate what we're going to do, but it's part of the plan.

"I want you to pull her," I say to my little jockey, Rattle.

What his real name is nobody knows, and he's never said. Just that folks call him that because he's so skinny seems like his bones are knocking together. But he's got arms like iron and legs that clamp down so hard you'd need a crowbar to pry him loose of a horse.

He stares at me. "Miz Belle," he says, shocked. "I can't do that."

"Yes, you can. Or you can go look for somebody else's horses to ride."

"But . . . !" He's honest, and I've never played dirty before.

"Just do it. I'm going to fix that Hargrove good. *And* get my hands on his horse. How'd you like to have that critter to ride?"

"I never pulled a horse," he says, still back where we started. Rattle's not strong on brains.

"There's always a first time. You let that black win by ten lengths, or you're fired."

"The money," he says. "It's five hundred dollars."

"Chicken scratch. Wait and see."

He sighs and gives in. I knew he would, me staring at him like I'd wring his scrawny neck if he didn't.

"It's your horse."

"You bet it is. And I'm paying you."

I give him a leg up, then go over, and place a bet. A small one, just for looks. Hargrove comes and stands beside me, smiling all over that nasty face and sweating, too. Kansas gets mighty hot in the summer.

26

"Looks like you don't have much faith in your horse, Belle," he says. "Want to call it off?"

I give him a look that would freeze a snake. "Not on your life."

Then I walk past him like he ain't there and go on down to the finish line where there's a grove of trees, and I can stand in the shade and wait for the fun to start. This is the first time I ever got a close look at the big black horse named Dirty. The names some people pick! A horse like this one ought to be named something noble, him standing at the starting line, shining like a beetle and tossing that big head of his so his mane blows out in the wind.

I look at him and feel my temper rise. Hargrove doesn't deserve an animal like this one. Hell, he's too fat to ride him and, even if he could, this horse would eat him up before they went a hundred yards. Rattle had better do what I told him, or I'll raise hell. I can do it, too. I want Hargrove's horse, and I usually get what I want — man or horse — and maybe not that much difference between them. At least not in the good ones. Strength and heart are what I look for. Without those all you have is a scrub, and Lord knows the world's full of them, too. Fools and scrubs — and every once in a while a flash of glory. You live for those. I do, anyhow. They make everything else worth it.

The horses are at the starting line, and what a picture they make — black and gold, and prancing. If my plan works, I'll have some dandy colts in a couple years.

They're off and running. Honey's ahead by a neck. She doesn't take to being slowed down, and she's fighting the bit, fighting for her head, for the right to run her race. Dirty's a big horse. It'll take him a while to get up to speed, but he's a runner all right. He's got his ears pinned back, and his neck stretched out, and he's going for broke. When I get hold of him, I sure intend to give him a new name.

Here they come down the stretch. Honey's about to bust in half, she's that mad. Looks like she'll blow and start bucking any second.

27

Well, she'll play hell getting rid of Rattle and disqualify herself if she does.

Dirty's big nostrils open wide like red flowers. He's a sight. It'd be a shame to see him sold to feed some farmer's hogs. He doesn't win by ten lengths, more like five, but that's enough. And here comes Hargrove, smirking like he just left the hen house with a full belly. I'll be polite, and get away as quick as I can. Honey'll need settling down after this day's work.

"Too bad, Belle," he says. "But she's still a good mare. I'll buy her from you. Name your price."

Sure he will — and run her till she drops. "She's not for sale."

His eyebrows come together over his eyes like a pair of caterpillars. "Every horse is for sale."

"Not this one." My heart's beating fast. Is the damn' fool going to make it this easy?

"Come on, Belle. I'll take her off your hands for the five hundred I just won. Then you can go get yourself a real horse."

I smile just as sweet as I can, like my mama taught me. She always said you could catch more flies with honey than with vinegar. "Tell you what," I say, still smiling. "Let's have a rematch. We'll each put up a thousand. The winner takes both horses and the purse."

He laughs. He thinks I'm touched and says so. "You're crazy. You're throwing your money away."

"I'd like her to have a second chance," I say in my best little girl voice. "That's all."

He has greed written all over him. "Sure," he says. "She can have a third and fourth chance, too. When do you want to run?"

"In a week. I want to rest her a bit."

He sticks out a hand like a ham. "Next Saturday then. And you rest her good. Maybe she'll make it to the finish line."

I'd as soon shake hands with a snake after that remark, but I do. Then I wipe my fingers on my skirt and go off to find Rattle before he gets drunk to forget his disgrace. He won't feel so bad when I give him the news, though.

He's washing Honey down, and he's upset. If his head and shoulders dropped any lower, he'd disappear. "We could've won," he says, when he sees me. "We could've got out in front and won."

"Cheer up. You'll have a chance on Saturday. I told you I had a plan, but you weren't listening."

He's listening now, though, and he's straightened up so he looks human again. He says: "Huh?"

When I explain, even Honey seems pleased. She stomps and twitches her ears at me, and I take the lead rope and walk her till she cools off, all the time talking so she won't feel bad and turn cranky on us. Some mares get cranky for what seems like no reason. Honey's never been that way, but this isn't the time to start, not with a prize like that in our future.

I'm laughing to myself all evening — even in town where folks keep coming up saying wasn't it too bad, and maybe Honey was just having an off day — and me nodding like I'm a good loser. But it's like I keep saying, there's a bunch of fools who don't have the brains of a doodle bug out there. Oh, well, it makes it easy for me, I guess, except there's precious few folks to talk to. Sometimes the world's a lonely place.

Seems like this week lasted ten years. I've felt like a kid counting the days till Christmas. One, two . . . damn it, hurry up and let's get it done! . . . three, four. . . .

And now it's race day, with thunder rumbling off over the Buffalo Hills, and the air heavy as mud. Days like this can take it out of a person. Honey don't seem to mind, though. She's been ready since breakfast, knowing the routine. Today she's going to run. Rattle would play hell trying to pull her today. She's had a week to think it over, and she's got her own ideas. Anybody that thinks horses are dumb hasn't spent much time with 'em. They know all they need to know, and that's better than folks can do.

Rattle's grinning. He's half horse himself and can read the signs. "She's gonna run today," he says.

"And you're going to let her. All you've got to do is sit there and steer."

His grin disappears. "Here comes trouble."

Hargrove is wiping his face with his handkerchief. It's all I can do not to hand him Honey's towel.

"You still got time to call it off," he says, and those little no-color eyes of his are all over Honey.

"I'll risk it."

He goes to touch her like she's his already, and her ears go back flat.

"She ain't yours yet," I tell him. "Leave her alone."

He goes off, mumbling something about women and mares, and I wish Honey had bit him. I wish *I* had. I'd as soon shoot her as let him get her. Hope I don't have to. . . . Now where did *that* thought come from, I wonder? All of a sudden I'm scared. Maybe I shot off my mouth once too often — outsmarted myself.

"Rattle . . . ," I start out and then can't say it.

He shakes his head. "Quit worryin'."

"I'll shoot her first!"

"No you won't. I'll just keep goin' and meet you at home."

That makes me laugh. Him and the mare on the run. "You do it," I say. "But I hope you don't have to."

"Me, too." He's grinning. "Hanged for horse stealin' ain't how I want to go."

"It wouldn't exactly be stealing," I tell him. Or would it? I hope I don't have to find out. "Honey," I whisper to the mare, "run like the devil's after you because he is."

She blows soft like she understands and, when she looks at me, I see the fire in her eyes. Damn, she does remind me of me! I wish I was riding her instead of Rattle — the wind in my face, and the big body moving under me, and both of us with only one idea: to run faster than anybody else. To win because there's no point to losing. "Honey," I whisper again. "Do your damnedest!"

Sometimes I think *I'm* the damned fool. Why'd I do this? Bet the mare? Just to prove I'm smart? I'm hating myself as they get to the starting line. Hating myself, and Hargrove, and all those folks out there so damned eager to see me make a fool of myself in public.

Belle, I say to myself, *Belle, sometimes I think you ought to take poison.*

Before I can answer myself, somebody says: "That's my mare, isn't it?"

I nearly jump out of my skin. I don't take kindly to being sneaked up on, and I have my pistol out of my belt before I turn around. The little dude's standing there under a tree. I recognize the hat. The hell it's his mare. "Not any more she isn't." I walk toward him holding the pistol.

"What I mean . . . she's the one, isn't she?" He's eyeing the pistol, and his voice is as squeaky as I remembered it.

If he has some notion of raising a fuss, of saying I stole her, he's going to be sorry. "That's her. You traded her, and I've got the paper to prove it. So, if you're thinking to make trouble, don't."

He opens his mouth then closes it again. Sure he was going to make trouble, but he ain't got guts enough.

"You have a problem with that, mister?"

He shakes his head.

From off in the trees comes a sound like a belch. Sure enough. Kiowa's tied there, and he's got his jaws around a branch, and he's sucking in air for all he's worth.

"You still have him, I see."

Another shake of that hat, this time up and down.

"I told you he was a good horse, didn't I?"

"Yes, ma'am. You did. But he's got this funny habit."

It's funny all right. "Bet he never dumped you though, did he?"

"We get along fine," he says.

31

"Then you got no complaints." I wave the pistol the littlest bit so he remembers who's in charge.

"Guess not," he says and sighs.

"That's real good," I tell him. Then I figure, what the heck? Might's well let the little grasshopper off the hook. "Tell you what," I say. "You go on and place a bet on the mare. And hurry up before they start."

That Adam's apple of his moves up and down. Then he says: "But that black horse is so pretty."

I have to laugh. Some folks never learn. "Pretty is as pretty does. You should've figured that out long since." I laugh some more. "Seems to me like you're overdue to win something."

"You're sure?" He doesn't trust me. Why should he?

"Nothing's sure in this world, and that's a fact."

He's still watching my pistol like he thinks I'll take a shot at him from behind. I wave it at him. "Go on. Do what I told you."

He runs off, taking little jumps over the scrub, not knowing I just did him the biggest favor of his life.

The two horses line up, and now they're running. Even from here I can see that Honey's grabbed the bit and has no intention of getting pulled again. She means business. She's out in front, and old Dirty's doing his best to catch her. But she's a little, golden wasp, slick and quick, mad clear through, belly to the ground, aiming straight for the finish.

"Come on!" I yell, though everybody else is yelling loud enough to drown me out. "Come on, Honey!"

I swear she hears me and moves faster, leaving the black to eat her dust as she roars on past me and out into the field, going another mile before Rattle can pull her up.

I go over to Dirty. He's sweated up but still prancing. Quite a horse. And quite an afternoon's work. "I'll take him," I say to his rider who gives me a look that could blister paint.

And here comes Hargrove, all three hundred pounds of him,

32

mad clear through. "You gave that mare something," he's yelling, loud enough for everybody to hear. "I know your type. Everybody knows . . . !"

He needs his face punched good and hard.

"What type is that?"

"You'll do anything to win. Lie. Cheat. Dope horses."

"I never doped a horse in my life." And God save me, that's the truth. What I've been is smart. I stand there, face to face with Hargrove, and yell: "She won it fair and square. And let me tell you something . . . I've never had to dope a horse. And I've never run them till they're only fit for the killers. Your horse is lucky, coming to me. Everybody knows what you are, too. Mean, greedy, pushing up to the trough. If I ever hear of you talking about me on the circuit again, I'll come back and stick you like the fat hog you are."

The little dude is standing beside me pop-eyed and holding a handful of money.

"I told you," I say to him. "Now get out and don't show your face around me again, or I'll blow that umbrella off your head."

Then I take Dirty's reins and walk away. The thunder is closer now, and the wind's rising. It'll rain soon, I think. Clear the air. "Well, old boy," I say, "We did a good day's work."

He nickers down in his throat.

"I think maybe I'll call you Thunder. That seems fitting."

He nickers again, and all of a sudden I'm laughing. Maybe I didn't win quite fair and square, but we won, Honey and me. Sometimes you got to use your brains. Sometimes you got to go for the dream and never mind what anybody thinks or says. Life's pretty short. If I don't break my neck on a green horse, or get hanged, or shot, I'll sit on my porch when I'm old and remember the good times, all of 'em, and how every once in a while I found glory.

A SMALL WAR IN LINCOLN COUNTY

This story is based on historical fact. There was, indeed, a family of Harrells (sometimes spelled Horrell) who, with their cohorts, were run out of Texas, and who, for a time, made their home in that huge and lawless county west of the Pecos named Lincoln. After the shooting of several of their men, the Harrells declared war on the Mexican population — shooting up a dance hall and killing Mexicans where they found them, including the American husband of a Mexican girl, an orphan who had been reared by Anglos. On a rampage they then murdered some innocent freighters and stole the horse herd belonging to Van Smith of Roswell, New Mexico. Smith, infuriated, tracked them down and shot four of the Harrell brothers. Horse stealing was, then, the equivalent of murder and was punishable by death.

Sister de Chantal was frantic. There was no garlic in the tiny pantry of the orphanage, and she could no more cook without it than run naked in the plaza of Santa Fé. Food was not plentiful — neither for the sisters of Loretto nor for the orphans in their charge — but what there was proved nourishing and tasty, for Sister de Chantal had an instinctive knowledge of herbs and spices, a way of turning even the most ordinary stew into a creation blessed by heaven.

"Delfina!" she called to the orphan girl who was her assistant in the kitchen. "Delfina, I need you."

The girl, who had been putting loaves of bread into the *horno* — the huge earthen oven outside — straightened her apron, smoothed her dark hair, and ran to see what had caused the nun to raise her voice in such a manner.

When she appeared in the doorway, delicate brows raised in a question over dark eyes, the sister mentally crossed herself. The child was growing into a beauty. Something would have to be done for her soon — a good position found or, perhaps, a husband. Surely there was a good man who would be grateful to take her in marriage even without a dowry. She was a good cook, able to read and write, and had a sweet, albeit sometimes fiery, nature.

She took some coins out of an earthenware bowl in the cupboard. "Here," she said. "Run to the market and bring me back some garlic. And go quickly and don't stop to gossip. *Jesu!*" She crossed herself again, outwardly this time. "The American traders are due this afternoon. Go now, and make sure you're away before the wagons come."

Delfina's eyes widened. The traders! Their arrival was the event of the summer! With any luck she would be able to watch the huge wagons coming into the plaza, see the blond-haired and bearded *gringos* unloading their wares — the bolts of many-colored cloth, the lace, shawls, beads, bottles of perfume, mirrors, pots, and pans that brought delight to so many. And what fun she would have describing the scene to the other, less lucky orphans detained behind the adobe walls.

Demurely she slipped the money into her pocket. "Yes, sister," she said. "I'll go quickly."

Once outside she stopped and looked up at the sky, made more brilliant by contrast with the white rain clouds that were pushing up from behind the mountains. She caught her breath at the beauty of it, the dazzle that made her half close her eyes so she could look long and remember what she had seen in those moments before she went to sleep, moments when she recalled the minute treasures of her day.

She stared, thinking how truly the sky resembled the turquoise so precious to the Indians, and then she walked on toward the market that lined the street and spilled out into the plaza, and which was filled with a different kind of treasure: red chilies strung in ristras, garlic in braids and baskets, the orange and green globes of squash, the shining skins of onions, golden corn and its coarse flour in sacks, beans like polished stones. There were Indians from the pueblos selling baskets and painted pottery, women hawking tamales, posole, sweet buns, fresh-killed chickens and turkeys and live ones in cages, sheep, pigs, goats. The sight, the sounds, the mouth-watering scents of cooking lured and delighted the girl, longing for a life she knew was vastly different from that behind the walls of the orphanage.

If only her parents had lived! If they had, perhaps she, too, would be selling things in the market, would be part of the vital, bustling scene instead of a mere shopper sent to purchase a lowly bulb of garlic. But the nuns were good, she scolded herself. They had taken her in when her parents died of the smallpox. They had bathed, fed, and clothed her, taught her to read and write, and to speak the English that, at first, seemed so harsh after the Spanish that rolled softly on her tongue. And she could cook, too. Perhaps one day she would have a job cooking for one of the *ricos* who lived in the big houses on Palace Avenue — who dressed in fine clothes and gave dinners of many courses served on delicate china. She herself had never seen these things, but the sisters had told her, so that in imagination she could see the white table cloths, the silver, the china, the goblets filled with wine, sparkling in the light of a hundred candles. The scene was another of her treasures. She saw it vividly as she stood in the middle of the noisy market, her feet in their woven sandals in the mud, her mind far away in a world she had never encountered.

"Hey! Delfina!"

The sound of her name brought her back to reality. She blinked and looked around.

"Nilda!" She crossed the street to the stall of her father's cousin who had been selling tamales on this corner for as long as anyone could remember.

"What're you doing?" Nilda demanded. "You look like you were seeing a vision."

Delfina smiled. "Perhaps."

"Better wake up. The Americans are due any minute. Keep dreaming, and you'll get trampled in the rush."

Nilda inspected the girl with curious eyes. *Dios!* She was ripening fast. Time she was married instead of mooning around in the street. A husband and children would soon cure that habit. Nilda sighed, thinking of her own brood, of her husband the hunter who came home only long enough to plant another seed in her. Maybe marriage wasn't the answer, after all. The child looked delicate. She fished a tamale out of the pot.

"Here," she said. "Eat. Do they feed you enough? The sisters?"

"Oh yes." Delfina bit into the succulent husk. "I have to buy some garlic, and I'm supposed to hurry, but I wanted to see the traders come."

"Stay here with me, then," Nilda advised. "You'll have a good view."

For more than fifty years, since Mexico had won its independence from Spain in 1821, the traders had been coming. Their arrival was an event, looked forward to as were the days of the saints, the rains of summer. The conestoga wagons came in with a flourish — heard before they were seen — the huge wheels rumbling over rocks and ruts, the jingling of harnesses, of the bells tied to the lead animals, the cracking of whips and the shouts of the traders, a rejoicing after months on the prairie, that vast land that stretched to the east.

Those in the market surged like a wave and carried Delfina, curious and small, with them toward the plaza. She saw them — wagon after wagon — like the ships the nuns had described, blown westward by the powerful winds of nature, of mankind. She saw them, and her eyes opened wide with wonder. So many! So many horses, mules, oxen, *gringos* in buckskins, flannel, linsey-woolsey that had seen better days.

She saw them and forgot her errand, let the crowd carry her to the very side of the wagons whose wheels towered above her head and whose osnaburg coverings snapped like sails in the wind. Buffeted but holding her place, she stood awed and silent and, when a young man swung down from a wagon seat, she did not move until his boot caught her foot, and the pain, the crack of bone, became a whimper in her throat.

Dios! How could she get home now? How walk? Fight through the mob? Explain? And without the garlic for which she had come.

He turned and saw her, white as bone itself, her eyes filled with tears, and he thought she was like a wounded bird. He thought — he didn't know what he thought, but only felt after months on the prairie in the company of men — he thought he had snapped a life in two, clipped the wings of a butterfly. And he picked her up, light and trembling, and carried her away from the mass of people to the edge of the plaza. He said: "I'll take you home."

"I have no home," she whispered. "Only the orphanage."

"Where?"

She gestured with her head. "That way."

"Put your arms around my neck," he said.

She did, feeling the movements of his body, smelling the scents of the long trail, forgetting for a moment her pain in the strange closeness of this man so different from herself. Later, much later, she remembered the feel of him, the touch of his hands as he set the bone in her foot. They were warm hands, strong and capable. Before she fell asleep she realized that she did not even know his name.

Andrew Tallant, like many young men before him, had come west for adventure and to make his fortune. Trading was in his blood, as was the land. He'd looked out across the High Plains en route to Santa Fé, and something in him rose up in response. There, he thought, somewhere out there he would make his home. With the money from the sale of his goods and wagon, he would go in search of land, put down roots, build a house, raise a family. No need to return to St. Louis. His parents were dead, his sister safely married. He was on his own.

What he hadn't counted on was that he'd lose his heart to a woman at the moment his feet touched the ground of Santa Fé. She haunted him — her eyes, her skin the color of a ripe apricot, the trust with which her body accepted his, and the musical way in which she spoke his language. He went back to the orphanage after two days, and he took her gifts, small things so the nuns couldn't object — a mirror, a length of red velvet ribbon, a sack of candy that she promptly shared with the other less fortunate orphans. He had to outwit the sisters who guarded their charges like watch dogs.

"We aren't accustomed to visits from strange men here, Mister Tallant," the nun assessed him with cool gray eyes.

"Madame," — how address a nun? . . . he had forgotten, if he ever knew — "Madame, . . . I feel responsible. I set the foot, and like any doctor I would like to see my patient."

"And that is all?" Her brows rose to her headdress.

He bowed his head, defeated as he had never been defeated in the world of men. He lied. "Certainly, Madame."

"Come with me. And mind you, we have rules here. This is a house of charity. A house of God. Delfina is a child in our care."

"I understand." He did not. What he understood was that he would cross whatever barriers there were, by any means.

She was lying in a small bed in a room of many beds, and she looked the child the nun had called her, but when he entered, her eyes showed a gladness like a light from within.

"*Señor,*" she said.

Such a little voice! Such music in two syllables! He knelt by the bed, took her hands in his own, felt them trembling. "I came to see how you are," he said. "To say how sorry I am. It was an accident. You know that."

She nodded. "Yes. An accident. But maybe a blessed one." Her huge eyes danced.

He couldn't grasp her meaning, but he seized her words. "Blessed. Blessed." He repeated himself, feeling like a fool. "Your foot," he got out at last. "Does it hurt?"

"Not very much. It is kind of you to come."

"Not kind. Selfish. I wanted to see you."

"Why?"

It seemed she was holding her breath as he held his while searching for words. How to find the words to say what he felt? Nothing seemed right. He shook his head, exasperated. "Because . . . because. . . ." God! It was agony, and the nun lurking outside the door like a black bat. "Because you don't need to be hurt. You need to be kept safe. Do you understand?"

Her smile said that she did, and the color that rose in her cheeks, but she said nothing, only watched him with those eyes that reminded him of dark silk.

"Here." He stood and patted his pockets, drew out his gifts, and handed them to her, feeling elation when she saw herself in the small mirror and drew a breath.

"Me?" she asked, filled with wonder.

"You," he said. "So beautiful."

There were no mirrors in the orphanage. Cautiously she stared at herself, smiled, then suddenly stuck out her tongue in a grimace, and laughed. "Not so beautiful, *señor*," she said playfully.

"Tsk!" The nun stood beside them, looking stern. "We do not encourage vanity, Mister Tallant."

"Not vanity, sister," Delfina said. "See me!" She grimaced again, then handed the mirror to the nun. "Here. Look."

Slowly the sister raised the mirror to face level. Heavens! She had aged since taking her vows. Why, there were wrinkles on what had been soft, white skin. And pouches under her eyes. She was old, ugly. Forty years of hardship showed clearly on her face. She sighed.

40

Vanity, indeed. Beauty never lasted, so let the child have her toy. Life was hard enough as it was.

She handed back the mirror with the admonition she felt called upon to give. "Remember, outward beauty isn't enough. One's soul must be beautiful, too. And now, Mister Tallant . . . ," she turned, "it is time for you to go."

"Tomorrow." He spoke to Delfina.

Her face shone up at him from the pillow. "Please," she whispered.

Before she slept that night, she sorted her day's treasures. Dwarfing them all was the man himself who had ridden into her life like a paladin, whose body she remembered, and whose eyes spoke more than words. He was unlike any man she knew or had ever seen, and thinking about him her heart seemed to swell in her breast until she thought she would die from the aching, the longing to reach out and touch his face. What had he meant when he said that about protecting her? Was she so helpless, so much the child still, that he thought of himself as a father? What she felt was not what a child feels for its parent. What she felt was a stirring, a need like a screaming in her body. What she felt, she could not speak, must never speak, at least not to the nuns who warned constantly about sins of the flesh. At that she laughed, the sound muffled by the covers. What nonsense. How could a feeling such as hers be sinful? How could what went on between a man and a woman be evil? The sisters were confused, but she was not.

She put her hand under her pillow and found the mirror. It was cool to the touch and reassuring. He would come back. He said so, and he was a man of his word. She sighed once, deeply, and fell asleep.

Again he returned, and again, and her eyes always showed her pleasure at the sight of "*Señor* Tallant," as she called him, a label he found at first a delight and then an irritant. He wanted to be called

41

something other. *Mi corazón. Mi amor.* He was learning her language quickly.

He put off leaving on his search for land until the aspens on the mountains were rivers of gold, and a skim of ice shivered over the *acequias* at dawn. At last he made up his mind. He would go, and return, and claim Delfina as his wife. When he told her his plans, she was radiant, and then in an instant fearful, reaching out a hand and touching his sleeve.

"Go carefully," she told him in a whisper. "Out there are Indians, not the Indians of the plaza but Apaches. And *bandidos.* They will kill you and leave your bones for coyotes."

He shook his head. He had, after all, crossed the prairie, had faced Indians, dust storms, tornadoes, hunger and thirst, and had emerged safely. "I'll be back," he said. "Wait for me."

Of course she would wait. It was a silly request. She would wait forever, if she had to, though that would be hard.

That night she dreamed of a hawk shot out of the sky. It lay at her feet, bloody and dying, and she was helpless. She awoke crying, with pleas to the Virgin on her lips. "Keep him safe. Keep him safe," she said over and over like a chant, the tolling of bells.

Winter deepened. Snow covered the mountains and seemed to burn in the sunlight, as if, in its heart, it was fire and not ice. The air of the town smelled of piñon fires and meat roasting, of the pungent chilies that were added to every pot.

Through the streets, the twisting *calles,* on the seven nights before Christmas a chosen group roamed, knocking at doors and being turned away — the ritual of *La Posada* that reenacted the flight of the Virgin and Joseph, their search for a birthplace for the miraculous babe. Delfina watched and prayed, although her heart felt broken. Surely by this time he should have returned. Surely.

Suddenly it was Christmas Eve, the holy night, and in the town, the adobe houses of the poor, the fine mansions of Palace Avenue, in the Palace of the Governors the governor himself — everyone was getting ready for midnight Mass. In the orphanage the younger children were excited over the lateness of the hour and over the promise of a cup of spicy chocolate after the service.

Delfina hushed them, remembering her own childhood — how she and her parents walked together to the church through the snow-covered streets, how strange it seemed to be awake so late, to see candles flickering in usually dark houses, to smell the incense mixed with piñon in the little church.

She sighed. More than ever she had been thinking about her life — its past, its future. Once she had hoped, but as the months passed that hope had dwindled to a small lump in her throat, a wish that probably would never be granted. She said his name silently. *Andrew.* Then she joined the sisters and the children for the walk to the church where, shortly, the bishop, Jean Baptiste Lamy, a tall man, slender as a reed but with the reed's supple strength, would bless his congregation and celebrate the birth of Christ.

Afterwards she was never sure at what point she noticed the stirring at the door, felt the draft of cold air that caused the candle flames to dance, heard the murmuring of the women behind her. The floor was hard. She shifted on her knees and turned her head covered by a *rebozo* toward the source of the distraction. And there he was with snow melting in his hair, so that he looked like one of the haloed saints, like an angel come to announce happiness.

Her lips moved. "Andrew."

Above the heads of the worshippers their eyes met and held, and danced like the candle flames.

"You love him? This *gringo?*" Nilda had not been able to believe the fact that the American had offered for the child, and her without a dowry.

"Yes, with all of me," came Delfina's answer.

"Not yet, I hope." Nilda was only too aware of the rush of young passion. "You haven't let him . . . ?" She stopped and eyed the girl.

43

Delfina shook her head. She hadn't, but only because there had been no opportunity.

"*Humph.*" Nilda wasn't fooled. Best get the girl married as soon as possible. "All right. I've brought you a gift. It belonged to my mother . . . your grandmother. All the way from Spain it came, many years ago. You should have something of your family to take along with you. We may never see each other again." She held out a package wrapped in a piece of burlap, and Delfina took it carefully.

Inside she found a shawl, a fragile, shining thing of blue and silver thread that lay in her hands as lightly as a spider web. When she raised her eyes, they were bright with tears. "Thank you," she said simply. "I'll wear it for my wedding, and I'll remember you always."

"Don't cry. A bride should smile. Save the tears for later. You'll probably need them." *Dios!* Nilda clapped her hand to her mouth. Her tongue was always clacking. What a thing to say, true or not. It sounded like a curse. She reached out for Delfina and hugged her. "Never mind me. Go with your *gringo* and be happy. He loves you. I can tell."

The sun seemed to rise out of a rift in the plains. She thought, if they went far enough, she might find the place from which it came and marvel at it as she marveled at the rest of the country they were passing through. They had left the Sangre de Cristo Mountains behind and were traveling on a high and endless plain. Antelope ran there in great herds, rippling in flight the way the yellow grass rippled, so that sometimes it seemed the entire world was in fluid motion. She gripped the wagon seat and stared in a kind of ecstasy, wishing she could join them, wishing she could run like that with the wind in her hair, her face, and no skirts to hinder her flight.

And then she remembered how it was with Andrew at night under a sky filled with stars, and how what they did was in a way the same, a wildness, a stampede, their hearts beating like the sound of hoofs, the country in which they ran the country of the other, unmapped,

44

joyful. And she who had been brought up to the sound of church bells, by the rigid discipline of the nuns, she who had stored up the tiny moments of each day had, suddenly, more moments than she could hold.

"I'm too small!" she cried, turning to Andrew who was watching her. "I can't keep it all, and I want to."

He reached out and pulled her close. She nestled there, small, indeed, but filled with life.

"No need to keep it," he said. "It's there all the time, and free for the asking. And it's not going away. It's ours . . . or some of it is."

"And is where we are going like this? So big? So beautiful?"

He nodded, and she was satisfied.

Home. They would build it together. A house. A garden. Cattle. And if they were blessed, children who would laugh and cry and grow up to be strong, good people, secure in the love of their parents.

Andrew had bought six hundred acres beside the Rio Hondo where it ran down out of the mountains and cut through the plain. *So much land,* she thought, used to narrow streets, walled courtyards, small rooms. And then, with a burst of happiness, *so much freedom!*

It was the women who built the houses, who came with their men — on foot, in wagons, on the backs of mules — and who smoothed and watered the dirt floors, layered the adobe bricks one by one into walls, laughing among themselves and gossiping, forming friendships while the men labored over the building of corrals and fences, the plowing of earth. They made the hearth wide and deep, the door heavy, the windows small and high.

"For safety," Inez said, inspecting her work. "Indians, thieves, many bad men come here. Can you shoot?"

Delfina, who had been scraping the floor with a flat shovel, stopped and looked at her new friend. "The nuns wouldn't let us," she said, attempting humor.

"The more fools they," came the response. "But your husband will teach you."

45

So much to learn! Delfina nodded and went back to work. He would teach her. She'd make sure of it.

Inez drove her point home. "When they come, the *bandidos,* you can run and hide and let them take everything, or you can fight. Me and my Juan, we fight. It's better than starving, let me tell you."

"Do they come often?"

Inez shrugged. "Often enough. And those Apaches. . . ." she grimaced. "They eat mules. That's why the corral is out there next to the house. So you can catch them. Maybe. If you have the ears of a hound and don't sleep too deeply."

Delfina shuddered in spite of herself. Freedom, happiness hung by a thread. Sometimes she thought of the security of the orphanage, the peace, the unchanging schedule of work and prayers, with a twinge of regret. But then she would think of Andrew, his strong arms, the tenderness of his passion, and how outside their door was the brilliance of a new world — sun, a sky pierced by the flights of birds, earth reaching to all the horizons. Ah, what was peace compared to greatness?

She laughed. "No one will take my white mule away from me," she said. "Or what we have, either."

"Let us hope it is so," Inez responded and went on with her work in silence.

When the house was finished and the corrals, when the beans, corn, squash, and barley showed green in the ploughed earth, it was time for a *baile,* a dance, a housewarming. Juan Citrón played his violin for the dancing that hardened the earth floor, the dirt in the small yard even more, and the music skittered out over the plains like dry leaves blown in the wind. Delfina wore her grandmother's shawl, and a skirt of red wool, and she laughed in delight as one man after another spun her around until she was dizzy, until Andrew claimed her, and her body melted into his the way it always did.

There was food, venison stew, *frijoles,* tortillas, tamales, pies, cakes, potatoes roasted in the ashes, and from somewhere a jug of whiskey that Juan Citrón sipped until his fingers danced wildly over the strings of his violin, and he threw back his head and sang *corridos* of his own — songs of love, betrayal, and death. And everyone clapped, danced all through the brief summer night under the light of a full, silver moon.

And while they were dancing, twenty men were riding hard out of Texas, following the moon and the dusty road that went west into the plains, across the Pecos River, into a country so large that even twenty men with the law behind them would be lost, would vanish, leaving no sign of their passage. They were the seven Harrell brothers and their companions, and they were wanted in Texas for murder, robbery, cattle theft. Dangerous men, violent, they knew no law but to take what they wanted, to do as they pleased, to kill when it pleased them to kill.

In the valley of the Hondo they bought a ranch, a rambling adobe with a portal for shade, and behind it the river gurgling its way east. Mountains rose to the north and south, and it was easy to watch the road for travelers or trouble. They sent for their wives and children and settled down, as much as restless men ever settle. Their herds of cattle and horses increased, some thought too quickly, but no one dared to ask or to check the brands. Twenty armed men kept curious strangers away.

Juan Citrón was worried. The Harrell brothers and their followers had declared war on the Mexicans. "They say they will kill all of us," he said to Andrew. "And they have already made a start. Five men and a woman at a *baile* in town last month, and two farmers and their families since. I'm sending Inez and the boy to her sister in Las Vegas. Perhaps it would be wise to send Delfina, too."

Delfina, who had been listening from inside the house, came out wiping her hands on her apron. "I won't go," she said. Her chin was set, her eyes serious. She hadn't been away from Andrew in two years. Separation from him was impossible to imagine.

47

The two men turned as she stepped out, both admiring her beauty which had changed, heightened into strength. She was confident now where she had been unsure. She was a woman, no longer a child.

She stood looking at them, and her eyes flashed. "You think because some men are killing us that I'll run away?" she demanded. "You think that I'm a coward? That I'll leave my husband, my home? If they come here shooting, I'll shoot back."

Juan shook his head. "These are mad dogs," he said. "And there are more of them than you know."

"What about the sheriff?" Andrew asked. "Can't he do anything to stop them?"

"*Amigo,* you know as well as I . . . this is a big country. The sheriff has his hands full of trouble in town. Out here a man must take care of himself and hope he does right. That is why I am sending Inez and the boy away. So I can do what I do, and if they kill me, at least my son can come back and take what is his. You understand me?"

Delfina's eyes flashed. "And Inez? What does she think about this?"

"Inez does as I tell her."

Inez, she thought, was the first to tell her she should learn to use a weapon. And she had. But of what use was the knowledge if she left her man to defend himself when he needed her most? When everything she loved was threatened?

Much to her sorrow she had not yet conceived a child, but perhaps that was as well with gunmen on the loose. And there was still much work to be done — fences to be built, more corn to be planted. The second room of the house stood finished except for the roof. The walls she had done herself, mixing the mud and straw, shaping the adobes, layering them meticulously one upon the other, and taking a deep satisfaction knowing that she, with her own hands, had built a dwelling place. And now she was expected to leave. She shook her head and planted her feet firmly. "I will not go," she said again, and her words came out with the hardness of hail.

* * * * *

The Harrells wanted blood. One of their men had been killed
a Mexican deputy while resisting arrest. The fact that their man wa
drunk, and that he had killed the deputy before dying himself, made
no difference to them. In the darkness, in retribution, they crept up
on a dance hall and opened fire on the Mexican dancers, wounding
five men and a woman.

The next day Ben Harrell was found dead. He was missing a finger
and the diamond ring that was on it.

"I'll kill every greaser between here and the Pecos," Sam Harrell
vowed, snarling like the mad dog Juan had called him. "They killed
one of mine. I'll kill theirs, and I'll keep on doing it till there's not
a one left."

It was the height of summer. Even the land seemed to be holding
its breath, waiting, waiting. The rains that gave life to the fields, that
nourished the grama grass to dancing seed, were late. Every day the
sun rose in a sky without clouds and, flaming, fell beyond the
horizon, its heat lingering long into the night. Among the scorched
plants, the drooping corn, the farmers waited, their ears tuned to the
sound of hoofs, their eyes alert for the dust raised by Harrell's
vengeful army. Rumors of more killings trickled down to those on
the plain, and still they waited, watched for a sign.

"Do you think they will come here?" Delfina asked. She was tired
of waiting, past the desperate moment, lulled into security.

"I don't know. I'm an American, so probably not." He spoke
carefully, hiding his fear. If they came by surprise, found Delfina
alone in the garden, what then? Women, children, youth, sex made
no difference to these men with blood lust in their hearts. Their
vengeance had no limits. *"Every greaser in the country!"* It seemed
he could hear the words like a violent echo, could hear them and
knew terror. He put his arms around his wife and drew her close, so
close he could hear the steady beating of her heart. "If they come,
you'll have to hide. It won't be me they're after."

49

She remembered his words later, too late to make a difference.

It was a dawn like all the others that summer — clear and brilliant, the light of the sun spreading like a giant grass fire over the swell of the eastern plains. Delfina heard the rooster crow at the first sign of light. Once, twice he greeted the day from his perch in the chicken house where she shut up her flock at night to keep them safe from coyotes. Usually she awakened early, was up and cooking breakfast before the sun cleared the horizon, but on this morning she lay still for a long while, savoring the quiet and the feel of Andrew's long body next to hers.

How lucky she was! All that she had ever wanted or dreamed of was here, most of it within reach of her hand. Andrew. A snug house. And outside the undulant plains with the river at their heart. She smiled, and Andrew awoke, turned, saw her face with its dark eyes shining as they had on that morning of his first visit to the orphanage.

He buried his face in her breasts, and she held to him, not wanting to let go. In the corral a horse stomped, blew. Another nickered. Neither of them heard or cared. Neither of them wanted to let go of the sweetness.

Later she heard hoofbeats coming up the rise away from the river. They were slow but urgent, like the sound of the blood in her ears, and she sat up, eyes wide, listening. She said: "Someone is coming," and pulled the quilt to her breasts.

"Stay here!" His command broke the silence. He struggled into his britches, took the pistol that always hung beside the bed into his hand. "Stay!" he said again, his voice harsh.

She heard his feet, bootless, crossing the dirt floor, the creak of the door on its leather hinges, and the sound of hoofs in the yard. And then the voices like the insane yapping of coyotes when they have surrounded their prey.

"Tallant!"

"Married to a greaser, ain't you?"

"What's it got you? You're as filthy as the rest."

The shots ripped through the gauze of morning. One. Two. Three. She counted them, rose, and ran to the door.

Three men, their faces masks of hatred and madness, stared back at her. Three men, one with eyes the color of shadows on winter snow. And Andrew, her heart, her love, on the ground, his face blown into nothingness.

The morning went dark. Everything was darkness. She was blinded and could not see, wounded and unable to move. Her heart lay dying in the yard, a thousand miles away, beyond her reach or comprehension. She dreamed the old dream — a hawk shot out of the sky, bleeding its life into her lap. She was dreaming. She knew she was dreaming. She stumbled into the yard where he lay, took what was left of him into her arms, keened, and the sound that she made was the sound of earth when it moves and splits apart at its core.

Why hadn't they killed her too? Without Andrew she wasn't alive. Without Andrew her purpose, her joy was gone. She recalled the depthless gray eyes of one of the men she had seen, the cruelty that distorted his face. She would see him in her sleep, would exist in the nightmare of his unfettered madness. She knew it, huddled there on the dirt with Andrew's blood draining out over her body.

It took her most of the morning to dig his grave in the hard-packed dry earth. She moved slowly, like an old woman, prying out stones, hacking at the ground with what strength she could summon. When she finished, she went inside and got her grandmother's blue shawl from the trunk. No need for it now. She wrapped what had been her husband in its warmth and began the task of covering him with the dirt she had moved.

She knew she should pray, but her mind was empty of prayers. She no longer believed — not in words, not in the God who had permitted murder. And, as she labored, she kept seeing the eyes of the killers, the color of ice.

The plan came to her slowly, not a conscious decision but a

flowing, like a tide. When she had finished, she went inside, stripped off her clothes, and put on Andrew's. They were too large, but inside them she felt better, as if he were there with her, lending her his strength. She banked the fire, loaded a sack with corn, another with bread. She dipped water from the barrel into a canteen, then she strapped on the pistol, retrieved the rifle from its place by the door, and filled her pockets with ammunition.

She put Andrew's heavy saddle on the white mule, Teresita, without apologies, swung up, and then, following the tracks gouged in the dirt, she rode eastward along the river. The Citrón house was empty. No smoke rose from the chimney. No children played in the yard. She laughed, a harsh noise like the croak of a raven. Juan was hiding somewhere, pistol in hand, too late to be of help to her. Well, she needed no help. Killing was easy, a matter of aiming, pulling the trigger. She knew how. Andrew had taught her well.

The tracks turned south into a country she did not know, and she shrugged her shoulders. What matter? Only the trail mattered, and the men who rode it.

When night came, she stopped in a small arroyo. She fed Teresita corn with her own hands, gave her water to drink out of her hat. For herself, she chewed on a piece of bread, sipped some water. Food had no taste. Perhaps it never would again. The future was blank. What she had was the present — a bed on hard ground, the star-swept sky, the warm presence of the mule hobbled close by. And her errand. It was enough. She thought she would never sleep until her purpose was accomplished, but sleep came to her swiftly, like a little death.

She could see the buzzards for miles, their great bodies circling, riding the air currents, darkening the sky. What she and the birds found was carnage — a pack train, its people slaughtered and left on the sand. Five Mexican drovers and two women lay stiffened in death.

"When I find you," Delfina said out loud, her voice shrill and

52

carrying, "when I find you, I will leave you like you left these poor people. I hope the coyotes rip out your hearts, and the buzzards eat your eyes."

Then she rode on into the blue waves of heat, moving slower now for the mule was tiring, and she herself was overcome by dizziness, so that she held to the saddle horn and hoped she wouldn't fall. The buzzards must not have her. Not yet.

The sound of running horses woke her, many horses, bunched in a herd. She shook the sleep out of her eyes, peeked out from behind the rocks where she had spent the night. Ten horses and four riders pushing them. She recognized them, and her lips drew back into a snarl. Murderers! Horse thieves! Heading for the border mountains where they could hide and return to kill again.

She drew her pistol, checked it, then turned and saddled Teresita who looked at her with mournful eyes. *So far from home,* the look said. *So far.*

"Soon now," she told her, patting the speckled nose. "Be brave, little one."

She took a bite of bread. It was stale and even more tasteless than it had been the day before. But no matter. If . . . when her job was finished, she would eat. For now, vengeance was sustenance enough.

Teresita pricked her long ears and looked off into the distance where more riders were visible, coming at a cautious trot. Delfina squinted into the sun. More of the Harrells? If so, she would have to stay hidden and follow behind. Teresita brayed. The riders pulled up and looked around.

"What the hell was that?" one of them asked.

Teresita shook Delfina's hand off her muzzle and brayed again. The men, pistols drawn, quickly surrounded the rocks and found her — small, filthy, defiant.

"*Señores,*" she said, staring at them out of dark-circled eyes, her own pistol steady in her hand.

53

"Put that damn' gun away," the first man said. "We ain't going to hurt you."

Delfina didn't move.

"Look," the man said, "we're after a bunch of murdering horse thieves and, if they get in those mountains, I'll never get my horses back. So put the gun down, and we'll all go about our business."

"Who are these thieves?"

"Those damned Harrells!" He was yelling, frustrated. "Now you go on wherever you're going, and we'll ride outta here."

She lowered her pistol. "The Harrells are my business, too," she said. "I'll go with you."

He laughed. "Little lady like you? What business you got with that bunch?"

The pain caught her, the loneliness she knew she'd carry for the rest of her days. She said: "They killed my husband. I will kill them. You understand me?"

He let out his breath in a whistle. "When? How long you been out here?"

She couldn't remember. It seemed she'd spent a lifetime on the back of a mule with one thought in her mind. She shook her head. "One day. Two. Forever. It makes no difference. I will find them . . . with or without you."

The three men looked at each other in silence, then the first one spoke. "Can that mule keep up?"

"She will keep up."

"Then come on," he said. "We ain't got time to waste. My name's Van. This here's Watt and Jake."

She looked up at him steadily. "Until a few days ago, I was Missus Andrew Tallant. Now . . . I don't know. You understand me?"

He moved uneasily in the saddle. "Yeah," he said finally, "I reckon I do."

She swung up on the mule. "When we find them, the man with the gray eyes is mine."

"That'd be Ed Hart. 'Little Ed,' they call him."

She shrugged. His name wasn't important. What mattered was the blotting out, the sealing shut of his eyes. Then, maybe, she could rest. Maybe.

The running horses left a visible trail, and the dust that they raised hung over the plain. Ahead the mountains looked rumpled, mysterious in the light of late afternoon.

"They'll have to hole up for the night pretty soon," Van said. "Those horses can't go forever."

They were his racing string, his pride, his life. He knew them each by name, knew their strengths, their weaknesses, knew that even conditioned as they were for running the best of them would break down in the hands of men with no regard for life of any kind. They had killed this woman's husband. What, after that, was a horse? He felt fury rise in him. The damned Harrells. All of them were better off buried.

Watt Mapson, riding in the lead, pulled up, grinning. "They're headed for Owl Cañon," he said. "Good place to hold horses. Narrow at both ends, and there's water."

Van grunted. "That's the first good news I've heard since yesterday. Maybe it's fine for horses, but it spells hell for the Harrells. If they camp under that big rock wall, we can get to the top, and they won't know what hit 'em." He turned to Delfina. "Now, I don't want any dumb moves from you. We'll take the east trail up the side, and be up there come morning. If you're set on this, do what I tell you and try not to get killed if they shoot back. You hear?"

She thought, if she died, it wouldn't matter. Not if she had finished her errand. But she nodded once. Maybe it was a good thing to have these men with her.

By nightfall they had reached the top of the cañon wall. Although she could hear the men below, they were out of sight, hidden by the swell of rock. She peered out, saw the horses bunched in a herd, tired from their long run — blacks, bays, one superb gray with a long neck and fine head. He was too good for the likes of those men who ruined everything they touched.

She tasted hatred like bile in her mouth and spat. Only a little while now, and there would be no more of them, and she could rest. She could go home and tell the people along the river that they need hide no more, tell Juan to send for his wife and son because the threat was over, because she had done what was necessary. Home. She found herself thinking of her house, her garden as home, perhaps because Andrew was still there, in spirit at least, his bones beneath the threshold.

"Mi corazón," she murmured into the night. *"Mi corazón."*

After all, the ambush was the easy part. The four men in the cañon were perfect targets in the clear morning light. She lay on her belly and sighted along the barrel of the Henry rifle, Andrew's weapon, well cared for and accurate. And then she saw him, the man named Ed Hart, sandy haired, lean as a wolf, wall eyed. She shivered then got hold of herself.

"Murderer," she murmured. "Viper." And she felt the wood and steel of the weapon against her cheek.

They were all in sight now, hauling out their gear, getting ready to ride. Out of the corner of her eye she saw Van lift his arm in the signal, and she took careful aim at her quarry's heart. He spun as her slug hit him, made a futile grab for his pistol before falling, face down, in the churned-up earth. She shot twice more, counting as she had counted on that other morning. "One. Two. Three." But this time it was the killer who lay bleeding in the dust.

Afterwards she felt nothing, only a numbness of body and brain. She lay with her eyes closed, the sound of her heart loud in her ears. She had come on a long journey — from the orphanage at Santa Fé to a cañon in the wilderness. She had tasted all the emotions of which humanity is capable — fear, love, anger, hatred. Now, like the child she had been, she felt wiped clean, empty, a traveler on the verge of yet another journey that would take her the rest of her life.

Her companions were rounding up the horses. Without a word she mounted Teresita and turned her face to the west.

"Come, my friend," she said to the mule. "We are finished here. Now we go home."

Teresita needed no urging. She knew the trail and took it, moving at a slow but steady trot.

It seemed that nothing had changed at the house. For a moment she felt that she had dreamed a bad dream, and that Andrew would come out to greet her, to help her off the mule and take her into his arms. So clearly could she see him, and hear the sound of his laughter!

She shook her head to clear it of ghosts, reached up to wipe her eyes on her sleeve, knowing that for the rest of her days she would see him there in the yard, hear his voice, the gentleness of it when, in the dark, they came together in love. She sat there and let the tears come, let out the grief that she had held in check for what seemed like years. When she could cry no more, she dismounted and led Teresita into the yard. Then she knelt on the newly turned grave.

"There will be no more war here," she whispered. "I have killed one of them, and some good men killed the rest. No one will come to harm me now . . . or you. No one. Sleep well where you are, *mi amor,* and pray for me."

When she stood up, she felt a faint flutter in her belly, so faint it seemed like the wings of a butterfly, the swift flight of a bird — once, and then again it came, demanding, insistent. She shifted her feet on the packed earth. A child! So a child would be born to her. It would be a son, she thought, a fine boy, and she would name him Andrew, and bring him up to be strong and proud and fearless.

Smiling then, she picked up the reins. "Come, Teresita," she said. "You and I, we have much to do, after all."

CORRIDO FOR BILLY

"Garrett, you big piss pot!"

That's what I called him, what I screamed into the night air startling everything — the crickets, the frogs in the river, the men gathered around the body, and Garrett himself, standing there like a scarecrow with the face of death.

And the men, Higinio, Manuel, Paco, they told me: "Hush!" They said: "What's done is done. Call the women and make him ready for burial."

But nothing was finished. Murder is never an end. Billy, my *chivato,* lay there with a hole the size of a fist where his heart had been, while Garrett lived. I wanted him dead, too, would have done it myself right there outside Don Pedro's house. I'd have done it with teeth and nails and the knife Billy dropped as he fell. I'd have pounded Garrett's brains into mush and stamped them into the ground, and no one would have stopped me, maybe would have helped me, for Billy was like one of ours.

We knew the meaning of friendship, of love, if Garrett did not. Hadn't Paco been hiding him in his sheep camp near the river, so that when he came to me he stank like a ram? How we laughed while I poured water over him and picked the ticks from his skin!

"*Chivato,*" I said, "you stink like a ram."

He turned and put his hands around my waist and said: "And have horns like one, too." And for a time we were lost to everything but our hearts, our pleasures.

Yes, we all knew he was the hunted, and we kept silent, went on about our business, feeding him when we could, pretending to be stupid when those others like Garrett came searching.

So, I thought, let this Garrett live a while watching his back trail. Let him be the hunted one, but without friends to watch like eyes and ears. Let him run. And run. And taste fear. "May you die as you have lived," I told him, and I looked into those pale eyes as I spoke. "May the *zopilote* pick out your eyes, your heart, and coyotes fight over your *cojones*. May you be without friends in life and in death."

He wasn't one to believe in curses. I tell you, that man had no soul. Who knew that better than I, whose sister died on her wedding night rather than bed with such a one? Still, he knew I meant every word, and he stared at me a long time, thinking, always thinking. Then he offered money to buy clothes for Billy. Oh, he was the sly one, thinking to win back our respect!

"Keep your money!" I spat at his feet. "You can't buy him back. We have clothes and shoes enough."

Half of Fort Sumner had gathered there in the summer night with the moths fluttering overhead and the flowers in the gardens turning their faces to the moon. Deluvina, Dona Luz and Pablita, Don Pedro in whose bedroom the murder happened, Paco, and Don Alejandro, the Justice of the Peace. They murmured assent to my words. Yes, we had clothes enough, love enough. We didn't need the help of this man without a soul.

But before we could take the body, Garrett had us all witness the death, had the men sign a paper. And then we, the women, took him into the house, already weeping for we had loved him, The Kid, the wild one called *El Chivato* who had danced with us, shared food with us, sometimes our beds. Who could say whose beds he'd graced? He took his pleasures and gave in return, and that's more than can be said for most. Always laughing he was. Always with the right words to warm a woman's heart.

And Deluvina brought water from the kitchen, and soft cloths, and we washed him and bound up the wound so it wouldn't stain the white shirt, the good coat, so he would be decent on his way to heaven. We did this murmuring to ourselves and to him. So young!

So alive only hours before! We spoke of death and betrayal, and the candles and lamps flickered so that he seemed to be smiling at us, and we thought he might wake and spin us off, each in turn, dancing.

Aiee! Never again!

Deluvina brushed his hair into neatness, pale hair and fine. How I had marveled at it, so unlike my own. She was sobbing. "He brought me this cloth." She looked down at the bright calico skirt that was her pride. " 'Make something pretty,' he said. To me, Deluvina, like I was a young girl and beautiful." Then she wrapped her arms around herself and such a sound came from her as to make the rest of us cross ourselves in fear.

Pablita, the youngest, the one of us who had, perhaps, suffered the greatest blow, put her arms around Deluvina. "Cry!" she said, and her voice cracked like a whip in the small room. "Cry for him . . . cry for us all." Then she went to Billy and smoothed his hair. "I remember," she said, "I remember how we would take Pedro's horses and ride out by the river with the wind in our faces. We ran them. We raced. And once the larks flew up from under us with every step. Thousands of them, singing and flying, and we laughed and laughed and had to stop. He made us stop, for fear we'd kill the little ones in their nests and leave the parents to mourn."

Deluvina's Indian face crumpled into itself like sand down a gopher hole. "Now we mourn for him, betrayed by his own. By that white man out there who looks like a snake."

She fumbled in her pocket and drew out her rosary, a heavy thing, a gift from Don Pedro upon her baptism. Each bead was carved from the seed of a peach, and the cross was of silver. And we all knelt around him, so many moths around a dying flame, and said our *Aves* with the taste of our tears in our mouths.

That we were there, that *he* was, seemed the devil's work. How else explain the greed of men? Dolan, Murphy, McSween, even the foolish Englishman, Tunstall — those men we had never seen but knew of, nonetheless — all had been gluttons wanting money, power, land. Could they not see that land belongs to no one? That it belongs to itself and that all must use it well and wisely?

No. They fought like a pack of dogs and killed each other, never thinking that they were the devil's tools, never knowing that when they killed the Englishman in plain sight, they made an enemy of Billy who was loyal to his friends above all. Always Billy — who laughed and danced and rode, who made love as if he knew his time was short and precious as water. Whose light fingers delighted me beyond all others so that I betrayed my own husband over and over again. And I not even ashamed!

No, I only ached in my heart so that my throat closed over the prayers, and all I could do was weep into my hands like a child. If I had not sent him out to cut the meat! If I had only kept him with me, laughing, loving! My guilt was heavy on me. I was glad of the curse wrung out of my womb and placed on Garrett's head. It was, after all, he who had pulled the trigger, he who had blood in his eye.

When the rosary was finished, we all knelt there on the cool dirt floor linked by pain, by sorrow, by knowledge that Billy would not rise, would never smile on us again. It was too much to bear.

Nasaria put a small hand on his white cheek. "So cold," she whispered. "He is so cold." And bowed her head till it touched his shoulder. When she spoke again, we could hardly understand her for her weeping. "At Anton Chico . . . at the fiesta . . . can you remember how he danced? How he brought the yellow roses for all of us? How we all danced and sang and never thought of dying?"

Yes, lightly, lightly he danced with each of us in turn, as if we were great ladies and he loved us all, and our skirts spun out like wings, and our laughter. But even then death hovered overhead. I saw it suddenly — the dark angel waiting in the night. Waiting . . . waiting, hungry for the youngest, the sweetest meat.

"It was there," I told her. "All the time. Death. Waiting for this night. Only we didn't see. He didn't want us to see."

Whoever looks for death? No one. But our lives hang from the thinnest of threads, as easily broken as the web of a spider.

I remembered him, dancing in defiance, though death slid through the sand hills, the tall grass, close on his heels. I thought of his hands, gentle and then not so gentle, hands that caressed in one hour, turned to steel in the next. He must have known they'd track him down, but he cared only for living. For the feel of a good horse, a good woman, for the sweetness of this land that stole his heart. He could have gone to Mexico, but he didn't, couldn't maybe.

It was here that he came to life — on these wide plains with the sky overhead burning his eyes, in the secret cañons, beside rivers and the grass thick and green, beneath the orchards in bloom like lace *mantillas* thrown across the valleys. The land was in his bones. We were in his bones, all of us, and here and there, so they say, are children with his look stamped upon them, fair-haired children full of grace and wildness.

So, it was done but not finished. The men were at the door, impatient, waiting to carry him to the church, and Garrett was behind them, a head taller than the rest, looking over them and into the room. Looking at Billy as if he expected not to find him, as if he still needed proof of what he'd done. At the sight of him my stomach turned. Bitterness rose in my throat, my mouth. He'd penetrated our sorrow, seen our tears, and it was as if we were naked before him.

"May God damn you to hell," I said, getting to my feet. "It's not enough to kill him, but you steal our tears as well." I tossed my head to get rid of his spell. Then I raised my arms over my head and began to sing and to sway with my own music. "Come," I said to the kneeling women. "We've sorrowed enough. Let us dance the fandango in celebration. Let's dance our Billy into paradise."

At first they were horrified. Then, one by one, they rose and followed, circling the body that was, after all, only a small part of the man. And so we danced. And sang. And clapped our hands. And our skirts rustled like the wings of dark moths as we drew death out of the shadows; as we took it, wrestled with it, and threw it back into the candles' yellow flame.

MIRACLES

Madril Ochoa was born with a birthmark. Not an ordinary birthmark, but one that covered half his face from hairline to chin and, when he cried, which he did as soon as he burst from his mother's womb and lay thrashing on the sheet, the mark turned a deep and angry red. The midwife, Apollonia, drew in her breath. Clearly Dona Inez had been bewitched while carrying, and the mark was left on the unborn child. She cut the cord and snatched the baby to her own breast.

"A fine boy," she pronounced, hiding his head against her. Then she carried him across the room and laid him in the crib.

First, she thought, she would attend the mother. Then, perhaps, there was something that could be done for the child, poor thing. Clucking her tongue, she bathed Dona Inez in warm water, filled with herbs, and fed her a potion of the seeds of the white poppy to induce a healing sleep. Clucking still louder, she picked up the statue of San Francisco that had attended the birth and carried him back to his niche in the wall.

"A fine piece of work," she said, addressing the saint with familiarity as she often did, though only in the privacy of her heart. "Who'll want this one with the mark of the devil on him?"

Quite clearly she heard the answer, so clearly that she started, nearly dropping the statue, and looked around her.

"He is blessed," the voice said.

When she recovered her wits, she peered at the saint who looked back at her with painted, unreadable eyes. "Is it so?" she asked.

No answer came. She heard only the whirring of locusts in the cottonwood trees by the door, the rush of the *acequia* beyond, the whimpering of the almost-forgotten child. Still, she had heard it —

the voice both stern and sweet, and not her own. She turned and went back to the infant, picked him up, and carried him to the door where the golden light of late afternoon came pouring down upon him like a baptism.

There was no denying the mark, but in the brilliant sunshine it seemed to fade. Perhaps a paste of herbs would bleach the stain — mallow leaves, or the crushed *yerba de la negrita* mixed with the whites of new-laid eggs.

She took him back into the birth room and busied herself, working swiftly and in silence, her ears attuned to the space around her, waiting for the voice to come again. None of her potions succeeded. The infant's face remained as it was — stained red down one side and crossing the bridge of his tiny nose with a shape like a hand.

Upon awakening, Dona Inez wailed at the sight and pounded her fists on the sheet. "A curse!" she cried. "Who hates me enough to mark an innocent child? Who? And how can I hold up my head in this place now?"

"Give him your milk," Apollonia said, putting the infant to nurse. "And listen to me. I have heard a miracle from the mouth of the *santo* himself."

"Miracles!" snapped Dona Inez. "Don't talk to me of miracles! Find me a wet nurse! Take the child away! I can't bear to look at him."

Blessed or not, miracle or not, Madril spent his infancy and his youth being largely ignored. Apollonia, after all, was regarded by some as a witch. Who could know for certain that she had heard the voice of the *santo* and not that of the devil? Perhaps it was trickery on her part.

After Madril, Dona Inez had other children, two boys and a girl, unmarked and handsome. They overflowed the house and kept the walled courtyard, the corrals, and stables ringing with games and laughter. Madril sometimes joined them. Most often he played by himself or wandered over the steep hills that circled the village, looking at the plants, the animals, the stones on the ground, enjoying the tricks the purple clouds played on the mountains, changing their shapes, their color even as he watched. Sometimes he went with Apollonia when she gathered the herbs necessary for her work. He carried her baskets and, when the way grew steep, or when she saw a plant she needed growing high above her head, he retrieved it, climbing nimbly.

"Little lizard," she would say and would give him a piece of licorice root to chew. Once, seriously, she asked: "Would you like to learn what I do?" Perhaps, she thought, he would become a great healer, a layer-on-of-hands, a spell-caster with power greater even than her own.

But he shook his head, his black hair falling over his forehead and shading the mark. "No. Thank you, but no."

"What then?" She put down her basket and lowered herself to the ground beside it. She was feeling old, stiff in the joints, and a little breathless, and she had no one in whom to confide or even talk to when the need came.

Madril shrugged and smiled. "I don't know. It's fun to go with you and find the herbs, though." He hoped he hadn't offended her. Witches, if indeed she was one, had ways of punishing insults. They turned into owls and frightened people to death, or murdered them on the lonely trails through the mountains where there were no witnesses. He didn't think Apollonia would do such a thing to him or to anyone, but you never knew. The children of the village were frightened of her and ran away, shrieking at the sight of her trudging toward them in her dusty skirt, her basket of medicines on her arm.

To hide his embarrassment he picked up a small piece of white stone and began to draw with it on another, harder stone. He drew Diego, the woodcutter's *burro,* coming down the trail with a load of piñon logs, hidden by her burden except for long ears and delicate, durable legs.

Apollonia watched him, saw the small creature taking shape in a

66

few scratches on stone. *"¡Dios!"* she exclaimed. "Where did you learn to do that?"

Madril shrugged again. As far as he knew, he'd learned nothing, done nothing, simply made a picture of what he and everybody else saw every day. "It's easy," he said. He smiled up at her, crouched on her rock like a grasshopper. "Look. I'll do you."

But she was vain. And superstitious. Who knew what harm could come to her from a likeness left on a stone? "No, no," she chided. "Do something pretty. Do the osha. Do you remember what it looks like?"

He closed his eyes. When he opened them again, they sparkled. "Like this!" He sketched the handsome plant with nimble fingers, then handed the stone up to her.

"What an artist you are!" she exclaimed, seeing that he had, indeed, captured the plant, its umbrels and delicate leaves.

He smiled, then frowned. "I like to draw. Maybe . . . maybe I would like someday to be a great painter. But my mama told Papa she wants me to be a priest. I don't want to be that. To have to pray all the time. Be locked up in a church and have to give sermons. But she says no woman will have me."

Dona Inez, Apollonia reflected, was a wicked woman, taking her wounded vanity out on this child. Apollonia was angry, but she swallowed her anger and answered gently. "Anybody can pray all the time, not just priests," she said. "Look at me. I always talk to God and the saints, and sometimes they answer. When you were born, San Francisco himself told me you were blessed."

"He did?" Madril looked at her open-mouthed.

"Yes. I'm surprised your mama hasn't told you that by now. It happened. I heard the voice out of the *santo* himself. What it means is for you to find out."

"How?"

She shrugged. "Who knows? Perhaps the answer will just come. Sometimes it happens that way."

"But how will I know?"

"You just will. Now help me up. *Dios,* I'm stiff as a poker! Getting old is hard!"

Several years passed, drought years in which the summer rains were few and even the winter snow lay sparsely on the mountain slopes, so that the streams dwindled, the *acequia* shrank to a trickle, the fields of corn, beans, squash and chilies withered. Madril began working with the laborers, hoeing, carrying water, anything to stay out of his mother's sight for truly, he thought, she wished he had never been born, had never disgraced her beauty. The fact saddened him, but for comfort and mothering there was always Apollonia with her good heart, her sharp tongue, her eyes upon the foibles of mankind. It was she, finally, who got him apprenticed to Salazar the *santero,* the carver of wooden saints.

At first Madril had resisted. Yes, he made drawings of plants and trees, whittled little animals and small figures. But Salazar! The old man was nearly blind! His milky eyes were terrifying to look at!

"And you are so perfect yourself," Apollonia commented slyly. "For shame! And Salazar a holy man."

"But. . . ."

"No buts. Salazar needs help. He carved the San Francisco for the church in the capital with six toes on one foot and four on the other, not that the *santo* cares but think how it looks! And to city people at that! With you to guide his hands, mix the *yeso,* this won't happen. Besides, your father has already agreed."

Madril shook his head. There was still a problem. Salazar had a daughter, Alma, a light-footed, laughing thing, graceful as a butterfly. All the boys talked about her, made excuses to be near her, hoping for a word, a look from her fine eyes, while he himself only watched from afar, turned his face sadly away when she came near.

Apollonia read his mind. "One day a woman will look into your heart. Maybe even this one," she said. "For now . . . you're too young,

68

and so is she. Go and learn to do something with those clever hands of yours and stop thinking about girls."

Madril, who had been experiencing stirrings of heart and body, focused on the first part of her statement and looked up hopefully. "Truly?" he asked. "Do you promise?"

"I promise nothing. You must make your own life happen. But it could be so."

More and more every day Apollonia was feeling age reduce her, make her irritable, especially when questioned about life and love, when begged for potions to stimulate desire. What, now, had these things to do with her? She had known desire, seen the results. It was the way of life, but life, suddenly, seemed very long and hard, and the posturings of male and female a wayward thread in a far greater tapestry. What, after all, was any of them — she, the boy, the *santero*, the laborers in the fields — compared to the fields themselves, the arc of sky above?

"Someday you'll know," she grumbled. "More I can't tell you."

"You always say that." Suddenly Madril felt himself to be alone, lacking guidance, an uncomfortable state that made him feel even more helpless than he was. He squared his shoulders, however, and looked at his friend. "All right," he said, "I'll go to Salazar."

Much to his astonishment old Salazar was kind, was good — almost, but not quite, taking the place of a mother. Like Apollonia, Salazar had a reverence for the trees from which he carved, for the earth that nourished them, for the saints themselves, those luminous personages who, quite often, he paused to consult. These consultations were akin to Apollonia's prayers, to her murmurings over plants and at sick beds, and in a short while Madril became accustomed to the constant sound of the old man's voice.

"So now, blessed Santiago . . . we have your horse except for the hoofs. He's a fine horse, don't you think? But the feet . . . the feet . . . where to put them in this wood that has no more room. Ah, Santiago, lend me your eyes, your holiness. . . ." And then: "Madril!

Are you here? Come help me with these hoofs — four of them that must go so!" A gesture with gnarled hands, a glance upward to heaven where the saints looked down upon their re-creator and lent their aid, a reaching out for the boy who had become his eyes, his fingers without any effort at all. The boy was good, possessed of an instinct, a knowledge in his bones. God and the saints be praised!

Alma was another matter. It was she who gathered the plants, the roots to make the dyes that were added to the *yeso,* she who stirred the whole mess in a pot to which horns and hoofs had been added to make the glue, all the while teaching Madril, talking to him as if he had no horrible mark upon his face.

"You see," she instructed, "wild plum roots to make the red of Santiago's jacket, ephedra for San Isidro's green one, sumac for the cloak of the Holy Mother." And, when his attention wandered, when he was dazzled by the vision of her hair, blue black and shining like a raven in the sun, she would stamp her foot. "Come back! Listen! My father is old. All he has left is us and the knowledge in his hands. We need you, Madril, so please pay attention."

And her voice, like the thunder in the mountains, like the softness of streams, the fact that she spoke of need, would bring him back to the job at hand. It was for her that he labored, learned, mixed the dyes and the foul-smelling glue into paint; it was for Alma that he sought out the pine trees, the pulpy cottonwood, and carved, carefully and slowly, terrified of error. It was for Alma that he prayed, awkwardly at first and then with gathering fluency. He prayed to the Santo Niño with His tiny shoes, His staff, to the Blessed Child who cherished the fallen and brought them hope; he prayed to Santiago, the mounted warrior who had fought the Moors, and to San Francisco, the gentle saint who spoke to and loved the creatures of earth, and who had decreed him, Madril, blessed.

Gradually, so slowly that no one noticed, it was Madril who became the *santero,* who freed the figures trapped within the wood, who applied the paint, murmured prayers. Gradually Salazar retired

70

to the shade of the cottonwood tree, his blind eyes turned inward on a vision no one but he could see. Gradually, Alma and Madril became two halves of a whole, their hands working in synchronicity, oblivious to everything but the pleasure of bringing the *santos* to life. Madril forgot that he was marked. The girl never mentioned it, looked at him without seeming to notice or care.

It was the third year of the drought. The sky remained clear; the winds were harsh and constant. The mountains, bare of snow, pierced heaven with purple shoulders, and the people of the village went hungry, their prayers unanswered.

Apollonia advised them. "San Isidro," she said, "you must take him out to bless the fields. To bring the rain and your seed to life. We must pray for a miracle, and never mind that the priest is not here. We must do for ourselves."

So the people unlocked the doors of the church and took San Isidro with his oxen and his companion angel from the niche where he stood. They dusted the cobwebs from the horns of the beasts and wiped the good saint's face. Then they went home to prepare for the fiesta, for the blessing of their fields.

Late that afternoon with the sun already behind the western mountains and long shadows marking the valley floor, Apollonia returned from the hills. Her basket was still half empty. The drought had brought hardship to her, too, for many of the herbs that she needed were gone, were withered, or had moved higher up the mountain where she could no longer go. Seeing that the wooden door to the church was open, she paused in the tiny courtyard. It was time to make a prayer, she decided, a real prayer, not like those constantly in her mind. She set down her basket, covered her head with her *rebozo,* and entered the church.

Inside it was cool and dark, and she stood a minute, squinting toward the altar. Someone had been here before her. A candle flickered at the feet of the Virgin and cast strange shadows along the white walls and over the *vigas* that formed the ceiling. Someone must

71

also have come to pray. Slowly she made her way down the aisle between the rows of rough benches toward the niche where San Isidro had stood for so many years. But the niche, when she got there, was empty. The saint, his patient oxen, the tiny angel were gone. Where could they be?

She glanced around, but saw no one. Perhaps the statue had been removed for a new coat of paint before the ceremony. Perhaps even now Madril and Alma were painting the *santo*'s green coat, polishing his high black boots, gilding the angel's wings, while Salazar sat on his bench under the cottonwood, listening to the music of their voices.

Apollonia genuflected, crossed herself, and hurried out of the church. At Salazar's the three sat over a frugal supper set out on the big pine table carved by the *santero* himself as a young man. As she moved toward them, they seemed, for a moment, to be surrounded by light like the radiance that surrounded the saints.

But Apollonia had no time for mysticism. "Where is San Isidro?" she called, stopping beside them.

They looked up, their faces questioning.

"Why?" asked Alma.

"Because he isn't in church. I thought you had him . . . were painting him. But if you don't know, then he's gone. Stolen. Taken away from us."

Only the trill of the mockingbird that had taken over the tallest branch of the cottonwood broke the silence. Then old Salazar stood, pushing back his stool and gripping the table edge. In the yellow light his blind eyes shone like opals.

"Thieves!" he quavered. "It was thieves! I know! I heard them and thought it was a dream . . . heard their running feet . . . and they sounded heavy like they carried a burden."

"Who?" Apollonia asked. "Who was it, *viejo?*"

He shook his head. "Strangers. Perhaps from some place that needs the saint more than we do."

"Curse them! Nobody needs him more. Another year like this, and

72

we'll all starve. And I won't be able to help with all the herbs and prayers that I know." She stood straight and waved her hand. "I hope San Isidro crushes their shoulders with his weight. And the oxen, too. I hope they scatter their own bones in their fields. Our children are hungry."

"Maybe he'll bless us for our intent," the old man said. "After all, in heaven they see everything."

Apollonia snorted. Faith was good, but it wasn't enough. You had to meet God and His saints half way. "Madril!" She turned to the boy who hadn't spoken or moved. "You will carve us a new saint. Get to work! Don't stand there like a stone!"

"But. . . ." His dark brows met over the bridge of his nose where the tiny red hand grew darker.

"But . . . but! You're always full of buts. Tomorrow is the Feast of San Isidro. Without his blessing we will all starve."

"I'll help," Alma said. She put her hand on Madril's. "You carve, and I'll paint. If we work all night, we can do it."

"I'll help, too," Apollonia said, removing her *rebozo*. "I'm old, but my hands are still steady."

And so through the night they worked — by the light of the lamps, under the brilliance of a moon that rose and seemed to hesitate overhead, striking silver from the leaves of the tree, illuminating the four laborers, Madril, Alma, Apollonia, and the white-haired Salazar who, sightless though he was, could still manage to make the platform upon which the *santo* would be carried to the fields. No craftsmanship was needed for that, only the feel of the wood becoming level under his plane.

Madril made the oxen first — two patient, wide-eyed beasts yoked together. Animals were easy with their rectangular bodies, their heavy heads and slender legs. When they were finished, he passed them to the two women who dipped their yucca brushes into the paint and gave the beasts color, spots, soulful eyes.

Before he began the statue of Isidro, Madril offered a prayer.

"Guide my hands," he murmured in imitation of Salazar. "Help me bring happiness back to our village."

Then, taking the knife with the sharpest blade, he began to carve. Slowly a broad hat, a head, wide shoulders, a long torso and longer legs emerged into the moonlight like a butterfly from a webbed cocoon.

Shortly before dawn, with the moon sinking in the west, and the east turning pale like the inside of a shell, Madril finished the *santo* and with reverence handed him to his assistants. Now there remained only the angel, a small radiance, the angel who, according to legend, had plowed Isidro's fields, leaving the saint free to pray. Happily, knowing that he would indeed finish in time, Madril carved a whimsical, laughing angel, one that would dance behind the yoked oxen, tread lightly on the furrows, bless the seeds, the fields, and on delicate wings return to the sky from which he had come.

"*¡Dios!*" Apollonia said, seeing the little figure. "This angel is laughing! You can't have an angel who laughs!"

Madril straightened up, irritated. Who was this woman to criticize what he had done? "Why not?"

"It's serious being an angel," she retorted. "Living with God, you don't laugh."

Alma intervened. "I think it's wonderful," she said. "Of course God laughs, and the angel is happy being with Him, being sent to guide the plow. He knows he'll make us a miracle, and so he laughs."

She smiled at Madril, willing her delight into him, and, amazed, he smiled back, aware of the leap of his heart.

Salazar awoke then and turned his head this way and that. "What's all the noise? Have you finished? Is it done?"

"The angel is laughing," Apollonia told him. "God help us all!"

"So?" the old man said. "This is a feast day. Even angels can enjoy it. Leave the boy alone. His hands don't lie. He is blessed."

At the familiar words Apollonia fell silent. Was this what San Francisco had meant? That the boy would bring prosperity back to the village through the cleverness of his hands, the simplicity of his soul? She smoothed her skirt and arranged her *rebozo*. "Finish the painting," she said to Alma. "I'll go and tell everyone that we have a new San Isidro. That the old one wasn't good enough."

She was aware of her persistent irritation, as if she had lost something, a power, a strength. Madril's fault, of course. He no longer needed her, had even challenged her opinion, and had been supported by Salazar, by that slender stem of a girl who was always making eyes at him. That's what was wrong with the young! They grew up, away from those who cared. They changed allegiances and left those who had loved them adrift.

"I hope," she said to San Francisco as she went out onto the dusty street, "I hope you know what's happening here. What you were doing when you marked that child and then blessed him!" Then she was shocked at her own audacity and quickly crossed herself. "I'm growing old and short tempered. He's a good boy. I know that. Please, San Francisco, forget what I said." The sun came over the mountain at that moment, turning the valley gold, touching the western slopes with flame, and she took the burst of light as a forgiveness of her shortcomings, a communication from the *santo* directly to her.

The procession into the fields was all that such a ceremony should be. Guitars, violins, flutes, drums accompanied the singing, and Madril himself was chosen as one of the bearers of the *santo*. Directly behind came Salazar, guided by Alma and Apollonia. In a long line the villagers crossed the *acequia* and wended their way through the drought-stricken fields, while high above their heads the *santo* in his fine green jacket swayed, the oxen looked out, wide eyed, and the little angel laughed in pure delight.

Later there were those who swore that he turned his head and looked down on Madril, and that San Isidro himself moved, smiled, blessed the boy with a special gesture. There were those who swore that the birthmark, from that day onward, began to shrink. Perhaps

75

this was imagination, or perhaps they had never really paid any attention to Madril in the first place.

Certainly after the rain came, there was too much work and rejoicing for anyone to take much notice of a mark on a boy's face. Even on the day of the wedding, when the priest came to make Madril and Alma man and wife, most of the attention was upon the bride who wore her mother's old lace veil and who carried a bouquet of flowers and herbs gathered by Apollonia. She was, everyone said, the most beautiful bride the village had ever seen.

The little angel agreed. From his niche in the wall, from his place beside San Isidro, behind the oxen, unnoticed by anyone, he stretched out his graceful hands and smiled.

GOOD MEDICINE

I fell in love with Jack Trader the summer I was thirteen and he came riding in with a bunch of horses, one of them for me. Jack Trader wasn't his real name, but out here in the Sand Hills in those days nobody asked questions about people's names or where they came from, especially not with men like Jack. Oh, he was friendly enough, and good to look at, too, with hair black as an Indian's and a pair of steel gray eyes that met yours straight on, but the fact is that Jack was a horse thief, and everybody knew it. And there were rumors about him having killed a man down in Texas, and something in those eyes of his told you maybe that was true and you'd better not push or you'd end up the same. Besides, all the ranchers, my dad included, bought those horses he stole from who-knows-where. They were good horses, unbranded, and good horseflesh was needed on places it might take a man two days to ride around, mending fence or checking cattle.

When I was little, I thought our place, the Circle B, was the world. There wasn't a town anywhere near, and we raised what we needed in the way of food, so there was no reason to leave. In fact, if anybody had asked me if I wanted to go to a city, I would've been suspicious and said: "No thank you, I'm fine right here."

I was, too. My mother died birthing me, and my dad never had time to find himself another wife. He brought me up like I was a boy — no frills, no gew gaws, no dolls to play with, although Mary White Tail, the Cheyenne woman who cooked for us, sometimes made me a dolly out of a corn cob with pieces of sacking for a skirt. Mary had been to what the Indians called "White Man's School," and she read the ladies' magazines and had her notions about the

77

little, motherless kid in her charge. I was more interested in horses than dolls, though. My daddy put me on a horse as soon as I could walk and turned me loose shortly after.

The hands looked after me, had the raising of me, and I like to think I didn't turn out too bad, though I still feel penned up in towns, and I have a habit of catching my heels in skirts and falling flat on my face. If you're born in the Sand Hills, you're never quite at home anywhere else. I don't know why, but it's true. There's something about the sky and how those hills reach up like they're trying to touch it or imitate the shapes of the summer clouds that build up on the edge of the world. The wind blows, and the grass rustles, and once in a while a lark sings so sweet it could break your heart. And when the cranes fly over, you wish you could sprout wings and go with them, it's that exciting — and lonely, too, like the silence after they're gone. Who'd want to leave a place like that?

Not me. I never even left to go to school. We had a hand who taught me my letters, and I learned to count keeping track of cattle. For the rest I had books and taught myself a lot, even though I did fall in love with a horse thief.

The spring I was to turn thirteen I was itching for a real horse, one of my own. I'd been riding a lop-eared, gangly gelding named Frying Pan since I could remember, and he was older than I was. Besides, I wanted a challenge, and the only challenge I got out of Frying Pan was trying to make him move.

Jack always liked to put on a good show when he brought the horses in, pushing them into a run down the lane and into the old post corral where they'd stop and blow and snort, curving their necks and acting spooked in general. That day he ran in six or seven head — bays and duns and a spotted critter spookier than the rest that just wouldn't calm down but went high-stepping around the fence, tossing his head and rolling his eyes, his black tail aloft.

I closed the gate and went over to Jack who dismounted. By way of greeting he said: "You're growing up quicker than a shoat."

I didn't have a ready answer for that, so I grinned and said: "Thirteen next week."

"You still riding that Frying Pan horse?" His eyes were twinkling.

"Yep." I sighed and looked up at him, wondering if I could get him to put in a word for me.

"Well," he scratched his chin. "Well, I got to thinking about that, and I said to myself: 'That old Frying Pan is just about ready for the pasture.' That's the truth, isn't it?"

I nodded.

"Well," he said again, pointing with his head toward the spotted critter snaking along the fence, "what do you think of that one?"

"He looks crazy," I said. "Is he broke?"

"Yep. But he's got a problem. He hates men."

"Why?" I asked.

"Fella that had him beat him. Broke a rake handle on him."

I could feel anger growing. Abuse of animals wasn't allowed on the Circle B. Any hand caught abusing a horse was off the place by nightfall. "No such thing as a mean horse . . . just people," my daddy always said, and he was right. And Jack agreed with him. I knew that.

"What'd you do?" I asking, knowing he'd surely done something.

He chuckled. "Broke an axe handle over *his* head and left him in the straw. Took the horse. It's a good horse. I tried him, and he's well trained, but it's not in him to trust a man any more. Then I thought, seein' as you're nearly thirteen and a girl, maybe you'd like him."

I stared at him in wonder.

"Cat got your tongue?" he asked.

I shook my head. Falling in love boggles a person. You can't think, can't get your mouth to working right, don't know whether to laugh or cry. Love is like that in general, part happiness, part tears. I knew that from the first, just like I knew that me, and Jack, and that spotted horse were all tied up together by a rope that went 'round our hearts.

I scuffed my boot toe in the sand. "I reckon you'll have to ask Dad," I said finally. The words sounded foolish, ungrateful, like I'd forgot my manners or never had any. I swallowed hard and looked up. "I'd sure like him, though. And thank you."

"You leave your dad to me." He handed his reins over. "Give this old boy a rub down and some feed when he's cooled off. He's had a hard couple weeks."

At that point I'd have done anything he asked me — cleaned his boots, done his laundry in the big wash tub behind the house, even cut his hair, a job I was pretty good at. A horse! And a real spirited one at that! I took extra care with the big bay, cooling him down and brushing the saddle marks off him before giving him his grain. By the time I got through, my dad and Jack had come out to the corrals and were watching the herd.

"I don't know," my dad was saying. "That gal thinks she can handle anything, but this horse looks like he needs a man's hand."

He and Jack knew I could hear and were waiting for me to take the bait. I did. "Please, Dad," I said, running up to him. "Let me try. He's a good horse except some no 'count beat him. Did Jack tell you?"

He nodded. "He did. And that's what worries me. It'll take you a while to win that one over. Look at him." He pointed into the corral where the horse was still wide-eyed and prancing like somebody was shooting at him with a pea shooter.

"Please let me try," I pleaded. "Give me two weeks."

My dad propped one foot on the fence. "What d'you say, Jack?"

Jack nodded once. "Big gal like Jessie needs her own horse, not that sorry bag of bones she's been hauling around. Hell, that horse is older than God."

We all laughed, then I headed for the barn to get a rope and halter. Nobody was more surprised than I was when that spotted critter let me walk right up and halter him. I'd figured on at least a little bit of fight. But that came later.

He stood gentle as a lamb while I brushed him down, bent his head for the bridle, and opened his mouth for the bit, nice as you please. Now a lot of horses will fight taking the bit till you think a good whipping is just what they deserve but, if you lose your temper with an animal, you lose your control, too. My daddy taught me that before he even put me on a horse, and I know it's true. Horses know who likes them and who doesn't, and they remember pain just like people.

He danced a little when I tightened the cinch, but any horse does that, and it's understandable. I wouldn't want a big strap tight around my belly, either. Anyhow, he stood still as a stone till I got on, and then the fun started. He arched his neck, rocked back on his haunches, and took off up the lane at a dead run. Somebody, probably the man who beat him, had ruined his mouth. It was hard as iron. He clamped his old jaws down on the bit, and I might as well have been riding without one for all the notice he took of me. I couldn't stop him, so I screwed down in the saddle for the ride.

And what a ride! That horse was fast. And sure-footed. And he had bottom, too. We were out in the Sand Hills before I knew it, moving so quick everything looked blurred. The wind was in my face, and I'd lost my hat, and that critter was running smooth as water under me. It was fun. No, it was more than that. It was like being alive for the first time.

"*Yippee!*" I yelled, and he caught my excitement, flattened his ears against his head, and ran faster. It was sure different from riding old Frying Pan.

We went five miles before he slowed down, and I could circle him back toward home. With the edge off him he was as good a horse as I ever rode. It was like he and I had become the same animal, one mind between us. For the second time that day I fell in love.

In the distance I saw Jack and my dad headed toward me, probably thinking I'd been thrown and dragged. I waved, and they waved back and, when we met up, I started talking before Dad could lay down the law. "He's a good horse," I said. "He's just fine."

81

"You call a runaway fine?" My dad, I could see, had been worried to death.

"He just had to get it out," I explained. "Watch us."

Right out there in the hills we did figure eights, we loped, jogged, stopped on a dime, side passed, like we had one body. "See?" I said, stopping in front of them. "See? He's fine."

Dad shook his head. "The day that horse kills you is the day he gets a bullet in his head. You, too, Jack."

Jack just grinned. "This little gal and that horse are made for each other. Hell, George, when you were thirteen, you could've ridden him."

"She's a girl," my dad answered. "And she's all I've got."

"Jessie and I will take our chances," Jack said. "Won't we, Jess?"

"Yep," I said, vowing that nobody would get that horse away from me, not if I had to sleep in the corral and him on a rope tied to my waist.

We started back then, just sort of moseying and me looking down at the spots that were all over the horse — black spots, no bigger than a dollar on a white coat. That, together with his black mane and sooty legs, made a pretty sight. I'd never seen a horse marked like him, and I said so.

That's when Jack explained about appaloosas, and how the Nez Percé Indians had bred them for a long time, longer than anybody could remember. They were tough horses, he said, and smart, and they were spotted all over like mine, or dark with spots on their rumps. Those Indians were proud of their horses, and careful about breeding them, and everything was fine till the Indian wars came with all the fighting and killing. Jack told me how one chief named Joseph had led his people on a long march away from the American Army, and how they starved and died in the cold because they didn't want to give up their freedom.

"Like some of those mustangs?" I asked. "The ones that'll die before they let themselves get caught?"

"Sort of," he answered. "It's a funny thing about freedom and living on your own home ground. It gets in your bones, and the idea of being penned in is like dying. Worse, maybe. Those Injuns didn't want to be locked up, put on a reservation in some strange place. They wanted back at Wallowa where they'd come from. So they fought. And ran. And died. And when they finally gave up, the Army killed all the spotted horses they could find. I guess they figured it'd keep the Injuns in one place. I'd say it damn' near broke their hearts."

"Killed horses?" My voice came out squeaky like an old windmill. I couldn't imagine anybody killing good animals.

He nodded, and his eyes were sad. I knew he felt like me — helpless and kind of sick. "Yep," he said. "They did. And the chief, Joseph, stood up and made a speech. He said: 'From where the sun now stands, I will fight no more forever.' And he didn't."

In my mind I could see it, though I wished I couldn't. The dead horses piled helter-skelter, and the coyotes and buzzards circling. And the old chief with a broken heart. I reached down and patted that spotted neck, ran a hand down the coarse black mane. "I'll call this horse Joseph," I said. "After the chief. It's a good name."

The thing about Jack was, he knew to take things I said seriously. He knew what I was thinking and feeling just like it was himself, and he gave me a look and a smile I still remember. Then he said: "It sure is a good name, honey. And it's honorable. That horse'll do you proud."

Of course he was right. Jack was always right about horses and usually about people.

It took only a few days before Joseph was nickering whenever he saw me, and a few more runaways before I figured how to hold him, and he got to understanding what I wanted. After that, well, I was hardly ever in the house till after nightfall. I was out riding, doing the work of a man, me and my spotted horse that loved me. Not that we didn't run sometimes. Joseph purely loved running, free as a bird, and the wind whistling in our ears like a song. He was a running fool, and he ran to win.

Sometimes on a Sunday, if the chores were done and time hung heavy, the boys and I would race down the lane and out into the hills. Joseph and I never lost, and after about three years the boys took it into their heads that I should challenge Colonel Buford's big hot-blooded chestnut, Chase, at the Fourth of July races.

Now, the colonel was from back East — Tennessee or Kentucky — and he had some fine blood horses, the best of which was Chase who'd never lost a race that I'd heard about. The colonel had a son, too, Randy, a few years older than me and downright spoiled. See, the Bufords were rich, and that kid had got everything he wanted from the time he was old enough to bawl for it. I hated him, and he knew it, although by that summer he was trying to change my mind, asking me to dance at parties and stuff. I hated that, too, and the fact that Mary White Tail insisted I dress like one of the ladies in those magazines she was always reading, and that, dancing, I had to touch Randy's hands that were always soft and wet like a dog had been licking them, when the plain truth was I'd given my heart to Jack Trader, and no brat could ever take his place.

I'd been half way considering staying home that year, but the idea of Joseph racing Chase and showing those Bufords a thing or two caught my fancy. "You think we can win?" I asked Hy Tucker, our foreman, who not only was good with horses but could call hogs with the best of them.

Hy took the straw he was chewing out of his mouth and gave me a look that said he thought I was a fool. "Think on it," he said. "That Chase has been racing Injun ponies and farmer's hosses and makin' himself and the colonel look good. But he's done in after a mile or so. Those long legs have been carryin' him, is all. Now, old Joseph here, he's just gettin' started when the rest of 'em quit. Besides, he can't stand to lose. You know it. I know it. It's only the colonel don't know it" — he put the straw back between his teeth — "yet," he added.

"And Randy?" I said

Hy gave me another look. "He's courtin' you."

"He can court me till doomsday!" I hopped off the fence. "I wouldn't have him if he was the President!"

"Good thing," Hy said. "He's worthless. I'm glad you got some sense."

I had sense all right. My only problem was how to get Jack to notice me. But I couldn't ask Hy's advice about that. It was my secret. Mine and Joseph's.

Everybody in the county went to the Fourth of July barbecue at the Bufords'. It was the social event of the year with dancing, tables of food set out on their porch, fireworks after dark, and, of course, the races. And the colonel and his wife, Alice, were good hosts even if, sometimes, they acted a little superior to some of their guests. Uppity was what people called them. They didn't fit into that country and never would, but folks came, had a good time, ate their food just the same, and talked about all of it until the next year.

Dad, Hy, and I drove over in the wagon with Joseph hitched to the back. The rest of the boys rode their horses, hollering and whooping, and leaving us far behind. Joseph's saddle was in the wagon alongside the box that held the new dress Mary White Tail had sewed and insisted I wear for the dancing. It had a long skirt with a flounce, and a ruffled neckline that I thought looked foolish on me, but she thought it was past time for me to get out of britches and boots, and be a girl, and she said so every time she got the chance. The only reason I agreed to take that dress was that she told me she heard Jack Trader was at the colonel's, and that he had as much an eye for a pretty girl as he had for a horse. And she smiled like a barn cat when she said it.

"Damn it, Mary," I said. "That's bribery, and you know it."

"You stop that cussin'," she retorted. "Men don't like women that

85

cuss. You been runnin' wild so long you've lost your manners."

Well, maybe I had, but I was comfortable with myself. And any man who wanted me would have to take me the way I was. Even Jack. If I could just get him to see that I'd grown up. I sighed and took the box. "Wish me luck," I said to her. "I'll sure need it."

She fished in the pocket of her skirt and brought out a smooth blue stone. "Good medicine," she said. "Just don't lose it."

Well, maybe it was good medicine, but it sure brought a bunch of trouble before luck finally set in. Or maybe that's how life is. Maybe you have to fight a lot of battles to win the war, otherwise you turn out like Randy, good for nothing and not able to help yourself.

Anyhow, we got there in good time, and I took Joseph around back to the corral where the horses were being saddled. The first person I saw was Randy, all dressed up with new boots, a fancy vest, and a red silk scarf tied around his neck. He looked like nobody I'd ever seen, and didn't want to. He said: "I've been looking for you."

"What for?" I was tired of being polite to him, and besides he was so swell-headed he couldn't recognize an insult if you spelled it out. He answered like he hadn't heard me, and that was probably true.

"What're you doing back here? This is the saddling arena."

Saddling arena, my foot! It was just a pen behind the stables. But Randy had another problem. He was always trying to talk like the Englishman who'd spent some time hunting in the Sand Hills. It was natural for *him* to sound the way he did, but Randy just sounded like he'd been reading a dictionary and needed to blow his nose. "I'm in the race," I told him. "Me and Joseph. And you make him nervous, so you'd better leave."

It was the truth. Joseph was dancing around and rolling his eyes at Randy like he'd like to take a kick at him, proving what I already knew. Randy was no good.

"Race?" His mouth opened so wide it looked like a blowout. "Race? You and this bronc are going to race Chase?"

He laughed until I wanted to kick him myself. "Go away, Randy,"

I said instead. "You're not very nice."

He was still laughing, but he said: "Use your head, Jessie. He's a good horse and all that, but you'll just make a fool out of yourself if you take on Chase."

"Thank you." I tightened the cinch strap

From across Joseph's back I saw Jack, and I swear my heart jumped into my throat. I waved, and he waved back and came over, laying a big hand on Joseph's neck. The horse nickered. He and I were still of one mind. "Come to win and give the colonel apoplexy?" Jack asked.

"Yes," I said.

Randy made a noise. "You're both loco. Wait'll Father hears." He said, "Fahthah." It made me sick.

"Best go tell him, then," I said, and stuck my tongue out at his back.

"Now, Jessie," Jack said.

"Don't 'now, Jessie' me." The words came out before I could stop them. "He's awful. Even Joseph thinks so."

"Horse sense." He grinned, then got serious. "If you're going to win, you'll have to forget about Randy. Concentrate on what you're doing. Don't take the lead if you can help it. Just stay on Chase's heels and push him hard. He's no stayer, and he'll fold after about a mile and a half. Then you open up. It'll be a two-horse race. You and him, and never mind the rest of 'em. Think you can do it?"

"I'll try," I said, wishing he'd kiss me for luck and wondering what it would feel like to be kissed.

What he did was cuff me on the shoulder like I was a boy, and I thought I should have listened to Mary, acted like a girl and prettied myself instead of trying to ride races. But I didn't have time for regrets. The colonel was calling us to the starting line. Jack gave me a leg up, though I didn't need one, and walked me toward the two-mile track. "One more thing," he said before we reached the others. "Watch out for that jockey on Chase. He's a pro, and he's mean. I've heard a few things about him being kicked off some tracks."

"We'll be fine," I said, and guided Joseph into the line.

While I listened to the colonel welcoming everybody, I looked around at the competition. There were a few kids on horses that'd be finished after half a mile, a couple cowhands riding the top of their strings, a rancher or two, but Jack was right. It'd be between Chase and Joseph, between me and that crooked jockey who looked like a grasshopper on that tall critter's back, and who was grinning at me with a look so purely evil I put my hand in my pocket to touch Mary's blue stone.

Under me I felt Joseph gather himself. He knew why we were there, and he was ready when the colonel dropped the flag. Chase with those long legs of his took the lead, but we were right behind him. I had my work cut out trying to keep Joseph back. That little horse was mad. He couldn't understand why I was pulling him, and he kept fighting for his head so he could run his rival into the dust. The rest of the horses were strung out behind us just like we'd figured. By the time we made the first turn, we were hanging on Chase's flank, aggravating that rider who kept looking back to see what we were doing.

By the time we'd gone the mile, Jack's strategy began to pay off. Chase was tiring, and Joseph was pure energy. All he wanted was permission to go and, when I gave it, he stretched out his neck, dropped his belly almost to the ground, and pulled alongside. That was when that jockey made his move, crowding us, bumping us, and throwing Joseph off his stride. He collected himself quick, but out of the corner of my eye I saw that rider raise his whip, and I knew what was coming. He caught me on the shoulder at the same time Chase rammed us again. Joseph stumbled and went to his knees, and I went off the other side like a rag doll.

What happened after that I only know from hearing about it. I hit the ground and was knocked cold. They say Joseph won the race

without me and then came back to stand guard, showing his heel
and his teeth to everybody who came close. It was Jack who finally
got him calmed down. And it was Jack who picked me up and carried
me to our wagon in spite of the Bufords' yelling about going to the
hospital at Fort Robinson.

What Jack said was it'd be a cold day in hell before he left me
with folks who let a crooked jockey foul a race and put me in danger.
"Send the sawbones out to the ranch," he told them, and then he went
out to the stables with blood in his eye, intending to take that jockey
apart piece by piece and feed him to the buzzards.

What I heard was that he said: "If that gal dies, there'll be a killing
in the Sand Hills," and he dragged that little insect around in the dust
for about five minutes. He might have killed him except that Randy,
who'd never fought fair in his life, came up behind and beaned him
with a two by four.

Half way home I came to, and the first thing I saw was Joseph
watching me over the tail gate of the wagon. Then I saw Jack
stretched out beside me. He had one eye black and swelled shut, and
a rag tied around his head. And he was still out cold. I ached all over,
and was seeing double; it was hard to sit up, but I managed. "Wha
happened?" I got out. "What happened to Jack?"

Dad and Hy turned around, looked me over for damage, a
grinned when they saw me awake.

"Thank God," my dad said. "Now you lie still, honey. We'll
you home."

"Is he dead?" My eyes were still blurred, but it was from tea

"He ain't dead. Ain't likely to be," Hy said. "That no-'count Ra
got him from behind. And then I got *him*. That kid'll be si
through a straw for months."

My dad laughed, but the sound had no fun in it. "Serve him
That whole bunch never heard about fair play. Winning's no
unless it's done square."

Just then Jack groaned, and I bent over him so I could see

89

My tears fell all over his face. "Why, Jessie," he whispered. "What're you crying for?"

I was so happy to hear him talk, I told the truth. "I thought you were dead," I said.

He focused his one good eye on me. "I don't die easy."

"How'd I know? There you were, all messed up, and it's all my fault, and I wanted to die, too!"

I cried harder, couldn't stop, because all of a sudden I got a picture of the world with no Jack in it. No more excitement, nobody to listen to me, to understand and encourage.

He reached out and grabbed hold of my hand. "Nobody ever cried over me," he said, like he was trying to believe it.

I was blubbering like a kid, I felt so bad for him, his saying that. "Why not? Didn't anybody ever love you?" I wailed out the words without caring how I sounded.

He took a long time answering. I could see my dad and Hy on the seat, sitting straight and stiff, pretending they'd gone deaf. That gray eye opened wide and stared right into my heart. "Not so I noticed," he said.

He smiled, and squeezed my hand tight, and Joseph stuck his head into the wagon bed and nickered, as if to say: "Hey! What about me?"

I lay down again, close up against Jack Trader just to make sure he didn't let go of my hand. Then I said: "Well, from here on, you'd better take notice of me . . . and Joseph."

He chuckled, though it must have hurt him. "I reckon I'd better," he said.

That's when I felt the stone in my pocket, Mary White Tail's good medicine, and thought how things in life — like people, and good and evil, and horses, and those summer green hills holding up the sky were all of a piece like a fine quilt or a story with a happy ending. I figured I'd be wearing Mary's fancy dress after all. To my wedding.

Then I sighed, and closed my eyes, and let the wagon carry us home.

MOVING ON

Nell Pomerene stopped on the edge of the stubble field and looked down at the house in the valley. It seemed lonesome in the middle of the bare yard where a few chickens scratched the hard dirt, and the sunflowers she'd planted in an effort to pretty the place drooped for lack of water. Their heads hung sadly, like hopeless faces, like the faces of her parents who had come here filled with dreams and seen them dashed, one by one, by the winds, the drought, the blizzards, the grasshoppers that cleaned off crops like a mowing machine and left bare ground behind them.

She stood on the sandy track for a minute, listening to the silence. Where *was* everybody? Where was her mother? It was wash day, but the big iron wash tub stood empty over the ashes of last week's fire, and the clothes — work shirts, diapers, shirtwaists that should have been drying in the breeze — weren't there. Where were her baby brothers, Luke and John, toddlers but active, so that the yard always resounded with the sound of little feet and infant squabbling? Where were the mules, Roy and Sally, their long ears cocked, their big mule heads hanging over the wire fence, waiting for supper?

She stood still and watched and listened, and when nothing familiar reached her but the sound of the wind in her ears, she began to run toward the house, her feet kicking up small spurts of dust.

"Mama!" she called. "Mama!"

No answer came. She stopped and stared at the blank face of the house, and then she was running again, terror at her heels.

"Mama! Mama!"

And the rustle of the prairie was around her — wind, crickets in the weeds, in the bending red grass. In the house there was nothing.

The pots and pans were gone, the bedding, the quilts, the trunks where clothes were kept. In the house was only the sweep of wind through the sagging door and the echoes of voices she could almost, but not quite, hear. In the house was a note scrawled in her mama's hand on a torn piece of brown paper.

We moved on.

That was all. That and the empty feeling in her stomach, the mockery of the silence that wasn't silence at all but a thousand small sounds that added to her terror. She was alone. She, Nell Pomerene, was all that was left, all that there was to prove that once a family had lived here, had laughed, and loved, and worked the fields, hoping for prosperity. She didn't cry. Couldn't. Tears never solved anything, and besides, only babies cried — her two brothers, their faces red and crinkled, roaring like healthy young animals. Luke and John, gone, with her parents, leaving her, Nell, fourteen years old, on her own.

She sat down on the edge of her bed and thought her way clear to her bones, and what she found was herself — alone, abandoned, but with a gut feeling that she wasn't meant to die for a long while. What lay ahead was struggle, and strife, and years. She knew that. Took it on her small shoulders, tried it, and found herself able.

After a long time she got up and went to the kitchen where she found an overlooked pot with dented sides, two shriveled potatoes, and a small onion in the back of the bin. Food first. Then sleep if it came. Trouble would keep until morning.

The sun rolled like a wheel on the edge of the plain, and the house creaked around her the way it always did except that, empty now, the sound was threatening. She lay still, wondering if she had dreamed it all, thinking that any minute now her mother would come in saying: "You going to sleep your life away?"

But no one came, and after a while she got up and went outside and drew some water from the well. She looked at her reflection in the bucket and saw blue eyes, brown hair in long braids — an ordinary face, nothing to be ashamed of or to gloat over, either.

"Why me?" she asked the girl in the mirror. "Why'd they go off and leave *me?*"

Of course, there was no answer. She hadn't expected one, simply had wanted the companionship of a voice, had felt the need to ask the question though she knew she'd never know the truth of it. She thought of going to school, then realized she never had to go again if she didn't want to. She could do as she pleased, now and forever. She, Nell, was boss, but somehow the idea was frightening, and she shied away from it like a new colt that sees the open field for the first time and sticks beside its mother. But she had no mother.

"We moved on." She said the words aloud, finding in their brevity a coldness that implied she didn't count, was as easily erased as a figure drawn in the dust, as quickly forgotten as a leaf blown from a tree. What to do? She sat on the splintered log that served as a step, chin in her hands, and thought, looking out over the rise and fall of the prairie. There were families who needed a hired girl and who would take her in. And they'd likely work her to death because she had no one to speak for her. She supposed she could go to the Reverend Mason. He'd see she was treated right, would probably ship her off to the orphanage, an uncertain fate at best. She wasn't clever with her hands, except around animals, so work as a dress-maker was out, too. So many choices, yet so few. She shook her head. Her hair had come loose from its braid and blew across her face gently as cobwebs. Without thinking, she rebraided it, splashed water on herself, and shivered because the October air was cold. Soon it would be winter. Too soon. And she with no place to go, alone, hungry for a family as well as for food.

She heard the wagon before it crested the hill and came slowly down the track, and she squinted against the morning light, hope like a sweetness in her mouth. Maybe they'd come back! Missed her! She stood up and trotted across the yard, stopped and leaned on the fence, a woman waiting for life to happen.

Levi Solomon had been on the road since he was fourteen. At first he had gone on foot, carrying his peddler's pack until it seemed he'd been born with it, like a hunchback, felt naked without its bulk. And then one day he'd gotten lucky. In the far corner of Kansas, where the plain stood drought seared and wind blasted, a homesteader was packing up, turning his back on dream turned nightmare.

"Take the damned mule!" he shouted at Levi. "Take the damned wagon! There's a curse on all of it!"

He stood by the grave of his wife and child, his beard blowing around his face, his eyes wild so that he looked like a prophet shouting doom except to Levi, who didn't wait to be told twice. He hitched up the mule and drove away toward the West, the poor farmer's keening growing fainter and fainter until at last it was no more than the wail of a coyote, the scream of a hunting hawk. After that he prospered, bought another mule, and replaced the wagon with one designed as a home as well as a place to store his goods.

The whole West was his for the taking: the sand hills, the prairie, the mountain passes and meadows of the Rockies, and he went where he chose with his pots and pans, his needles and thread and bolts of cloth, his seeds and saplings, tablets, tools, and patent medicines, and the stories that flowed out of his mouth like honey. He was welcome at all the farms, the ranches. He brought news, gossip, messages, a touch of the theatrical for wives starved for the sound of a voice, to husbands bored with the sameness of it all.

The night before he had camped out and lay watching the stars and sniffing the frosty air like an old hound that feels the approach of winter. He was feeling old for the first time in twenty years of traveling, and he allowed himself the odd pleasure of imagining a home in a town, a store that wasn't ambulatory, a fire in his own hearth during long winter nights. "Ach, Levi," he had said out loud because he often talked to himself or to his mules that listened stolidly. "And what would you do in a house without the land for company?" He had shaken his head. The road was what he knew, the road and the land beckoning, he and his mules and wagon bobbing along like a small ship on waves of grass in a prairie sea.

He had climbed into the back of the wagon and slept, and in the morning had had a cold breakfast of bread and cheese. Then he had hitched his team and driven on until he had reached the stubble field and saw the sad house, the figure that leaned on the fence.

"No money there," he said, assessing the barren yard, the sagging roof. But the woman — at least he thought it was a woman — seemed to beckon him, standing alone in the center of it all. He clucked to his team and headed down the hill. "Good morning."

He tipped his old straw hat as he spoke, realizing that the person he had thought was a woman was a young girl and a frightened one, if he was any judge. In his years on the road he'd seen many such, women and girls, some with bloodied faces, some whose men had gone away, burying their dead. But none had aroused the compassion that this girl did, with her blue eyes the color of sky and her shoulders squared as if she would take on the world in spite of her fear.

"Hello." Her voice was low, but there was music in it, back in her throat like a songbird.

"Are you the lady of the house?" He spoke jokingly, hoping to put her at ease.

She shook her head. "No," she said. "No."

"Well then, your mama. Is she home? I have needles and good thread. And some fine wool for winter." He stepped down and came to stand beside her.

"She isn't here." He had to tilt his head to catch her whisper. "They left. Moved on."

Mein Gott! he thought, *to leave a child, a girl-child, out here alone. What kind of people were these?* "This is true?"

95

She nodded. "It's just me now." Her voice broke, and there was a glint of tears in her blue eyes, but she lifted her chin proudly.

"You have friends? Relatives?"

"Nobody who'd want me."

It got worse and worse. If he had sense, he'd get back in the wagon and leave, but he knew in his heart that he'd remember how she looked, standing in the yard with the empty house behind her, knew that she would haunt him no matter how far away he went. He said: "This is very bad."

She scuffed the toe of her worn boot in the sand then looked at him, at his mules, at the wagon with its water barrel, pots and herbs and harness bells strung on the outside like a Christmas tree. "Take me with you," she said.

"I can't. It isn't possible. People would talk. Say bad things."

"What people?"

She was being deliberately hard headed. What people, indeed! "My customers." He raised his voice. "Good women. What will they say when Levi Solomon comes to trade with a little *shiksa* sitting in his wagon? What?"

"Why should they say anything?" she wanted to know. "What you do isn't their business."

"My business is everybody's business. I have to be careful. People trust me. But they won't if they think they have to look out for their daughters in case I kidnap little girls."

Her head shot up. "I'm fourteen."

"And that makes you a grown-up?"

"My mother was married at fifteen."

" 'Marry in haste, repent at leisure,' " he quoted. "Look what happened. She left you." Then, seeing the hurt in her eyes, he wanted to cut off his tongue.

Strangely she came to her mother's defense. "She probably had reasons!"

He put a hand on her shoulder. "Listen to me," he said. "There is no good reason to leave a child, a daughter, out here alone. It was a bad thing. Wrong. But I won't make it worse. Get your clothes. You can come with me. At least," he added, "until we get to a town. Some place where maybe you can find work. Maybe even find your mama, who can tell?"

The look she gave startled him. He had thought her a plain little thing, but her eyes suddenly blazed with blue fire, and she smiled, it seemed with her whole body. "You won't be sorry," she said, breathless. "I can cook, and drive a team. And I'm good with animals. They like me. And you can say I'm your daughter. We'll be a family. I don't want to find mine. I don't want to see them again. Not ever!"

He thought how he would give anything to see his mother once more, but then she had never abandoned him, not until her death. Bitterness was a disease. It ate at a person from inside, and this child with her stubborn chin and fiery eyes was too young for such knowledge. "What's your name?" he asked her.

"Nell," she said. "Nell Pomerene. Not that I'm proud of it."

"So then, Nell," he said. "Get your things. Me, I'll catch some of these chickens to take with us. It would be a shame to leave them for the coyotes."

She stopped on her way back to the house. "Do you have anything to eat?"

"I have enough," he said. "And tonight we'll have chicken. Hurry now. We have places to go."

They headed southwest. Levi wanted to put distance between them and the coming winter, but she was too relieved to care where they were going — and a little doubtful, too. Maybe it was a foolish thing, what she'd done. Maybe she should have stayed at the house, waiting and hoping instead of going off with a stranger, this black-bearded man sitting beside her on the wagon seat. "You think I did right?" she asked finally. "Coming with you?"

He was annoyed. She could tell by the way his mouth tightened. "What would you have done?" he asked. "Tell me. With winter coming, no food, nobody? Anyway, it's too late now. I don't go backwards."

"Why not?"

"A waste of time." He flipped the reins. "Rocinante! Sancho!" he called to the mules. "Walk faster! Don't be lazy."

"What did you call them?"

He told her.

"Those sure are funny names," she said.

His annoyance vanished, and he smiled. "Not so funny. They are out of a book. About a man and his servant who wandered around Spain and had adventures."

"A book?" she said. "You have a book?"

His smile broadened. "Ach, child, I have many. A life without knowledge is no life at all, and knowledge is written in books."

"Can I see them? I'll be careful. Honest. All I ever had was the reader in school, and it wasn't mine."

"Not only can you see them, you may read them," he said. "And we'll talk about them afterwards, if you want." Which, he reflected, would be quite different from talking to himself. Life on the road was often a lonely thing, knowledge or no.

She gave a little bounce on the seat and turned toward him, her eyes once again filled with that strange fire. "I want to start now, please," she said, and her voice, polite but determined, told him she intended to do just that.

He pulled up and got down. She didn't wait for him but hopped out and followed him to the back of the wagon. Slowly he opened the trunk where he kept the things that were precious to him — a tintype of his parents, the certificate of his birth in a city he had forgotten, and the books that had been his friends since his youth.

She peered inside, then carefully lifted out the books, one by one, caressing them as if they were jewels. "So many!" she whispered.

"There are libraries with thousands of books," he said. "More than you can count." She set her chin. "Then I better get started." Her excitement was infectious. Back on the seat he found himself singing, and the mules whose names had started it all laid back one long ear each to listen.

He felt the storm long before it was visible, felt the darting tongue of wind against his cheek and smelled the dampness of snow. It was a day of such brilliance, of a flood of sunlight from a sky so empty of clouds that a newcomer to the prairie would have laughed at the notion of an approaching blizzard, made fun of his sudden attention. He drove down into a small dell that was protected by the coming together of two hills. Wild plum trees, bare of leaves but with thickly laced branches, formed a screen there, and a pond reflected them as they moved to the music of the wind. Levi was no stranger to weather. He knew.

"What's happening?" Nell stuck her head out of the wagon. "Why are we stopped?"

In answer Levi gestured to the north where a cloud, purple and black, had appeared suddenly on the horizon. "We'll stop here," he said. "There's good shelter. Maybe we have a couple hours before it hits."

He unhitched the mules, watered them, and fed them corn before picketing them on the lee side of the wagon. Nell, with the instinct of one born on the prairie, made a fire. "Dinner," she said. "Probably we won't have another hot meal for a while."

He gulped his coffee and eyed the storm that was closing in on them now, the edges of the clouds curling and misshapen. "I'll need to sleep in the wagon tonight," he said carefully, wondering how to bring up the subject.

"Where else? Only a fool'd sleep under it in this weather."

"Thank you," he said.

"What for?"

"For trusting me. I didn't want you to think. . . ." Embarrassed, his voice trailed off.

She didn't understand his hesitation. People froze to death in blizzards, or got lost in the blowing whiteness only a few feet from their doorsteps. Storms such as this one was going to be were no time for fancy manners. "Levi," she said, "it's *cold,* that's what I think. And we'd better clean up these dishes and get inside before it gets colder."

They made their beds at opposite ends of the wagon with the lantern flickering in between. She put on mittens and a knitted cap and pulled a shawl close around her shoulders, all the while listening to the roar of the wind driving the first particles of snow against the board and canvas sides of the wagon. If she were home now, she'd be doing the same thing, trying to stay warm, the snow coming through cracks in the walls and no voice but her own to drown out her fear.

" 'Blow, blow thou winter wind. Thou art not so unkind as man's ingratitude,' " she quoted across the space that separated them.

"You've found the Shakespeare," he said, his eyes gleaming.

"Yes. And I just now thought I'd never really thanked you. That maybe I seemed ungrateful. But I'm not. If it wasn't for you, I'd be back there alone and likely freezing to death."

"That can happen here," he reminded her.

"Yes, but at least there's two of us. That makes a difference."

It did, indeed. Two people could keep the world at bay, could bring a faint warmth to the inside of the fragile little shell that was all that stood between them and death. Two people could laugh and drown out the wolf howl of storm.

"It's a good thing I came along that day," he said gruffly. "Your being here is a good thing."

She fought down a happiness so intense it nearly choked her. "I think so, too," was all she said. She lay down in her nest of blankets and curled in upon herself to keep the warmth of it all. And she never noticed when he placed another blanket over her and blew out the lamp.

She awoke to gray light and the soundlessness of snow falling on snow. "Levi!" she called.

No answer came. To her it seemed that she had always been calling for someone who wasn't there, who would never be there again. She sat up and threw off the blankets.

"Levi!" she called again and heard the death of her own voice in the deepness of snow.

"Out here."

She stumbled down the narrow aisle toward the rear of the wagon. Outside was a white curtain, blank and thick as cotton, but she thought, if she put out her hand, she would touch the hardness of stone. "Where?"

"Feeding the mules. Don't come out. It's drifted."

Levi's head appeared in the opening, then the rest of him, his breath making clouds in the air. Icicles hung from his beard, and his eyebrows were white.

Unexpectedly, she laughed. "You look like Father Christmas!"

He laughed with her. "But I have no gifts."

"Yourself," she answered. "You've brought yourself."

"Such as I am." He wiped his beard and looked down at his boots and trousers that were coated with ice.

She followed his glance. "Take them off," she ordered. "Get dry. If you don't, you'll get frostbite. You'll get sick." She tugged at his arm and forced him to sit. "Do what I tell you."

It was pleasant to be fussed over, to have her chafe his frozen hands and feet, to be handed dry socks, and all the while her voice swooping like a flock of sparrows. Do this! Do that! Take care of yourself! When will it stop? Will we ever be warm and on our way again? At that her tears came, too many to be turned to ice, and he held her, patted her, said words of consolation and hope.

"Yes, yes. Soon the sun will shine, and we'll be moving. Don't worry. Levi Solomon has weathered many storms."

But she felt their isolation, knew her own. Always, in the past, there had been four walls and a roof, parents, her little brothers beside her in the bed, giving and taking warmth. There had been the old stove, casting its inadequate heat through the curtain that separated the rooms. There had been many bodies, not just her own and this man's — still a stranger. Yet she stayed in his arms, needing the closeness of another, the beating of a second heart in a world empty of all but the falling snow.

It seemed a miracle when the blizzard passed and the sun poured out of a sky as blue as turquoise. The white world seemed to absorb its light and give it back, sparkling and radiant. She looked out, held her breath for a moment, and put out her hands as if she could preserve the beauty, could capture the blue shadows of the plum trees, the erratic tracks of a rabbit, the blackness of a raven overhead, his wings defining the sky.

Beside the wagon Rocinante and Sancho stomped and blew, and looked toward her, hopeful, their ears and whiskers still coated with ice. Behind her Levi coughed, and the sound filled her with sudden dread. She turned, blinking in the dark, trying to see him where he lay in his blankets.

"You're sick," she said.

"Just clearing my throat." His voice was hoarse.

She stumbled toward him, knelt down, put her hand to his forehead. "You've got fever."

"A cold. Nothing more." He tried to smile but a violent shiver wracked his body.

And she had thought she was safe! She had rejoiced in the sunlight, the coming of day! Perhaps never again would she trust life or believe in its innate goodness. For all purposes she was alone again, marooned in a sea of snow that was too deep to travel over. Once again everything rested on her shoulders — her life and this man's to whom she was beholden. "Lie still," she commanded. "I'll see to the mules. And then I'm going to start a fire and get you some tea."

"You can't. . . ."

"Try me." She stood up, looking tall and determined.

"Child, child," he said.

And she answered. "I'm not a child. I already told you. Not any more. Not since *they* left me. Now lie there and keep warm."

Even when she was an old woman with much of a happy life behind her, she never liked to remember the time that followed. How she dug down through the drifts and struggled to build a feeble fire, scarcely hot enough to warm water, how she searched her mind for remedies her mother had used and pulled patent medicines from Levi's stock, how she piled blankets on him, washed him, and finally, in desperation, slept beside him during the long, cold nights, warming him with her own warmth, willing him to stay alive so hard that it hurt. And when the snow melted enough to travel, she hitched the team and drove on in search of a farm, a town, the winter camp of Indians, she didn't care as long as whoever was there had the ability to cure.

She shot rabbits for food, she who hated the killing of animals. She skinned them, gutted them, wiped the blood on her skirts and cooked them, forcing the meat and gruel through Levi's dry lips and trying not to hear the rattle in his lungs. Sometimes she read to him, straining her eyes in the lamplight, the words of the Bible resonant and somehow comforting, though she never really felt their meaning. It was the sound of her voice that was important, a link between her and the man who lay in rumpled blankets burning with fever.

And then one day, far in the distance, she saw mountains rising up out of the plain, and she stared at them in wonder and wished that Levi was beside her to share her excitement, to tell her their names. As it was, she had only herself to talk to, only her own questions that she could not answer. Was the whole country empty? Where were the people? She had seen only the rabbits she shot, and antelope, and once a herd of buffaloes like a dark river passing over the land. And there were always a few small birds buffeted by the wind that never stopped, that sang in her ears like the deepest notes of a fiddle, dark and mournful.

How long a time she spent on the road she was never able to determine later, but it was long enough to turn her into the woman she knew that she was, supple and tough as a sapling, and as determined to live. When she saw the little settlement tucked against the side of the mountain, she didn't change her pace, just moved toward it, not blinking, watching for fear that, like the mirages of the plains, it would suddenly lift and disappear, a trick of light and distance.

People came out to meet her, and she said without thinking and before the world went dark: "Please. My husband is very ill. Please help us."

She awoke to warmth and the rich scent of roasting meat, and for a moment she struggled to remember where she was. A tall woman crossed the room and stood, looking down at her.

"You're awake," she said.

"Where's Levi?" Nell held her breath, waiting for the answer.

"In the other room."

"Is he . . . is he all right?" She hated how she sounded, weak and babyish.

"He'll make it. But it was close."

She forced back tears of relief. "Can I see him?"

The woman smiled. "Sure. He's been asking for you, but I told him you were asleep."

"How long?"

"A day and a night. You were worn out. Must've been quite a trip."

Nell closed her eyes. She felt a thousand years old. "We were caught in a blizzard. That's when he took sick."

"You were lucky," the woman said. "That storm wiped most of the cattle off the range. Killed some people, too." She shook her head

104

as if she was casting off memories. Then, abruptly, she changed the subject. "I'm Lucy Wickers. I run the post office, such as it is. My husband's a freighter."

"Oh." Nell was quiet a minute, picking at the quilt, her own words echoing in her head. *My husband is sick.* Had she really said that? And if she had, how could she explain such a lie? "I'm Nell," she said finally. "And he's Levi . . . Levi Solomon," she added.

"Well, Nell, have some breakfast. Then you can take some to him. You both look half starved. How long've you been on the road?"

It seemed like forever since that day when she climbed into the wagon and left her past behind. She shrugged. "A long time. I kind of lost track."

"You poor kid. You ought to settle down some place. Open a store. You could do it here. There's enough in that wagon of yours to get you started."

"I guess," Nell said.

What happened next really wasn't up to her. All that she owned were the clothes she had with her. She was shocked when she saw Levi. He was pale, and his eyes were sunken in their sockets, and someone, probably Lucy, had trimmed his beard so that it clung to his thin cheeks like a shadow.

"How do you feel?" she asked, suddenly shy, remembering how she had slept beside him in the wagon, held him close night after night, keeping death and the cold away.

"I'm alive," he said, his dark eyes glowing. "And I thank you."

"I didn't do much."

"Yes," he said. "Yes you did. You saved my life."

"Then we're even," she said.

He thought he didn't want the slate wiped clean. With a clear conscience she could leave, go out into the world where he would never see her again, never hear her voice, reading his precious books aloud.

She said, so low he wasn't sure he understood: "I told a lie. I didn't

105

mean to. It just came out. But you'd better know."

He cocked his head at her. "Was it very bad?"

"Bad enough." She twisted her hands in her lap. "I said . . . I told them . . . you were my husband."

"So? So what's wrong with that?"

"Because you're not. I'm not your wife."

But she could be. If only. . . . He sighed. "Would it shame you if you were?" he asked.

That startled her. "Why should it? Why should I be ashamed?"

"I'm a peddler. A Jew. I have no home, no place. Some people laugh at me. Call me names and throw stones. Maybe even you once."

"I never," she said, indignant, although part of what he said was true enough. She'd seen it happen, so long ago she'd almost forgotten. She'd been sitting beside her papa on the wagon seat. They had driven to town, and she saw the boys, three of them armed with sticks and stones, and they were shouting at a peddler, an old man with a pack. What they said she couldn't recall, but their faces were clear in her mind, ugly and twisted, unlike the old man's with his white beard, blood on his forehead, his face filled with sorrow. "I never," she repeated, fiercely this time. "And if it happened . . . to us I mean . . . why, I'd stop them. I'd throw stones right back. What does anybody know about you? How good you are? How kind?"

He watched her face, and the quick flame in her eyes, and knew she was telling the truth. She would fight, for herself as much as for him. Had she not brought them through illness and storm to safety? Suddenly he couldn't imagine going on without her, just him and the mules and his own somber thoughts. "What shall we do then?" he asked and thought his heart would stop waiting for her answer.

When it came, it wasn't what he'd hoped. "Lucy says we could stay here and open a store."

"And? Would you like that?"

She folded her hands in her lap and sat quite still, looking at him, at his hollow cheeks, his eyes that seemed to be pleading with her.

Running a store would mean staying in one place, building a home, having neighbors like Lucy to help when help was needed. It would mean the comfort of four walls, a fire on the hearth when the storms drove out of the north. But then she thought of the miles they had covered together, the land rolling away in front of them calling, always calling. She thought of the cold nights, of days filled with the dazzle of sun, and how, without him, she was empty, a water jug holding only the sad music of the wind. And she found she didn't want the life without him, didn't want life the way it had been before in that lonely house on the silent prairie.

She spoke slowly, awed by her knowledge. "I think," she said, "I think you and I should move on. Together. If you wouldn't mind."

He held out his arms, and she went into them, carefully but surely for it was where she knew she belonged.

"Ach, Nell," he whispered. "I wouldn't mind at all."

ASYLUM

Flossie Carmichael was released from the state asylum for the insane on a rainy afternoon in 1877. She got out of the hack that had taken her away from that lonely place and stood uncertainly on the wooden sidewalk, her face tilted up, letting the drops fall onto her cheeks, into her open mouth. How long? How long since she had stood like this, tasting the rain, the scent of new leaves and blooming things? How long since she had listened to the world's ordinary sounds, so different from the mumblings and screams of the inmates?

Her tears mingled with the rain, and with the taste of salt in her mouth she set off down the street, her progress noted by many who stopped to stare, to pull aside curtains and whisper to one another. *"See there! It's Flossie Carmichael. Remember when she tried to kill herself and her husband? Not that he didn't deserve it, but still. . . ."*

At the corner she bought a newspaper from a pimple-faced boy who never noticed her out-of-date black cape, her hat squashed down over her head, or the wonder in her round blue eyes. He was too young to remember her shame, and how she had been taken away from the only home she'd ever had, her hands manacled, her every move watched by the cold eyes of two attendants.

Taking courage from the boy's ignorance, she looked around in astonishment. The town had tripled in size in the five years she'd been inside. Five long years in which to think back over her life, ponder her mistakes and illusions. That's what they'd been, of course — illusions of happiness, of married life. She knew that now, knew she'd been naïve, a child believing in the ecstasy of fairy tales.

She had lasted ten years with Jim Carmichael, until he found the widow who ran the millinery shop on Main Street. Little, she was, with a mop of golden curls, and a well-rounded figure, as much unlike the tall, lean Flossie as chalk to cheese. At first she hadn't noticed Jim's excuses for his absences from the farm. She was running it as she had since childhood. She'd been milking cows, feeding chickens, cutting hay, cooking at the big iron stove since she could remember, she and her grandmother Arnold, a widow who farmed as well as any man, whose cows gave the richest milk, whose chickens always laid, even in winter.

Flossie couldn't remember her parents, killed in an accident when she was two, but her granny had been enough, her granny and the farm. Then Jim Carmichael had walked into their lives on a rainy evening much like this one, appearing at the back door and asking for work.

"Plenty of that," Granny had said, eyeing him through the crack, a tall boy, almost a man, with broad shoulders and nut-brown eyes. After a minute she opened the door. "Come in and have some supper."

People didn't fool Granny often. She had a way of seeing through them down to their hearts. But Jim Carmichael had fooled them both with his willingness to work, his good manners, his slow smile that brought a kind of warmth into the lives of the old woman and the young Flossie just turned sixteen and eager for more than the companionship of her grandmother. Oh, he had a way with him, had Jim, once he knew what he wanted. He'd courted her slowly, carefully, right under the old lady's nose. A touch here, a word there, a bit of flattery that had made her blush and catch her breath.

"Pretty Flossie," he'd say. "Pretty little thing."

He had brought her wild flowers from the fields, a ribbon or a bag of candy on pay day. "The ribbon's for your hair. Your hair's so fine. Like black silk." And his hand would reach out slowly, gently, and touch her hair, the back of her neck, making her shudder with the need to touch him in return, to hold on and not let go.

Then Granny was dead, taken suddenly in the hay field. They had laid her out in the parlor, and Jim had proposed right there alongside her body, beside that bony face set in death. "Marry me, Floss. We'll be good together. I'll take care of you just like she did."

It seemed obvious now, looking back, that what he had wanted was not her with her eager heart, but the farm. Eighty acres of prime land that the Arnolds had owned for seventy years and that had kept them prosperous. Well, it was his now. His and that woman's whose hair curled around her face like a flowering vine, and whose laughter never seemed to stop. She remembered the signing of the papers, remembered how, terrified, drugged, quivering from shock they'd brought her out of her cell and handed her a pen — Jim, his lawyer, and Dr. Baines.

"Can you sign, Flossie?" the doctor asked. "Do you remember your name?"

Of course she did. She wasn't crazy, only confused, hurt, and with an anger in the core of her that broke out now and then into uncontrollable rage. That was why she was there. She'd put her hands through the window, sawed at her wrists on the jagged glass. Then she'd gone for him, the husband who betrayed her, mocked her, saw her as less than human.

"A man wants a real woman in his bed," he'd said. "A family. Not some old dry cow."

He still had the scar of her attack. It ran down his cheek and disappeared under his collar. She'd missed his jugular. Too bad. He should be dead now, and she should be free and standing on the porch where the lilacs rustled, their heart-shaped leaves holding the sun, and roses scenting the evening air. She should be in the cornfield, checking the harvest, watching the full ears bend down the stalks, and feeling sudden joy at the sight of a fox hunting in the shade of the rows. She, and she alone, not this stranger she had married, this man with cold eyes and a red scar that pulsed with the beating of his heart.

Could she sign her name? Of course. They were tricking her, trying to keep her here in this place filled with the screams of the damned. She picked up the pen and wrote her name with a careful flourish. Flossie Arnold Carmichael. And she smiled at her tormentors.

Later she understood what she'd done, and the knowledge had released another fit of rage. They had locked her away then, in a room without a window, and had kept her there in the dark until weariness and drugs forced her to sleep. They had given her treatments that left her shaken, bewildered. They had packed her in ice until she believed she was dead — or dying — and had wished that she was.

Crazy woman. *Crazy*. The words played round in her head. But she wasn't crazy. She knew that much. She was anguished, in pain, torn and clutching what there was left of herself with desperate fingers.

Now she stood on the street corner in the rain, suddenly confused by the normality of the scene — the horse traffic, the new, more permanent buildings that blocked her view of the country beyond. Once she had been a part of it all; now she was merely an onlooker, frightened by a world she no longer recognized, and by the knowing glances of the passersby.

Well, she knew when she was wet and getting soaked through, that much was certain. She knew enough to get in out of a rainstorm. She chuckled to herself and, seeing what appeared to be a restaurant, went inside.

Someone showed her to a table and handed her a menu. She stared at it in amazement, at the words that leaped from the page and conjured up a feast. Fresh ham. Eggs. Oysters. Beef steak. Roast chicken. Applesauce. Peas. Tomatoes.

She found her mouth watering. So much choice! Such riches for her, used to the dry oatmeal and watery stews of the asylum. She wanted one of everything. But no. Someone was sure to be watching, waiting to report her conduct. Any foolish act and they'd have her back, for good this time.

Swallowing hard, she ordered a steak, a salad, a dish of peas. And coffee. Suddenly she wanted coffee, steaming and fragrant and laced with cream.

She settled back in her chair to wait and opened the paper she had kept dry under her cape. Goodness! It wasn't only her own small town that had grown and changed. The whole world was different now, having passed her by while she had simply endured and fought to keep her kernel of sanity. Something called a telephone had been invented by a man named Bell, and a new game, tennis, was being played across America. Rutherford B. Hayes was President, though she'd never paid much attention to politics, having no say in what was a man's world.

DESERT LAND ACT IN ARIZONA TERRITORY. The headline caught her eye, and she read on. Why, for merely digging ditches, irrigating fields, a person could claim as much as 640 acres! What she couldn't do with 640 acres! Even in the desert. She'd dug her share of ditches, plowed, pitched hay, moved rocks. She was young yet and would get strong again, even though her black hair had turned pure white, and her heart annoyed her with its tendency to speed up when she was frightened.

Could she do it? Her hands, clutching the paper, trembled. Away from here no one would know her shame or conjecture about what she might do in the future. In the clear desert air she could regain her health. She would be free of it all — of the gossip, the quickly silenced laughter, of the possibility of meeting Jim, and that woman, and the child he had fathered.

What she needed was money. Not much. Only enough to give her a start. And then, out of the haze of a memory distorted by five years of mistreatment, she heard her granny's voice. *Always keep something back. For yourself.*

And she had! She had! In the bank there was a box that she'd never mentioned to anyone, not even Jim. It had been Granny's, and twice a year they'd gone to deposit a few dollars. How much was there she didn't know, but at least she wasn't penniless.

She was almost too excited to eat when the meal came. Almost. The scent of gravy and meat, the juicy red of the tomatoes seduced her, and she ate heartily, lost in sensual delight and in a dream of land that she had never seen.

She entered the bank and hesitated just inside the heavy doors, searching for a familiar face and finding it. Lyle Pickett sat behind his oak desk, looking the same as he'd looked when she'd been here the last time — gray hair, bushy mustache, spectacles that kept falling down his nose. He looked up, saw her in her old black cape and felt hat, and pushed his spectacles high. "Flossie?" he said. "Good Lord. Is that you?"

She nodded once. "Yes sir," she said and inwardly chided herself for sounding like a child.

He came toward her, opened the gate that separated him from the customers, and led her inside. "Sit down. Sit down. How are you . . . uh . . . feeling?"

"Fine." She wished she hadn't come. He was making her nervous. Her hands shook, and she clasped them in her lap.

"I heard you were . . . uh . . . home again." He frowned. "It was a terrible thing, Flossie. Terrible."

"I was never crazy," she said. "Not ever."

He nodded. "Tell the truth, I never thought you were. But nobody asked me."

"I've come on business," she said then. "My granny's box. Is it still here?"

"You remembered that." He looked at her in astonishment. "Funny. I paid the rent on that box while you were . . . away."

"It's mine, isn't it?" she wanted to know. "Whatever's there?"

"I'd certainly say so. I had the greatest respect for your grandmother. And I know how you worked that place. It's not what it was, Flossie. Not at all."

"Never mind," she interrupted. "I'd just like what's in that box if it's all right. I want to leave here." Her voice was louder now. It echoed through the old building, and customers turned to stare. "I want to go somewhere where nobody knows who I am."

He sighed. "A good idea. And there's over six hundred dollars that's yours as of right now."

Her eyes widened. "That much?"

"That's right. Where did you plan on going?"

"Arizona territory," she said, her words firm.

His spectacles fell down his nose, and he pushed them up to stare at her. "That's no place for a lone woman," he commented.

"Neither is where I've been, Mister Pickett," she said. "Now, may I have my money please?"

She stood once more on the street, looking at the town for almost the last time and glad of it. There was nothing here for her now, nothing she wanted to keep or take with her except . . . she took a quick breath. The rosebush! She and Granny had planted it, watched it grow and spread, harvested the petals that scented the air every June with a perfume so heavy it made her dizzy, gathered the hips in the fall and with them made rose-red jelly and scented tea. Suddenly she wanted that bush more than she wanted freedom. It was hers. Tangible proof of . . . of what? That she'd been here, lived here, suffered and nearly died here, and now was setting out on a great adventure. Quickly she made up her mind. *I'll just go and get me a root.*

At dusk she set out on the old road to the farm. She knew every rock, every tree. Old friends, they were, and she spoke to them quietly, knowing that, if she were seen, they'd think she was crazy for sure, slipping along in the twilight, greeting trees, murmuring to the creek that flowed under the plank bridge.

"Hello," she said. "And good bye. I'm going away, you know,"

114

and the ache in her throat threatened to consume her as she spoke, for her roots were here, mingled with those of the forest, and her childhood, her time of dreams.

She took the turn-off down the lane. The house was ahead in its grove of pines, the house that had been hers. Sternly she choked down tears. This wasn't the time to succumb. Later she might, after she'd gotten what she came for.

A light shone out of the kitchen window. She pictured them sitting around the table — the man who had been her husband, the woman and child who had taken her place, had seen her committed, and never said a word.

"God damn you all," she whispered. "God damn you all to hell. That's where I've been. See how you like it."

At the sound of her voice the old dog on the porch raised its head and listened, nose in the air, then got up and came toward her, wagging its tail. She got down on her knees in the dirt and gathered him in. "You remembered. You knew it was me. Good old boy. Good old Crackers." She wished she could take him away, too, for he was hers, had always loved her best. But that was only a wish, impractical but loving. "Don't give me away now," she said in his ear. "Be quiet." He obeyed but stayed close at her heels.

The rose had spread farther than she remembered, forming a hedge as high as her shoulders, putting forth long roots that, in turn, became new growth and thrust up toward the light. She knelt again and dug with her fingers deeply into the damp earth. The roots were easily found and taken, and she had to force herself to stop, to overcome her sudden greed to take and carry away the whole hedge, a witch making magic in the darkness.

Carefully she packed the plants into a sack, keeping as much earth around them as she could and, when she was finished, she stood up and looked around. Beside her the dog whined, sensing another departure, another loss, and she dropped a hand to his big head in a blessing. "Stay," she told him. "Stay and don't forget me." Then she trotted away down the lane and onto the road that wound through the forest.

She took the train as far as it went, and then the stage, and with every mile she felt her happiness growing. Nobody knew her, no one snickered behind her back, or gossiped about what she had done. Here, it was the land that ruled, miles of it and empty, making the lives of humans seem small and inconsequential, herself most of all. So much land! She reveled in it and in her anonymity, spoke with her fellow passengers as she would have done before her downfall. Most of the travelers were men, and they were full of advice which she filed away for reference.

"All the good land around the Gila's gone," the man beside her said. "It was first come, first served, and the Mormons was first."

Disappointment rose in her. Had she come this far only to be defeated? "What'll I do, then?" she asked.

"Plenty good land left. Go on down south. Toward the mountains. File on a homestead. Put in some cattle."

She shook her head. "I don't know anything about range cattle."

He grinned at her. "Just put 'em on grass. They'll do the rest."

"Where should I buy some?"

He grinned harder. "Most folks rustle their neighbors'. Or run 'em out of Mexico."

"Be serious!"

"Missy," he said, "I *am* serious." He looked at her in her new bonnet chosen for longevity and not fashion, her serge traveling coat, dust covered now and wrinkled. "Maybe you better turn around and go back where you come from. Or settle down in a town some place. Ranching, farming . . . that's men's work."

She looked out the window, saw mountains rising out of the plain, and she felt, for an instant, as if they rose out of her own body, barren, aching, tough. "This here's home now," she said.

At the land office she filed on 160 acres in a valley she'd never seen.

116

The clerk shook his head. "This really isn't the time for a woman alone to be out there. It isn't safe. Snakes, rustlers, Injuns jumping the reservation, who knows what could happen? You know how to use a gun?"

She ignored his fussing. What she couldn't explain was that she *wanted* to be alone, in the silence, with the land spilling out around her. After what she'd seen of cruelty, Indians held no threat. If she died, well, so be it. Life hadn't been all that wonderful.

"Suicide," he said. "That's what it is, plain and simple."

She folded the paper and the map he'd given her and put them in her purse. "One way or the other," she said, "at least I'll have some peace."

She bought a wagon and team from a Mexican up from Sonora. The horses were broke to saddle as well as to harness and were probably stolen. They needed feeding up but seemed sturdy enough, and she had an eye for horses. She bought an axe, a shovel, a pick, a hammer and nails, rolls of rope and wire, barrels of flour, beans, coffee, salt and molasses, a sack of onions, and a string of dried red peppers. Then, thinking ahead, she bought potatoes and seed corn, though it was probably too late for a crop. She bought herself a Winchester rifle, wishing she could have reclaimed her own, probably gathering dust over the door at the farm. And then, on a whim, she bought two sapling apple trees from a peddler who handed them over as if they were gold.

"Keep them wet," he advised. "And plant soon."

"Soon as I get where I'm going," she promised, and stowed the slender things carefully behind the wagon seat beside her sack of roses.

Then, on advice from the clerk at the land office, she joined up with another family, also headed for the valley to the east. Like her the Cobbs had been lured by the promise of land. Also like her they had no real idea of what to expect once they left the safety of the town.

"But I guess we'll do what we have to," Nancy Cobb said. "We come out here for a chance, and we'll take it." She was a plain woman, big boned with a powder of freckles across her cheeks.

"Me, too," Flossie said. "And I guess we'll be neighbors."

"A couple miles away, but that's neighborly."

Brewster Cobb nodded. "You need anything, you come ask. That's what neighbors are for."

Flossie smiled. It was good to know there were folks of her own kind close at hand, but a couple miles was as close as she wanted them. Solitude drove her; communion with a world that made no judgment, asked no questions. "I'll holler," she promised. "And you do the same." She picked up the reins and clucked to her team. The quicker she got where she was headed, the better.

Driving east, the land changed from harsh desert into rolling plains where the grass was as high as her wagon, as the shoulders of the horses. The valleys, and the mountains that separated them, ran north and south, and each had a character of its own. She saw sand hills, shaped by wind and rain into arches and rose-colored bluffs, and cañons where the stones had shivered and cracked into a billion strange fragments, as if someone had hurled a clay bowl and it had shattered against the mountain. The mountains themselves were never the same, changing in the blink of an eye from sunlight to shadow, from the dazzle of light on red stone to the dark purple of passing clouds. And watching, feeling with all her senses and the skin that covered her bones, Flossie knew a kind of joy that was like music — the music of a strange land in the emptiness of her womb where there had never been life but where now something seemed to rise up — not a babe but the expectations of her heart as she looked and gloried in a place that existed for no other reason than it had been conceived and born.

She saw the moving dust cloud long before the detachment of buffalo soldiers came into view.

"Best turn around, folks," the white lieutenant said. "Victorio jumped the reservation a week ago. Nobody's safe out here."

Flossie set her chin, and he noticed.

"Go back," he repeated. "You're crazy to risk it."

That word again. She looked at his men on their lathered horses. She looked at him, his face caked with dust. Then she laughed. "Lieutenant," she said, "do you have any idea where these Indians are?"

"No, ma'am. Probably south of here, but we can't say for sure."

Her voice rang clearly in the high desert air. "Lieutenant, I think every Indian for a hundred miles knows where you are by that dust cloud you've been making. If you want to catch Victorio, I think you should change your tactics. As for me, there's no place to go back to. I'll take my chances."

She'd made him angry. A snicker from one of his men hadn't helped. His mouth tightened under the mask of dust, and he pulled on his reins, making his mount prance. "Thank you for the advice, ma'am," he said, his voice harsh.

"Good luck." She nodded to him, clucked to her team, and rolled past without looking back.

Better to face death here, in these valleys of yellow grass, on the purple slopes of stone mountains. Better to be whole, if only for a moment, than deprived of the becoming.

She found her homestead — tucked into the flank of a mountain with a stream running through it, and she said her good byes to the Cobbs without regret, for this was hers, this stony ground dotted with oak and juniper, where the grass with its sickle-shaped seeds danced in the wind, and where she would build a shelter under the fern-like leaves of a mesquite.

"Mine," she said when the Cobbs had driven away to the south, the sound of hoofs and wheels growing fainter, swallowed up by the great jaws of the valley. "Mine." And she sat down on the warm earth and laughed and cried for the freedom of it, the pleasure of aloneness.

119

Morning came early, colored lemon, rose, apple green. She had slept in the wagon bed after picketing the horses in the moving grass by the creek, and she woke still laughing at finding herself in a new place, wearing a new skin, with happiness rippling up from her toes. She built a fire, ate a quick breakfast, and then bareback rode her boundary, planning a fence, a corral, a pasture, and finally the site of the shelter she would build with rocks hauled from the creek.

God, it was hard work! All of it. Had she made the wrong choice? After a week she began to think so. Her hands were cracked and bruised; the body she had always taken for granted was stiff, sore, and balky. Often too tired to eat in the evening, she simply washed cold biscuits down with water toted from the creek and fell asleep in the wagon where she lay without moving until morning. No time to savor the dawn now, not even the wish. Daylight meant more labor, forcing herself, often to the point of tears.

"Why?" she mumbled. "Why did I think I could do this?" Her lips and face were sunburned. It hurt even to talk to herself, and her white hair, hanging down her back, suddenly seemed a burden — and likely filled with pests.

She took a knife and hacked it off, and then, appalled at what she had done, sat down and buried her face in her hands.

Someone was watching her. She knew it with the instinct born of years of surveillance but, when she straightened up and searched the hills, she saw nothing, heard nothing. "I wish they'd come out, whoever they are," she said.

Nothing moved, no answer came, and she went back to loading rock into the wagon. After a month she felt lean and fit, enough so that she took pleasure in watching the wall of her house rise — rock cemented with mud that she hoped would hold. Now she bent, picked up a rock, and threw it into the wagon with fluid ease. Then the man behind her spoke.

"If I was an Injun, you'd have an axe in your head."

For one brief moment she was so frightened she couldn't move. Then she whirled and came face to face with the ugliest man she'd ever seen, so ugly that he gave her courage. "How dare you sneak up on me?"

He chuckled, showing brown teeth in a mouth almost hidden by a filthy beard. "Taught you a lesson," he said. "You think you're alone and safe out here, but you ain't."

"I was, till you came along." She glanced over at her rifle that lay in the wagon.

He read her thoughts. "Forget it. I didn't come to hurt you."

"Then why did you?"

"Smelt that coffee, and it set my mouth to waterin'. Thought maybe you'd like some fresh meat in exchange."

Her supplies were getting low. She'd been working so hard she hadn't taken time to hunt. "I'd be grateful," she said. "My name's Flossie Carmichael."

"Hugh." He muttered the one syllable, and she looked at him curiously. "That's all?"

"That's enough."

She laughed, losing all her fear. The old man was no crazier than inmates she'd known. "All right," she said, "where's the meat?"

He gestured with his chin. "Up yonder. I'll fetch it soon's I have some of that coffee."

"There's cold biscuits, too," she offered with the good manners put into her by her granny. Anyone who appeared out of nowhere in such a state was hungry.

"That would go good." He gave another hideous grimace that passed for a smile, then said: "What in blue blazes are you doin' out here by yourself?"

She could be as tight as he was with information. "Homesteading."

He was squatted by the fire where the coffee pot boiled. "You're crazy," he said without turning around. "Plumb loco is what."

121

"Oh, no, Mister Hugh," she answered. "I am definitely *not* crazy."

He looked at her then, caught by something in her tone — desperation, perhaps, or a plea — and he saw determination and strength, and the shadow of an old anguish in her blue eyes. No stranger to sorrow himself, he nodded and raised his cup in a toast. "Then here's to good luck," he said, and drank.

Hugh Magoffin had been wandering for more years than he could count, living off the land and learning about its justice, its cruelty, its beauty that even now had the ability to stop him in his tracks. He'd had a wife once, a small, slender whip of a wife with the heart of a wildcat and a daughter who was like her mother, a wife who had enchanted him with her energy, the warmth of her body next to his.

He had come home eagerly that day. A week was too long to be gone from where his heart was. She'd have a stew cooking, and the yard swept, and little Mae would be dancing with excitement, knowing he was due home soon and watching the wagon trace where it came over the rise. He flicked the whip over the back of his team and urged them into a trot, and then smelled smoke from an old fire, and saw the buzzards honing in on a feast. That's what he remembered in his nightmares — the buzzards with their black wings and scaly heads like reptiles — and how they defied him, clustering over what was left of the bodies like the savages that had been there before them. A raiding party, perhaps. He never knew. Knew only that his heart was buried in a grave in Texas with the charred bones of his past. From that time he became a wanderer set on revenge, a killer of Indians regardless of tribe, a lone wolf howling in the arroyos, the mountains, the valleys of bending grass.

For a week he'd been camped in a cave watching Flossie, protecting her if she'd known it. A band of Apaches had passed just west of her, headed for Mexico. They hadn't stopped to investigate, and he'd let them move on, knowing a better time would come for his purpose. He thought Flossie was mad to be doing what she was doing — staking a claim, building a house as if she were the only person in the world, and there was no danger. Damn' fools had no place in this country, and he wished he hadn't come across her, didn't feel, somehow, responsible for her now that he'd watched and accepted her coffee.

It was that sense of responsibility that made him walk into her camp. To teach her a lesson, he thought. That her life hung by the slenderest of threads, and that innocence was a danger, not a state of grace. But now that he'd talked to her, looked into her eyes, he recognized a kinship. Like a wounded animal, she had retreated to nurse herself into a kind of health. Understanding that, he nodded to himself. The choice was hers, and she'd made it, even as he had. A person's life was, after all, his own.

"I'll help with the rocks and the house," he said. "Build a corral for the horses, too, or them Injuns'll steal 'em out from under your nose."

She figured he wouldn't stay long. "Thanks," she said, and with that one word sealed a lasting friendship.

Neither of them talked much, for which both were grateful. He'd forgotten how, and Flossie craved silence. She wanted to lose herself in doing, in the lessons taught her by her senses. She stared into the hearts of rocks at the flecks of mica that glittered in the sun, at bands of color that seemed like a miniature landscape — ocher, lavender, the pink of a dusky rose. She wanted to look, and touch, and feel the pulsing of earth, to taste the juice in the stems of grass, the water in the creek that sang in her mouth with the coldness of stone. What she wanted was knowledge of something other than people, perhaps the flowing of a time that existed without clocks or calendars or any human assistance at all.

So they labored, sometimes side by side, sometimes apart, and in their unspoken communication formed a bond. Hugh built a fireplace into one wall of the house and, as he fitted the rocks together, his hands seemed to go on by themselves. His mind was elsewhere, back in the past and building another house, another hearth, a chimney that was all that was standing after the massacre.

He wanted to tell her of it, to warn her, but he couldn't summon the words or the courage to begin, and besides she wouldn't listen. Stubborn she was, and set on the notion. And something else, besides. He'd been wounded and knew the signs. They were his own. She was building a bolt-hole for herself and would take her chances. He sighed. The world was a rotten place, though it had its moments. He'd seen her watching the mountains like she wanted to take them apart stone by stone and put them together again inside herself. That was a hunger he understood, like he understood the rest, and maybe, with her, he was being given a second chance. Maybe he could see her through, keep her safe. Maybe. He sighed again and went on fitting stones.

He went up into the mountains and came back for the horses to drag down a ridge pole for the roof. He hunted, going off without comment and returning with wild turkeys or venison. Like smoke from the fire he was there and then not there. Flossie never knew when she'd find him gone, or when, noiselessly, he'd reappear, stepping into the clearing as if he'd never left.

He was gone the morning she found the baby in its cradleboard, hanging from the limb of a tree. It was awake and watching her with dark eyes that had no bottom, that betrayed nothing, neither fear nor curiosity. Flossie looked around, saw no one. But someone had to have left the baby, an Indian on stealthy feet. She shivered at the thought, then searched the ground, but whoever had come had left no sign except this living proof of passage.

"Hello, sweet thing," she said. Her voice startled a jay that flew up, squawking. The baby remained still, its eyes unblinking. Indian mothers, she knew, taught their infants never to cry by pinching off their breath. This one, it seemed, had learned its lesson young and well. "Don't be afraid," she whispered, and put out a finger and stroked the brown cheek. It felt like velvet, like the tenderness of a petal, and with the touching something inside her ruptured — a dam, a wall erected between self and self went down until she thought the noise would deafen her. She had never had a child, not even the beginnings of one. Now, like a miracle, here was an infant left to her in the night. She put out her arms and took it, cradleboard and all, into the house.

"Daughter," she said after she had unwrapped the lacings, discarded the moss that served as a diaper, "I'll call you Mariah, and you'll be mine. No one else's. Just mine."

At the sound of her voice, Mariah yawned, stretched, and cooed softly, like the fluting of a dove.

"Oh, my pretty little girl," she cooed back.

Hugh stood in the doorway. "What in God's name is that?"

"A baby."

"An Injun."

"Her name's Mariah." She picked up the child who did not protest.

"Best drown it in the creek."

"She's mine! My daughter."

He stared at her as she cradled Mariah to her breast. "You're a damn' fool," he said. "They'll come back for her and take your scalp."

"Mariah won't let them, will you?" she asked the child.

He swallowed hard, unable to watch any longer, to blot out memories — the old one and the new. "The Army caught up with some of 'em a couple days ago," he said. "Just north of here. Kilt a bunch of women and kids. Must've missed this one."

"And somebody gave her to me to keep safe," she responded. "And I will." She challenged him with her eyes, with her posture — a white-haired Madonna holding a black-eyed infant.

He had the last word. "Nits breed lice. Don't say I never warned you." Then he turned and walked away.

He was gone for what seemed like a month. Flossie didn't notice at first, she was too busy learning to be a mother. Mariah made that easy, never crying, amusing herself with whatever she was given — colored stones, twigs with leaves on them, a doll that Flossie made out of a corn cob. And Flossie talked. It seemed like she never stopped talking to this small creature who listened with wonder to the words that poured out.

One afternoon, after a thunderstorm had swept over and deluged them, she began to dig holes for her apple trees and for the rosebush. The time was right; the moon was coming full. She believed in planting on the waxing moon, except for root crops. Those she planted when the moon was dark. She explained all this to Mariah who was sitting on the doorstep, watching and listening, her once secretive eyes bright with intelligence.

"This here's a rose," Flossie said. "All the way from Ohio I brought it. It was my granny's. And mine. And now it's ours. It'll grow big and strong, just like you." Then she turned, hearing hoofbeats on the trail.

"Flossie? You there?"

Nancy Cobb rode up the hill on the back of a mule. "Come to see how you're getting on," she said, looking around. "Goodness! You got a house already, and we're still camping out." Her eyes fell on Mariah who was watching her with interest. "Who's that?"

"My daughter. Her name's Mariah," Flossie said grimly, knowing what was coming.

"But . . . but she's Apache! How . . . ? You can't. . . ." Nancy broke off, horrified.

"What should I do? Bash her head in with a rock?"

Nancy shuddered.

"See?" Flossie said. "You wouldn't do it, either."

"Well, no, but . . . are you sure you're doing right? After all. . . ." Her voice trailed off again, and she stood there, perplexed.

"Murder's not right," Flossie snapped. "I know that much." She went back to her planting and hoped the subject was closed.

But Nancy, like Hugh, had the last word. "If I come up someday and find you scalped, is there anybody I should write to?"

Flossie slammed her shovel point down in the damp ground, then faced her neighbor. "Just bury me," she said. "Right here by the rose will be good enough."

And she wished with all her heart that, if it happened, Hugh would find her before the buzzards did, or this freckle-faced creature who disguised her lack of charity in the name of friendship. But when Hugh did come back, she faced him with anger.

"Where've you been?" she demanded. "You go off, and never a word, so I don't know if the Injuns got you or what. Or if you're ever coming home again. I don't know if I should cook you dinner, or save it. It isn't fair!"

It was the word "home" that struck him, deep in his belly, so he didn't know how to answer. "I've been off thinkin'," he said.

She swished her skirt and went to the fire. "Thinking!" she said. "What do you have to think about you can't think about here?" He stood there, silent as the mountain, knowing she'd turn back to him. "What've you got there?" she wanted to know. "What've you brung?"

He opened the sack, and the puppy tumbled out, snarling and showing white teeth. She stared at it, at him, off balance if the truth were known, because once more he'd taken her by surprise. "Figured you could use a dog," he mumbled. "Nobody'll sneak up on you when he's grown."

"It's a wolf," she said.

He nodded. "And young enough to raise. His mother got killed. You treat him right, he'll guard you till he dies."

The pup looked around and saw Mariah by the fire. On unsteady legs he went to her and lay down by her side.

Flossie was amazed. "Look at that!"

"Two young 'uns," Hugh said.

"Hungry?" she asked.

He nodded.

127

"I think it's time we had ourselves a talk," she said. "I have to know where I am, and what's going on. You hear me?"

He nodded again.

"Good. Now eat. Then we'll talk."

She ladled stew into a bowl and set it out, wishing as she did that he'd go bathe in the creek, trim his beard and his hair, and change his clothes. Having him in the house was like having a wild creature around. Oh, it was all a problem she could do without, except she'd gotten used to him, relied on his presence and his knowledge of the country. She sat down across from him and rested her chin in her hands.

"Ladies first," he said, when he'd scraped the bowl clean. He was still wondering if she had meant what she said, and what he was going to do about it if she did.

"All right," she said in a way he knew meant trouble. "What I have to say is, simply, I want to know your plans. You've helped me. God knows I couldn't have done all this without you. But I have to know . . . are you staying or going? Winter's coming on, and you'd better think before you answer. Or," she grinned at him, "is that what you were thinking about that kept you away so long?"

It was as long a speech as she'd ever made, and he took a while to digest it. Then he said, surprising himself: "You want me to stay?"

"Only if you're willing. And I'm not . . . I'm not proposing anything but a roof over your head and food, and that's only if you take a bath. How long's it been?"

He shook his head slowly. "What year is it?"

"You don't know?"

"I lost track," he said. "It hasn't much mattered."

"Why not?"

He told her then, all of it, the story he hadn't dared think about even to himself, and, when he finished, she sat quietly, biting her lip and thinking that no matter where she went pain and sorrow followed,

128

and people doing things to other people because it was in them to inflict wounds.

"It's Eighteen Seventy-Seven," she said abruptly. "And I was in the insane asylum for five years."

"You?" His eyebrows rose in shaggy Vs.

"Me." She smiled grimly.

"I know I called you loco," he said, "but you ain't crazy. Not that way."

"I know." She looked around the room — at Mariah, at the pup that was chewing on a piece of leather, at the man across from her. "A bunch of misfits, all of us," she said. "We'd best stick together. I'd like it, if you'd stay."

He looked at the child, asleep by the fire, and at the woman across the table who said she was crazy, and he felt, suddenly, as if he *had* come home, as if he'd walked a thousand miles just to find his place.

"I'd like it, too," he said.

She was awakened a few mornings later by the sound of cattle bawling, a lot of cattle judging by the noise. Beside her Mariah still slept, and on the floor the pup lay flat on its side, its belly bulging with the stew it had eaten. "Some watch dog," she murmured, and went cautiously to the door.

Where the creek spilled into a natural tank, a herd of scrawny cattle was pushing to water. Four men on horseback stood guard.

"Hugh!" she called.

No answer came.

"Damnation," she muttered. "Never around when I need you!"

She took her Winchester and stepped out, shutting the door quietly behind her. By the time the herd moved on, she'd have a mud hole instead of the place she used for bathing.

"Hey!" she said to the nearest rider who spun around, drawing his pistol so that, when he faced her, she was looking right down the black barrel.

She swallowed hard and stepped back, all the warnings, all the advice she'd heard rampant in her head. *A woman alone. Danger. Indians. Outlaws. Rustlers.* What would happen to Mariah if she were gunned down?

The rider had the drop on her and was looking at her out of the coldest, palest eyes she'd ever seen. Carefully she raised her free hand.

"You going to shoot a woman?" she asked, though her throat had gone so dry it was hard getting the words out. He didn't move, and from the look of him she thought he'd as soon shoot her as a snake. "Well," she demanded. "Are you?"

He lowered the pistol but didn't put it away. "You're lucky I didn't blow your head off, sneakin' up on me like that," he said.

Bit by bit her courage was coming back. "That's my water," she said.

One corner of his mouth twitched. "Nobody owns the water out here. Not you. Not nobody."

That was true, and she knew it, but still it rankled, those cows in what she used as a bathtub. "Where you headed?" she asked then.

"Nosy, ain't you?" His mouth twitched again, and she thought it was possible he was laughing at her.

She shook her head. "I just wanted to know how long you'd be. That's all."

"You alone?" he asked, looking at her more closely.

If he was trying to scare her, he was succeeding. But she lifted her chin and stared back at him. "Nosy, ain't you?" she mimicked.

Suddenly he laughed, a short burst like an explosion. "Yeah," he said. "I reckon so. We're headed north. Just stopped for water like always. You're new here."

"I live here now," she said. "Me and my daughter and Hugh."

"Then you'll likely see a lot of us. Next time, don't come sneakin' up waving that rifle."

She looked past him at the herd, contented now and resting. Most were little more than skin laid over jutting bones, the sorriest looking animals she'd ever seen. "Wherever you're headed," she said, "there's some that won't make it. Like those calves there." She jerked her head in the direction of a few young stragglers that were hardly able to stand.

"They'll fatten up," he said. "Once they get on good grass."

His words were familiar. Someone else had said something similar. She was quiet, thinking. Range cattle. Run out of Mexico. It had been the man on the stage, and she had been shocked. But standing here, facing a man who was surely an outlaw, she grabbed at an idea. "*If* they get there," she said. "Leave them. And you're welcome to stop when you want."

She knew by the sudden glint in his eyes that she'd passed a test, was made one of them, an outlaw, the misfit that she — and they — undoubtedly were. Well, for the sake of those half-dead calves and for her homestead — she wasn't given to self-deception — she'd go along, take advantage of what came. One lesson she'd learned in her years shut away was that she had to help herself. Nobody was going to do it for her. Not even Hugh, wherever he was. If grinning at a cow rustler helped, then she'd do it and be damned. So she grinned. "Leave those strays," she repeated. "If they die on me, so be it. If they live, then they're mine. And you're welcome to stop any time."

The rider tipped his hat and curled his lip. "Yes, ma'am," he said. He reined his horse in a wide circle and left her wiping sand and gravel off her face.

"Now what?" Hugh stood by the horse pen watching her nurse the calves that were licking up some of her precious molasses. "What'd you go do now?"

"Got us some calves," she said.

"Who from?"

"Rustlers, I guess."

"I go off half a day, and you take up with outlaws. You're gonna get us in trouble. Turn them calves loose!"

She let him rave into wordlessness, then said: "Use your eyes, man. These babies won't make it without help. But if they do, I got us some beef."

"Rustled!"

"Does that mean I should let them die?"

"You ain't got enough pasture." It was a dumb argument. He knew it as soon as he spoke.

"I got the whole valley."

"For now," he said. "But you'd best brand them. Then go file on more land and make it legal, even if your cattle ain't."

More land. She looked beyond him to where the grass waved, golden, cured on the stem, so that the valley seemed alive, rippling like the hide of an animal. And she could make it hers. "Why not?" she said.

He frowned, his brows meeting over his nose. "One thing I never liked was a woman gettin' too big for her britches."

"And I never could put up with a man who knew it all," she shot back. "Telling me what to do."

"Somebody better," he said. "But I'll prove up your claims. Get out of your hair. Besides, that way folks won't talk about me livin' here with you."

She chuckled. "No folks around that I can see," she said. "And there won't be. Not on this place. Not for miles."

Then she closed her eyes and pictured it all — her land, her cattle grazing fat and slick, and the rain clouds crossing over, their bellies filled with moisture. She chuckled again, low in her throat, thinking of Jim back on the farm, thinking maybe someday she'd write a letter, not to him, but to someone, telling what she'd done, she, Flossie Carmichael, all by herself with the help of an old renegade and a bunch of cowboy crooks.

"Who's going to town to file?" she asked. "You or me?"

* * * * *

Two days after Hugh had gone, clouds broke over the mountains, and snow swept down in a dense curtain, obliterating all familiar landmarks. Flossie was delighted. She took Mariah and Wolf into the yard and held up her face to the falling flakes. "Snow," she said to Mariah. "Can you say 'snow' for Mama?"

Mariah chuckled, grabbing at the flakes with chubby fingers. "Mama," she said suddenly and then, pleased with herself, repeated the word. "Mama, Mama."

Flossie's heart moved in her breast. Denied everything for so long, it seemed that now she had all that she had ever wanted. A daughter. A friend. And a place where hope flowered.

"Let's go in," she murmured, her face against Mariah's cheek. "Let's go in and have a party to celebrate." And after she spoke, she noticed the thick silence and shivered a little, remembering how once silence was all she desired and how now it seemed menacing, as if the world was holding its breath and waiting. But for what? "Nonsense!" she said. "Soon as I'm happy, I have to go and drag up ghosts."

She called the pup and went inside, closing the door firmly. If something was out there in the storm, it could stay out. She was going to have a party.

She and Mariah played games by the fire, and then Flossie sang, all the old songs her granny had sung to her, and at last, picking up Mariah, she waltzed around the room to the sound of the child's laughter. Just when that laughter stopped, she was never sure afterwards. But suddenly she felt a draft, heard Wolf growl low in his throat, and saw the curiosity in her daughter's eyes as they watched something over her shoulder. She turned slowly, filled with dread.

The Apache stood in the doorway, a broad-shouldered man but thin, as if at the edge of starvation. His eyes glittered; she could read nothing in them, not even her own death. She hugged Mariah tighter. "Come in," she said, her voice shaking. "Come in, and shut the door."

133

He didn't move, just stood as if he were carved from dark wood or out of the same stone as the walls. So she gestured with what she hoped was a welcoming motion and repeated herself. "Come in."

Who was he? she wondered. Mariah's father? Some lone renegade looking for vengeance? Or simply a man suffering from cold and hunger who had found his way through the storm to her fire? Since there was no way of knowing, she walked carefully to the hearth where the kettle of stew was cooking. "Hungry?" She pointed to the kettle, then to him. "Eat?"

Oh, he was hungry. She knew it by the widening of his eyes, quickly subdued. But instead he pointed at Mariah.

Flossie shook her head. "Mine!" she said loudly, too loudly, she thought, because slowly he came toward them, still expressionless.

For one moment she thought she would faint. Then she clenched her teeth and stood facing him ready to fight — to kick, bite, scratch, kill if she could, or at least get in her licks before she herself was killed. He put out a hand and touched Mariah's cheek, and he and the child stared at each other out of unblinking black eyes. After a long while the child turned and hid her face in Flossie's shoulder. "Mama," she whispered.

Triumph surged through Flossie, obliterating fear. "She loves me," she said to her visitor. "And I love her. Would you kill me for that?"

He said something she didn't understand, and she shook her head. It was horrible not being able to talk, to communicate even the simplest concepts like love and death. But one thing she did know. He was hungry. And cold. Still holding Mariah, she put three bowls and three wooden spoons on the plank table.

"Eat!" she invited again.

This time he needed no urging, picking up his bowl in two hands and drinking the rich broth. When he had emptied it several times, he lay down beside the fire, closed his eyes, and slept, a gesture of trust that Flossie found overwhelming.

"I'll be," she said. "And here I was shaking in my shoes."

He slept all day. At sundown she went out to check the animals. Snow was still falling from a sky as gray as smoke. When she went back inside, he was awake and helping himself to the last of her molasses. Mariah sat beside him, licking her fingers. In spite of her irritation Flossie smiled. "I hope Hugh remembers to bring some more of that," she said.

"Good," said the Indian.

Her eyes widened. "You speak English?"

"Good," he repeated.

"Guess not." She busied herself cleaning Mariah's face.

Was he going to stay all night? How would she ever sleep with him there by the fire, perhaps waiting for her eyes to close before stealing Mariah and taking her scalp? She put out more stew and some cornbread she had in the cupboard, and again he ate as if he were famished. "I'm glad I don't have to feed you every day," she said pleasantly.

He made no response. She hadn't expected one. But she was easier now, watching him across the table. He was a fierce-looking man with a jutting nose and cruel lips. Not a lovable face, but an honest one, and in a strange way she trusted him. He hadn't done anything to her, at least not yet, and his affection for Mariah was obvious. It must be hard, she thought, being forced to live on a reservation when the whole world had once been yours, being made an outlaw because all you sought was freedom.

"I know how you feel," she said to him. "Like a hawk in a damned cage." She surprised herself by saying: "It's still snowing. You'd best stay the night." She pointed to the hearth and pantomimed sleep.

Then, since she usually sang to Mariah at bed time, she did so, taking pleasure from the warmth of the small body and how sleep came gently to the child's vital face. The Indian watched, humming low in his throat his own lullaby, tuneless but comforting like wind in juniper branches. When she had finished, he got up and laid a gnarled hand on the sleeping child's head.

135

"Good," he muttered again.

"Yes, good," Flossie said. "I will take care of her always, and that's a promise. You understand me?"

He stared at her, and she felt that he was penetrating into her skull, divining her person down to blood and bone. She held her breath and stood motionless, hoping he could read her intentions and the message loud in her heart. Slowly, from around his neck, he lifted a small buckskin pouch on a leather thong and held it out, pointing to Mariah as if to indicate that the pouch was hers.

"Medicine," Flossie said, nodding. She'd heard of the Indian belief, knew that each carried a medicine pouch given soon after birth and filled with symbolic objects. Obviously this belonged to Mariah and had been brought to her at considerable risk.

She took the pouch and laid it close to the sleeping child, then turned back to speak and found that her visitor was gone, had disappeared into the snow as if he were himself snow. Only his footprints, fast filling in, proved that he had come on his errand and gone again.

For a long time she sat by the fire, watching the flames and musing about this new world she had found and made hospitable. It was, she thought, truly a place of misfits, a true asylum for herself, Hugh, the orphaned child, the calves that belonged to no one, and the strange Indian who had come only to assure himself of Mariah's well-being. Perhaps the whole West was like this one homestead, filled with those who sought a place of belonging, a place where trust and hope and hard work made paradise of the ordinary, where dignity was a blessing and self-reliance a necessity.

The fire was burning low. Carefully she banked it, preserving the coals for morning, then she went once more to the door and peered outside. The storm had blown away. Under an almost full moon mountains and valley caught and reflected the light as if from a silver mirror. The footprints of her visitor had vanished. He could have been a dream except for his gift to Mariah and her own vivid recollection of his face.

She stood transfixed in the doorway, overcome by memories and by the perfection of the scene before her. Nothing stirred, not even the wind, and the shadows the junipers cast seemed carved, like shapes she could learn with her fingers, carry in her hands. Orion stalked the sky to the east, while overhead a billion stars echoed the fallen snow. She felt joy rising in her, a wild elation. She had faced danger and emerged unbroken, stronger than before. Now she felt as big as the valley. If she were to lie down in it and stretch out her arms, earth's contours would become her own.

Here she would live — and die — and be buried, her bones crumbling into the soil, the thatch of her hair mingling with the roots of grass, the stems of flowers. Here she had become herself, and the knowledge formed her rising prayer. Flossie Carmichael, at last, was home.

LADY FLO

"How long will it take? This . . . this roundup of yours?"

Lord Charles is standing on the porch of what was *my* house, looking at me like I'm some kind of criminal when all I want is to get what's mine. I'm up on Apple, a big sorrel gelding, and looking down on him gives me a nasty kind of pleasure.

"It'll take till I find my stock. All of it," I say and snap my mouth shut before I really lose my temper and disgrace myself.

It's hard acting like a lady when all you want to do is strangle somebody, when all you have is your own dignity to keep you from doing it. Some folks think money will buy anything. Take this brother of James's. He thinks handing me a check can make twenty years disappear, even my own cattle, even what was between James and me. He'd rather not think about that at all or deal with me, either. I'm just a black woman who "stole" his brother and laid claim to these ranches we built with our own hands.

Well, what he doesn't know is I loved James like he was part of my own body, like he was made out of my bones, and them as white as his. And he felt the same about me. What does anybody know about love who hasn't felt it? What do Lord Charles and his pinch-nosed lawyer know? A pair of fools, both of them. "Here's a check," they say, standing off a ways like I got something catching, "for keeping house all those years."

It makes my blood boil just looking at them. Keeping house! Of course I kept house. That's what any woman does for her man, and herself if she has any pride. I took pride in our ranches, too. Worked hard as a man, learned to ride good as any *vaquero,* had my own brand, W. E. James gave it to me as a birthday present. Gave me my own cattle and horses to raise. We bred this horse I'm sitting on, and we had fine horses. Steel Dusts, mostly, bred tough in Texas, and Thoroughbreds brought over from Ireland.

James came from Ireland, and he always said how the Irish had an eye for a good horse. He taught me all he knew — and that was plenty, and not just about horses. He taught me how to laugh and have fun. How to play. Things I never had time for growing up in Illinois with no daddy around to help out, only my mama who worked herself near to death to keep a roof over my brother and me and food on the table.

No, we never played. Living was serious business. You scrabbled to keep alive and, when that got too much, you laid down and died. Soon as I was old enough, I got a regular job, cleaning house. I was fourteen and strong and presentable looking, and I knew my manners. My mama saw to that. She'd been raised in Virginia and set a store by good behavior. *Her* daddy was a white man and mine was part Indian, and I guess that accounts for how we look, not black *or* white but in between, which makes it hard because nobody lays claim to you. Under the law, though, I'm black. Under the law any white man married to a black can go to jail and the woman with him. So it's no wonder we stayed in Mexico, James and me, the Irish Lord Beresford and his black Lady Flo.

Neither of us intended what happened. In my craziest dreams, a kid in Illinois, I never saw my life turning out like it did. There I was cleaning houses, and all of a sudden I got asked to go to Mexico as nursemaid for the Anthonys' two children. Now that's a step most folks would take a day or two to think about, but not me.

"Yes, sir. I'll come," I said to Mr. Anthony, soon as he asked. "It'll be an adventure."

He laughed. "For all of us, I imagine."

He got that right. Mexico sure isn't Illinois. It's deserts, and mountains, and cañons, and rivers that are dry most of the year. It's hot, and dusty, and the plants, most of 'em, have stickers or thorns.

And it's poor. Lordy, most folks are poorer than my family was, and no chance of getting ahead, what with the government the way it is — rich men getting richer, and *bandidos* stealing all they can from whoever they can.

But don't get me wrong. I love this country. The happiest years of my life were here. It's beautiful, see? The kind of beauty that catches you so you want to cry over it. The way the sun graces the rocks at sunset and turns them pink as a rose and then red as fire. How the wind always smells from some sweet plant blooming, and in summer the grass weaves in and out of itself, a carpet of green and yellow thread.

Oh, I'm all mixed up! I'm trying to tell about James and me, and how we met and loved, and here I am going on about everything else. Maybe it's because I'm scared to remember. It'll hurt too bad, and I'll have to admit that being alone will be like I'm dead, too, half of me missing, cut off and buried, and not even in the place I called home. They took James's body back to Ireland. Never asked me what I wanted, what *he* wanted. Never even gave me a chance to say a proper good bye.

All I've got is a piece of paper with numbers on it, my clothes, and those horses and cattle with my own brand on them that the boys and I are ready to round up. Nobody's going to cheat me out of my cattle, and they can't really take the land away from me because it's in me like James is. Can these things fill up the emptiness? Take the place of eyes that were always soft and laughing? Talk to me in that funny way he had — or touch me — gently like a Mexican touches the strings of a guitar and makes music?

I'm sitting here in the front yard of Los Ojitos Ranch, remembering how we trailed our first herd of shorthorns down from the railroad depot. Talk about wild cattle! Those critters had been penned up so long that, when they got out, they hit the ground, running. It took us a week to round them up and get them moving toward home. I rode with the men, and there was a kind of glory in it, maybe more for me than for anybody, even James. It was like I'd been born again into a different world. I wasn't a black woman any more. I was Lady Flo, riding a big sorrel horse that's kin to this one I'm riding now, and I was doing a man's job. The wind was in my face, and the sound of hoofs and cattle bawling like to made me deaf, but I loved it, every minute. And there was James, grinning through the dust and saying: "You ride like you were born in the saddle, my lady."

Oh, I was proud! And happy. I never had an unhappy minute on these ranches. Not a one. Until last month when they brought word that James had died in that train wreck up in Canada. Grief comes slow sometimes. It hasn't quite caught me yet. I've been too busy fighting for what's mine, what I helped build, fighting for the glory, for the past.

Oh, get on with it, Flo! You're like an old woman mumbling back history and getting no place. Get on with it, get it out and done!

All right. This is how it all started, how it was. We were in Chihuahua City, and it was 1885. Mr. Anthony had a job with the American government, and he rented a nice house built around a courtyard in the Mexican style. My job was easy. Taking care of the two children, Grace and Tom, seeing they ate their dinners and minded their manners and had on nice clothes when they met company. For schooling, they had a tutor. My school was the town — the streets, the market, the people.

The first thing, I set about learning the language because, not being able to talk to anybody but the kids, I was pretty lonely. Even the maids were Mexican, though one of them, Alicia, had a little English and helped me as best she could. It didn't take me long before I could chatter with the best of them. I've always been a talker. My mama always said I spoke my first words at nine months and never stopped after. Except around James. Try as I might, I couldn't seem to get words out that meant anything. I was scared, see? Even after twenty years I couldn't come right out and say I loved him. Seemed like saying it would make it all disappear, and I'd be left there on the ranch with only the wind for company. He was a man. And he was white. He had the power.

The first time I laid eyes on him, though, he was anything but powerful. He'd caught himself one of those Mexican bugs, and he was out of his head and just plain sick. At that point Lord Delaval James Beresford, fifth son of the Marquis of Waterford, lay in his bed, looking bad off.

"You know what to do, Florida," Mrs. Anthony told me. "You have to nurse him. You're the only girl here who knows how and who speaks English."

I hadn't been trained to refuse. Besides, he looked so small laying there. So helpless. I put a hand on his forehead. "If we don't break this fever, he won't be needing me," I said.

If he hadn't been so helpless, like a kitten you'd save from drowning, like an orphan lamb, maybe it'd all have been different. But looking at him, my belly twisted in a knot, and my heart seemed to swell up in my breast. I felt like, if he died, I'd be guilty of a sin so big it didn't have a name.

So I sat by that bed for nearly a week, sponging him off, keeping him clean, squeezing lemons in water for him to drink, and sending Alicia for soup that I spooned into him whether he wanted it or not. Then I remembered the herb-woman, the *curandera,* who sold potions at the back of the market and who all the maids swore was a witch. She'd have a medicine, I figured. Born here, she'd know what cure was best.

I took off my apron, washed my face, put on a hat. Then I called Alicia. "You sit with him," I ordered. "I'll be back quick as I can."

Alicia had black eyebrows the shape of horse shoes, and they lifted up over her eyes. Her skin wasn't any darker than mine, I noticed. Funny. And a funny time to have such a thought. "Where are you going?" she wanted to know.

"To the *curandera.*"

She made a noise half way between a squeak and a breath. "Altagracia?"

I nodded.

"Be careful." She put out her hand. "Be careful of that one that she doesn't fool you and make a spell."

I laughed. I knew all about those old herb-women and their reputations, just like I knew that they mostly got blamed for what was already in people's heads. "Don't worry," I said. "You just watch him till I get back."

She crossed herself when she thought I wasn't looking. Silliness. Superstition. That's what her fears amounted to. I ran out the door and down the street to the market.

Any other day I'd have stopped to enjoy the booths where the people were selling everything from live chickens and goats to the platters and bowls where they'd end up. I loved that market. A friendly place, full of gossip and laughter. But that day I didn't waste time. I made my way through the crowd to Altagracia's little stall where she sold herbs and salves, and those silver *milagros* folks bought and hung in the church as thanks for prayers that were answered.

Altagracia sat in the middle of it all, wrapped in a shawl and looking dried up and shriveled like a mushroom that's been in the sun too long. One thing I knew; nobody ever hurried her. She demanded respect, and got it, partly because of her reputation as a witch, and partly because she'd been born knowing who she was and had dignity as a result.

So I said good morning and asked how she was, and said I was fine, too, all that ritual we go through, never matter how anxious we are or what we're feeling, and all the while her sharp little eyes watched me and tried to guess my errand. Finally she asked: "What can I do to help you?" smiling like she already knew and showing the stubs of her old teeth.

"I need something for fever. We got a visitor who's bad off."

143

She smiled again and made a little humming noise. "Ah, ah, ah." Then she said: "The white gentleman from across the ocean, yes?"

"How'd you know?"

"Oh, I hear, I hear," she said, turning around and poking through her baskets and pots like what was inside them was jewels, taking a pinch of this, and a sprinkle of that, all the time humming under her breath. Finally she handed me two little packages in paper so old it looked like it would split apart before I made it home. "This you give to the gentleman," she said. "The other is for you."

"Me? I'm not sick."

"And you won't be. Do what I tell you." Her eyes looked as black as storm clouds.

I felt the hair on my neck prickle. Maybe Alicia was right. Maybe the old woman was putting a spell on me. She grabbed my wrist. "Lady," she said, "you take this. It won't hurt you." She brought out an old mug and filled it with water, and I found myself laughing. She'd called me "lady" like I was white. Like I was a *rica*. "I'm no lady," I said.

She sprinkled the powder into the mug and stirred it up with a finger that looked like a bone. "I know what I know," she said, handing me the mug.

I drank it all, like I was taking a dare. Whatever it was, it tasted of cinnamon and cloves and something bittersweet like a lost dream. "What do you know?" I asked when I finished.

She shook her head. "Wait and see, lady. Wait and see." Then she turned around and left me standing there.

Who knows? Maybe she did put a spell on me, that old woman. And maybe she put one on James, too. If she did, it was sure powerful. It lasted more than twenty years.

That night I gave him the medicine and fixed a chair by the long doors that opened out into the courtyard. "Either the fever breaks or, if it doesn't, we lose him," I told Mrs. Anthony. "But I'll sit up and call if we need the doctor to come."

What I didn't say was that the doctor was worthless — a drunk, usually passed out cold in a *cantina* somewhere and not worth the powder to blow him away.

Mrs. Anthony wasn't good in a pinch. Actually she was a silly woman. She fluttered her hands at me. "Do your best, Florida. I know you will. We need men like Lord Beresford in Mexico." Then she ran like she was scared she'd catch the fever next.

So there I was in the room with him asleep, the lamp turned low, and me in my rocking chair. It looked like a long night. A little skittish wind came up and blew the curtains in and out with a sound like somebody breathing, and after a while moths flew in and danced around the flame in the lamp like the fools they had to be. I brushed them away, but they kept coming back, all of them different, but all of the same mind — to jump into that fire. Then the biggest moth I ever saw came in on a puff of wind and landed on my hand. Just like that it touched down and laid there, so light I could hardly feel it, and so beautiful all I could do was stare. It was creamy white and pale green, like a piece of lace, and I wanted to touch it but didn't for fear it would break in two. All I did was sit and look, and breathe easy so as not to scare it off.

"What do you have there?"

The voice seemed like it came out of nowhere. I jumped, then looked around. James was sitting up, watching me.

"The biggest moth ever," I said when I got my wits back. "And don't you get uncovered."

He chuckled. The sound of it made me glad. Then he said: "It's been you here with me, hasn't it? All the time."

"Yes sir," I said. "It's been me. There isn't anybody else."

"How long?" he wanted to know.

I counted back. " 'Bout a week now."

"Ah." He nodded. "Bring that moth here. Let's have a look."

I eased myself out of the chair, holding my hand steady.

"I thought I was dreaming," he said. "Seeing you there."

145

"It was the fever. You been out of your head."

"What I meant was, I thought I'd dreamed you, but I didn't, did I?" He was smiling, watching me.

I figured maybe he was still feverish and felt his forehead. It was cool as spring water. "I'm real," I told him.

"So I see."

He looked at the moth that seemed like pure light, like water running over stone. Beside it my skin seemed even darker than it was, and I sighed. For a minute there I'd felt like somebody else.

"How perfect it is." He was whispering, like he felt he'd scare it if he talked loud. "What will we do with it?"

"I'm putting it out and closing the door so it won't get burnt to dust, that's what. Then you're going to pull up those covers unless you want to take sick again."

"I'm fine, thanks to you," he said, watching while I put out the moth and latched the door. "Did you know?" he asked when I'd finished, "did you know that a moth will fly thousands of miles to find its mate?"

I thought that one over. Then, because I didn't know how to answer, and because for the littlest second I felt that prickle on the back of my neck, I said: "Sometimes there's no telling about things."

"An elusive remark, if ever I heard one," he said. He pulled the covers up to his chin and sat there, grinning. "I'm hungry enough to eat an ox."

"I'll get something. But you got to promise to be good while I'm gone."

That grin burst out into a chuckle that made him sound like a wild child. "Promises, promises. All right. But bring something for yourself, and we'll have a celebration."

Now, I'd never sat down at a table with white folks in my life, celebration or no celebration. That's the way it was, see? Servants ate in the kitchen, not with lords in the dining room or any place

146

else, either. "I ate already," I said.

"What's your name?" he wanted to know then. Lord, he was full of questions!

"Florida," I said. "Florida Wolfe."

He settled back against the pillow. "Well, Florida, bring enough for two, and we'll see."

"This is baby food," he said, when I got back with a tray. "I meant it about the ox."

"It's all you get till we see if you keep it down."

He looked surprised, then unhappy. "It must have been awful for you. I'm sorry."

I shrugged. "You were sick, and I'm used to sick folks. Now try and eat those eggs."

What I didn't want to talk or think about was how I'd washed him and changed his clothes. How I knew his body like I knew my own — the broad shoulders, the long legs, and everything in between. Sick, he was just a patient. Well, he was a man, and he had a way with him, and he bothered me with his talk and his questions, and how he watched me with those eyes of his — dark brown, almost purple, the color of an iris I saw once and never forgot.

I sat down in my chair and looked at my hands. It felt safe that way. That wasn't to his liking. He squinted at me, trying to see in the shadows. "Come, sit here while I eat. I can't be shouting across the room and eat all at once."

It was an order. I knew the difference. I moved. Slowly. Still thinking about him as a man and trying to hide it.

He didn't notice. "Now," he said. "Tell me about yourself. How old you are. Where you were born. Who you really are." He took a bite of egg.

"Why you want to know?" It sounded bold. It *was* bold. I wasn't supposed to ask questions, just answer them.

He put down his fork and cocked his head like a bird does. "We're

147

practicing the fine art of conversation," he said. "I haven't had much chance at it lately. Besides, it's my turn to find out about you. You've had a week's head start."

Lord, he must have suspected what I was trying not to show! But knowing a man's body — or a woman's — isn't the same as knowing their minds. I figured to put him off and answered his question. "I'm nineteen," I said. "And I was born in Illinois. Folks there are like they are anywhere. Rich and poor. Black and white. Me . . . I was black *and* poor."

"Nonsense," he said. "You're not black. More like a good cup of strong tea. With milk."

"Maybe so. But that doesn't make me white. You better learn that first thing." He gave a sigh. I thought he was tired and took advantage of it. "Best go to sleep now," I told him. "You don't want a relapse."

He didn't argue. All he said was, "Will you stay?"

I settled into the chair. "Till you don't need me."

Then I blew out the lamp and left the room in darkness.

The next evening, when I took him up a proper meal, he was waiting for me. "There you are. Scheherezade," he said.

I know I just stopped in my tracks, thinking he'd gone off his head and was saying nonsense.

He laughed. "Put the tray down, Florida. I see I'll have to explain." While he was eating, he told me the story. About how there was a sultan who wanted revenge on women. How he married them and then cut off their heads. Except for Scheherezade who told him stories every night for a thousand and one nights and saved her life. "So you see," he said, "you'll have to stay and talk, or I'll chop off your head."

"You'll need to get a lot stronger first," I told him. "You couldn't lift an axe if you tried."

"I will. I have to. I want to get on with it." His eyes shone with

148

that wild look I was getting used to. "I'm buying land, Florida. Lots of it. And I'll raise cattle and horses and be rich. What do you say to that?"

"I thought you already were rich."

"Comparatively I guess I am. But I'm the youngest son. There's nothing left for me at home. Can you understand that?"

It sounded strange to me whose family from first to last never had a nickel to spare, but finally I said: "Yes, sir."

He leaned over the edge of the bed. "Florida, stop calling me 'sir.' My name is James."

I thought the fever had come back sure. Either that or he was as innocent as a baby. "I can't do that," I told him. "Now you lay back and behave."

"Why can't you?"

"That's not the way it is. Not here, probably not any place. Do the folks who work for you where you come from call you James?"

That stumped him. But he was always ready with an argument. That man should've been a preacher or in government the way he could twist things to suit himself. "This is the New World," he said. "We're both free to do as we please."

I was right. He was innocent. "That's what you think," I said.

He laughed. "Stubborn. That's what you are. I bet your mother had to beat you."

"She never!"

"Then she should have." He laid back and looked pleased with himself, like he'd won out over me.

I had to laugh in spite of myself, and that seemed to please him even more.

"I made you laugh," he said. "I didn't think you knew how. You're always so serious."

"Not much to laugh about."

"Not true. The world's a sorry place without it."

"It's sorry, all right," I said, feeling, all of a sudden, like I was carrying a rock on my back, so tired I could have laid right down on the floor and slept for three days. It wasn't just that I'd been sitting up, nursing him. My whole life seemed heavy on me, and my mother's life, and my granny's, though I'd never known her. All of us women, all of us hurting. "Let me tell you something," I began, and told him all of it. How my own mother had been born a slave, the daughter of the man who owned her. How she married another slave, and him killed fighting alongside his white owner in the war, and her with two children. How she left the South and raised us kids by working till she was ready to drop, and how that was all we knew. Work and more work, freezing in the winter, sweating in the summer, and hungry most of the time. And how there wasn't any place for laughing or for gentleness in our lives. When I finished, I sat back in the chair like I'd purged something, got rid of it once and for all. That's what talking does sometimes. It frees you, lets out the badness and the pain.

He said: "Good God, Florida."

I rocked a little in my chair, then said: "It was hard, but I lived through it."

"I'm very glad you did, my dear," he said.

Maybe it was the words, maybe the way he said them, but my heart started pounding again so I could hardly breathe. "My dear." Nobody had ever called me that, not even my mama. She'd never had the time. Sitting there, it seemed I'd lived my whole life waiting to hear him say those two words, that I'd been born and survived just so I'd be here on this night, with this strange white man who was looking at me out of soft, dark eyes.

"I'm glad, too," I said after a minute, and meant it.

James got better fast. In a week he was up and around, and then he went off looking at the land he'd come to buy. And I was back with the children, wishing I wasn't. I knew what was wrong with me, but that didn't make me feel any happier. I'd

"Your family . . . ?" I got out.

"They're not here. I am. You are."

But they could come, all of them, those strange rich people used to funny ways, and every last one of them white. "It's against the law!" The words came out like to strangle me.

He laughed. "Where we're going, I *am* the law. Do you understand?"

I didn't. "No," I said. "All I know is that nobody's gonna marry us. Not in the States and not down here."

"Then we'll marry ourselves."

Maybe this was how my granny had felt — light headed and heavy all at once, and the warmth in her, the tears back of her eyes. It was like saving myself only to jump off an edge into some other danger. And there wasn't anybody to give me advice. All I had was me. I looked him square in the face and saw hope there, and kindness, and that little shine of mischief that always did me in. "You're sure?" I asked.

"I'm sure." His voice was smooth and deep like a good whiskey.

"All right, then." Just saying the words lifted the weight off me. The misery of the last month was gone, and the fear.

"You won't change your mind?"

"What's done is done," I said. "I won't change it."

"Thank the Lord." He put his arms around me and hugged me close.

Oh, it was a scandal! The whole town talked, and the Anthonys dismissed me.

"Nobody will receive you," Mrs. Anthony told me, and her tone was as nasty as the look in her eyes.

James thought that was really funny. "Where we're going, we'll be doing the receiving," he said. "And we'll be very careful whom we choose to entertain."

Then he swept me out as if, really, I was a lady and she was a nobody. It was a good feeling, and I kept it close inside me, hoping

gotten *used* to the man, to talking to him, doing for him. He was in me and would be the rest of my life. That notion didn't help, either. What good was loving, if I had to pretend it wasn't there, keep on like I always had for no reason except to stay alive? I tried to talk myself out of it. I scolded. I made fun of me, Florida, who was fool enough to love a white man, and a lord at that. Nothing worked. It seemed like my own body resisted, dug in its heels and argued back at me.

"What's done is done," it said. "Might as well try to unstitch a quilt."

I looked in the mirror. It was true I wasn't any darker than a lot of the Mexicans, and my hair was straight as a rope, but that didn't change the fact that I was a black woman, in a long line of black women stretching back to Africa. Their blood was mine. Had my granny loved the white man who took her for himself? Had she welcomed the sight of him? Talked to him? Nursed him when he was sick, and taken him into her body where color didn't matter? I didn't know. All I knew was that I had to go through the rest of my days, pretending I didn't hurt.

"Are you sickening with something, Florida?" Mrs. Anthony wasn't worried about me, only herself and her family.

"No, ma'am."

We were out in the courtyard, keeping cool in the late afternoon.

"Well if you are, you go straight to bed. Alicia can look after the children."

"Yes, ma'am."

I wished I would get sick. I wished I would die and be buried in the dusty ground of Mexico, under the hot sun that was like a burning eye.

Two weeks went by, then three. The summer rains started. I remember that. How the big clouds would build up till they got so full of water they burst open and dumped on us. How afterward the air was cool, and the flowers in the yard bloomed and made my nights worse than the days.

And then one afternoon came the ringing of the bell that hung by the front door. Lunch was over, and the whole house was taking a siesta. Everybody but me. I'd stopped trying to sleep. I went down the hall and opened the little window that was cut into the door, and there he was, smiling at me, all lit up with excitement.

He took my hands as soon as he got inside. "Flo!" he said. "I'm glad it's you. There's so much to tell. Where is everyone?"

"Taking siesta."

"Ah, yes," he said. "I keep forgetting."

Just then Mrs. Anthony opened her door at the end of the hall and called out. "Who is it, Florida?"

"Mister James, ma'am."

"Back so soon?" She was all in a tizzy, I could tell, him being a lord and all. "Show him into the parlor. I'll be a few minutes."

He looked at me and grinned, then held out his arm. "Shall we, my dear?"

I had to laugh, him escorting me as if I were the lady of the house. "One of these days you'll get me in trouble with your fooling," I said, but I took his arm anyhow, just to see how it would be.

"Nonsense," he said, and swept me into the parlor. "Aren't you going to ask where I've been? What I did?"

"You tell me. You will anyhow."

That made him laugh again. "You know me too well," he said. I thought, he didn't know how well. "I bought a ranch. Thousands of acres. Grass. Water. Scenery!" He spread his arms. "You should see it. I missed you, Flo. I kept wishing you were there with me to see it. There's a little house, too, but I've already got men started on a bigger one."

Sure, I thought. He'd need a big house. He was a lord, and pretty soon there'd be a lady, and children, and all the time I'd be some

place else. I swallowed hard, so busy hiding my misery I sto[p] listening.

"Will you?" he was saying, watching me with those eyes.

"Will I what?"

"Come there with me?"

That's all I'd need! Nursemaiding his wife and kids! "I got a[ ] job here," I said.

He took my hands again and pulled me so close I could fe[el] breath on my face. I was scared and tried to pull away. [Stop] wriggling!" It was one of his orders.

I stood still as a stone, trying not to think about the littl[e] glowing down deep in my belly, the banging of my heart. "M[r.] James . . ."

"And stop 'mistering' me!"

Best let him have his say, I thought. Get it over with. "Yes[,"] I said and looked down at the floor, at our feet, his in high le[ather] boots, mine in worn-down house slippers. They showed the d[iffer]ence between us better than a mirror.

"You haven't heard a word I said! I said I want you to com[e with] me to the ranch. To be my Lady Flo. Damn it, woman, are you d[eaf?]"

For sure I was deaf. And dumb, too. Couldn't move to save m[e.] I let myself look at him. "What're you saying?"

He tightened his grip on me. He said: "I'm saying I misse[d you.] I'm saying I don't want to go out there without you, and wi[ll you] come with me? Damn it, Flo, I'm proposing, and you're sta[nding] there like a lump!"

He meant it. I knew he meant it, and I wanted to bawl, to [stamp] my feet, to tell him fever had addled him, and I'd rather take p[oison.] But that fire in me wouldn't let go, and I couldn't let go of his [hands,] and all the time my heart jumping like a frog in my throat. H[e was] giving me my wish, but I was scared to take it for fear it woul[d turn] out to be only ashes and I'd end up the same as I was.

"Well?" he said. "Can't you talk? What do you say, Flo?"

life would always be like that. For twenty years, it was.

Running a ranch isn't so different from running a house — a big house. What you have to be is organized. And you can't sit home and expect anybody else to do it for you. I saw that right off, as soon as I realized how big six hundred thousand acres really is. But there was a happiness in the doing of it, in the setting off at first light to check cattle, mend fence, any one of the hundred chores that need doing on a ranch.

"You keep the books," I told James early on. "I'll do the rest."

My head isn't good with book work, but I can count cows quicker than anybody and be accurate, too. And after a while, with lessons from James and our Mexican *vaqueros* who could sit a horse like they were born on one, I could ride as good as they could, and not on one of those ladies' saddles, either.

"I won't break in half," I said when James brought me my first horse, a big black gelding I named Sacaton. "But get me a real saddle. I want to ride, not hang off one side like a sack of wood on a *burro*."

I guess riding sidesaddle is an art. James said how in Ireland ladies ride to the hunt on those contraptions, and jump fences, too, but I dug in my heels. He just laughed. He liked seeing me take a stand and, when I did, he always had the same answer. "You're the boss, Lady Flo."

That's what he told the hands on that first day — those men who are riding with me now on roundup — Luis, Manuel, Sixtos. He told them: "Do what the *Señora* Flo tells you as if I were telling you."

They did, too, and not because they were paid to do it, either. I understood how it was to work for somebody, and I treated those *vaqueros* like people, not like slaves. What they did, I did — brand, doctor, swallow dust, hunt cows, help in birthings, and take a drink of good whiskey at the end of a long day. Love of the land was bred into them, see? . . . was that part of them that was Indian like me. It's not something you can help, any more than you can help any kind of love. It's just there, and it shapes you, makes you hard and gentle both at once.

Now I tell them in Spanish so that pompous lord up there on the porch won't understand: "We're rounding up everything out there that has my brand. Cattle and horses. Every one of them, if it takes us a month."

They look at me with serious eyes, and they smile, that bitter kind of smile that tells me they know as well as I do what's going on, that the *ricos* are cheating all of us and not just me.

Manuel, the foreman, gives me a kind of salute and says: "Every one, *señora*. We won't let this rattlesnake bite you." He sounds like he's laughing.

We head out together, kicking up dust for Lord Charles to choke on. I hope he does.

It does take us nearly a month. There are more horses and cattle than I thought. Many more. I go down to the big pens to take a count.

All those horses! Mine! Only now I've got to sell them at auction in El Paso or Juarez. Sell all those fiery eyes and quick hoofs. All the colts that come up to me curious and prick-eared. Not that I'd ever have the chance to ride them all, but, still, they're mine, and I love them like the children James and I never had. Here comes Belle, one of our best brood mares with a little critter tagging along. He's got a fresh brand on his hip that he keeps twisting around trying to see or sniff. My brand. W E.

I'm thinking something that makes me smile, the same smile I saw on Manuel's face when we left home, and I go over to the cattle pens and stand there looking at what seems to be a thousand head. I'm counting all the fresh W E brands.

"Many cattle. Many good horses." Manuel's beside me, trying to look innocent, but he knows he can't fool me.

He and the men have been branding every critter they could catch, and they're doing it out of loyalty, out of love, out of their belief in right and wrong. No *gringo* lord is going to come in here and cheat me, not if they can help it. Not if they have to round up half the cattle in Chihuahua and Texas and brand each and every one with my mark.

Oh, I wish James was here! How he'd laugh. He always loved a good joke, even on his own people. How he enjoyed introducing me to some of them as Lady Flo and making them be polite, even though I must've been a shock and a hard pill to swallow.

Now come the tears. I can't help myself. They fall and fall and splash into the dust and don't stop for what feels like an hour. I wipe my face on my sleeve, then hold out my hand to Manuel who takes it in his two hard ones.

"How do I thank you?" I ask him.

He shrugs. "You have thanked us, *señora*. You have been good to us. Now, what we do, we do."

We stare at each other. I hear what he said. And I hear old Altagracia in the market so many years ago. "Lady," she had said, and it came true — Lady Flo. That was James, and me on his arm everywhere we went — El Paso, Mexico City, our big ranch in Canada where nobody cared what I was anyhow.

One thing left to do. There's no way I'll sell my babies at auction to strangers. I call the men, and I tell them to take their pick of these horses they love the same as me. "You take them," I say. "And you take them far from here and hide them. When you come back, I'll be here with the cattle, and we'll drive them back to the ranch."

They look at me, these loyal men, and I see the light in their eyes, the glory of having fine horses of their own to ride. I'm hoping that years from now they'll see horses and remember, that maybe we have left a mark on this place of sun and wind and a thousand horses, running. Lord Beresford and me. His Lady Flo.

Lord Delaval James Beresford was killed in a train wreck near Enderlin, North Dakota in December, 1906. Florida J. Wolfe died of pulmonary tuberculosis in El Paso on May 19, 1913.

OLD PETE

The way I had it figured, my mule would go first so I could give him a decent burial and so he wouldn't grieve for me too hard. But Old Pete's going on thirty with no signs of dying, and they got me in this hospital bed, and they're a-running around making tests and prodding me like a calf that don't want to be rounded up nohow.

Pete and I have been together longer than most folks stay married these days. He was a two-year-old when I bought him but, young as he was, he had trail sense and savvy. The day I went to see him he looked me over just as sharp as I was looking at him, and he took a couple of sniffs at my hand so he'd know my smell. Then he stood while I mounted, one eye and one ear cocked sideways, just watching me. He was the best riding mule I ever sat. He had an easy walk, a jog like running water, and a lope you couldn't get in your favorite rocking chair.

I bought him there and then, not knowing I'd bought a watch dog and a best friend for next to nothing. So maybe it's better this way, me going first. I just won't come back, and after a while I hope he'll stop looking for me, watching the road for the truck. He'll nose around Daisy, the mare, until it dawns on him I'm not coming back, and then maybe he'll lie down and dream about the way it used to be — the roundups, all those trails up in the mountains, all the things he and I have kept to ourselves for fear folks would come running to take a look and ruin it. And maybe he'll go out that way, easy and dreaming.

Used to be I could find places no one had ever seen, Pete's making his own trail over the rocks and through the pines. There's a spot up there that has twenty-pound trout living underground. They're blind from being in the dark so long and, when they surface, right under the roots of an old juniper, you can pull 'em out barehanded.

Farther up there's a meadow where the lady bugs come every summer thick as locusts, breaking down branches and crawling everywhere, even up a man's pants and into his boots. That whole mountain top is red with them, and the air's just a-buzzing with their little wings. Old Pete always walked careful there, putting his feet down slow like he didn't want to disturb them. I don't know what they come for, whether it's to mate or to die, but they come every summer for sure, and it's something to see.

These are things I keep to myself. In the last twenty years there's so many people come out here that nothing's the same. I don't resent them, but I sure don't need any more of them. I wish the land could stay the way it was — open, empty, green. When I was a boy, this whole place was green. There wasn't any rainy season or dry. We had rain twelve months a year, and the wash was full up and running unless it was froze in the winter. We had grass then that was as high as a boy's head. Good grass that grew so thick you never walked on the dirt but on the stems and roots. And I could look out and see it bending and blowing and waving just like the sea. It was a sight. I can close my eyes and see it, see the cattle moving through, and the seed heads of the grass so heavy the stems bend down.

Old Pete, he was something on a roundup. Knew what those dumb critters were going to do before they knew it themselves. And he was sure footed. He never went around a mountain after a steer, or zig-zagged down like a horse will do. He'd just sit on his rear and slide to the bottom, with me holding on for dear life. And he never got tired. He was as fresh at sunset as he was at first light. He knew how to take care of himself. A mule does.

I recollect one time when I was foreman on the Running W and working with a green kid, somebody's city relative who wanted to be a cowboy. A couple cows and their calves broke loose, and I had to go round them up and get them penned, so I told the kid to stay by the gate and wait, and help me drive 'em in when I came. The first time Pete and I come down with the cows, the kid was nowhere to be seen. He'd gone off somewhere in the brush, thinking he was helping me look. The cows split up and took off, and I had to find the kid and give him a talking to. Told him to follow orders and stay put. Then Pete and I went off and rounded up the cows and brought them back again. Same thing. The kid wasn't there. He'd got bored and was settin' off a ways under a tree. I gave him what for, and got back on Pete, but Pete, he just planted his feet and wouldn't move. He just looked at me and at that kid and said: "No, sir!" I whupped him, spurred him even, but he'd had enough fooling around. He knew that kid was worthless, and he just quit.

And there's no man can make a mule change its mind once it's decided. I led him home and left him alone for a week, and then got on and rode him hard. No trouble. He'd just figured there was no point wasting any more time with a fool kid.

Well, seems like everything's changed. There's no big roundups now, and not much open range, neither. And the good grass is dried up and gone with the change in the weather. A steer's got to roam for its dinner and then get sent to a feed lot to fatten. And what's worse, we've got big business and the government and a bunch of playboys from the cities telling us what we can and can't do with our own land so all the freedom's gone out of life. Seems like a man can't even spit without somebody tellin' him, and that takes the pleasure out of it.

Used to be a man had good neighbors, folks he could depend on even if he never saw them from one month to the next. Nowadays that road outside my fence is filled with folks I never saw before and don't much care to see again. Folks who don't know how to get along with the land, don't know what it's for or how to take care of it or themselves.

Old Pete, though, he keeps them away. He watches that gate and, if someone he don't know or don't like gets close, he'll snort and holler and block the way, and he'll show those yellow teeth if they get ornery. Mules have long memories. Pete knows his friends, though they might not come but once a year. He smells 'em all over like a dog and remembers in that old mule brain of his.

He's got that mare to look out for, too. He loves that mare. He'd kill anyone laid a hand on her. I've seen him shove her away from rattlers and test water before letting her drink.

He's got a lot of words to tell me what's going on, too. The other day he found a rattler up against the house, and I could tell from the sounds he was making what he'd got. He'd stomped it before I could get there, but he was ready to talk about it to anyone who'd listen.

Like I say, he's a watchdog and a friend. I never had a better. He doesn't intrude but lets a man be, and there's not many people know that. Everybody knows everybody else's business. Folks don't seem to know how good it is just to be quiet, to sit outside and listen to the sounds of the land. The land has a language, too, but you got to listen, and listen good before you know what it's saying.

Sometimes I think the whole world's gone deaf and blind. Everybody fighting everybody else, and for what? For the land, and it belonging to itself. Oh, it's happened before. It's all in the Bible, but nobody reads the Bible any more, except for a line here, a psalm there, a piece on Sunday. But that's not the way to do it. You got to read it straight through like a history book, because that's what it is. Back history. And anybody who wants to know what's coming can find it in there repeated over and over.

I've read the Book through more times than I can count. Took it out on the mountain and read it out loud, and watched the trees blowing and the clouds going over, the whole earth running on, and I knew what it was — poetry and literature and history all in one book, and that's the way a man should read it. High up somewhere, close to God, touching the land and the sky all at once, with time to listen and think things through.

I don't know but what I'm glad to be going. There's nothing a man can call his own any more without paying for it twice over. Except friendship. And maybe love. But it's been my experience that even love depends on what's in a man's pocket.

I was courting a girl once, trying to put enough by to set up my own place. A man can't live with his family or his in-laws when he's married. Being married is hard enough without everybody giving advice, although Kate said she'd be happy with me anywhere. And maybe that was true. She was a happy woman then, round faced and always laughing. But she said she'd wait, and she did for a while. I worked cattle all over the state, even did a stint in the mines, though that wasn't work I was used to or liked. But those were hard times. I lost a horse and had to replace him, and I was off a lot on the cattle trains and didn't get home often. But I'd taken her at her word. Didn't think I had to keep coming back to make sure she still believed in our life together.

In the end she caught Crane Whittaker's eye, and maybe it was his money caught hers. The Running W's a big spread and a good one. She did her duty by him and it — five boys and as neat a house as I ever did see. But the laughter went out of her. I knew because I worked as Whittaker's foreman for a good many years, and I never once saw her lay her head back and laugh like she had with me. Truth is, I didn't go out of my way to see her. It rankled, her saying she'd wait and then going back on her word. Women are funny that way. Changeable.

Come down to it, only the fact of the land doesn't change. You care for it, and it takes care of you. That's what folks nowadays have got to learn. But I haven't been able to make anybody see. They come out here and say how beautiful it is, and I want to tell them to go back home. I want to say, when I was a boy, there were trees and flowers and animals that are gone now, disappeared because we're pumping out the water and tearing up the mountains and the flats just so everybody can have a piece and take from it without giving anything back.

Well, the land's still here, rock and soil, and at home I can wake up and look out and see the mountains running clear to Mexico and changing colors with the clouds and the sun, the hawks and buzzards riding the wind currents, and the mule and the mare off in the shade.

I hate to let Pete down, not go back. It's not right. And a place like this hospital is no place to die. I can't even see a piece of the sky, and there's never a time when it's quiet, when a man can lie back and think. The Indians had the right idea. When a man's time came, he just went out alone somewhere and waited for the spirit to go out of him, back into the wind or the mountains where it had come from, where it belonged.

Maybe that's what I'll do — lie here a while and get up the strength to go home, and never a word to those doctors. Pete will understand why I've come. He knows my mind like I know his. He knows I've never gone back on my word. A man's word has to count for something, and that's just about all I've got left.

So I'll go home, and maybe the two of us can go up the mountain to where the ladybugs go. We can sit there and watch the meadow turn red as fire, watch the sun go down over the purple shadows of the valley. And when the night comes, we'll count the stars, name them — Orion, Betelgeus, the Pleiades. And when we close our eyes, we'll still see them. With any luck they'll light our way.

LOU

It was how Charley Barnes died that set folks talking, not that some didn't think it better than most ways of departing this earth.

"That was Charley," Jake Wiggins said, when we were all sitting around talking and remembering. "Always after a woman."

"If I had a choice between livin' alone or dyin' in Lou Simms's arms, I'd sure choose livin' alone," I said.

We all laughed, but as far as I was concerned that was the pure truth. I'd seen better-looking faces on cows out on the range.

"You must be gettin' old, Luther," Tom Eakin said. "Now, Charley, he knew how to keep young. He just changed women every so often."

"Time Lou Simms starts lookin' good to me, you'll know I'm old. And blind, too," I said.

Thing was, we were all the same age as Charley. We'd all grown up together, been working and socializing together since we were boys. And now there was Charley laid out in his front parlor, waiting for the preacher. It kind of made me stop and think. It made me feel mortal, like maybe someday soon I'd be next, just by doing something purely natural.

"Thing about Lou," Jake said, "is she's peaceful. She don't talk too much."

"Don't have to," I said.

Jake grinned. "That's so. And Charley had a belly-full of talk from Jo-Etta anyhow."

Everybody up Horse Creek remembers Jo-Etta. She was Charley's second wife — yellow headed, full breasted, with the damnedest little feet that were always on the move just like her mouth. After

164

ten years those little feet ran off with a dentist from Phoenix, leaving Charley wide open for Lou who'd had a crush on him since she was ten.

"Jo-Etta had a laugh just like a crazy person," I said.

Tom looked at me. "You're the *pickin'est* son of a bitch," he said. "I sure don't know how Kate ever caught you."

"Me neither," I said, and meant it. I'd been a widower about five years by then and liking it — the quiet, the freedom, no one telling me to shave, or wipe my feet, or stop making music when I damn' well pleased, even at two in the morning. Thing is, a man don't need all that much sleep as he gets older. A nap here and there does it. A snooze midday when the sun gets hot, in a chair out under the trumpet vine with the wings of the hummingbirds all around, blurry, fast moving, making your eyes want to close.

I never knew nights were so interesting, either. Farming, ranching, feeding four kids and a wife don't leave time to appreciate the dark. A man's tired come nightfall. Now, though, I set up a lot, watching the 'coons that come by looking for a handout, and the skunks, all bright eyed and sleek as cats. And once in a while, if I set right still, I'll catch the coyotes, drifting past like smoke, so quiet it's hard to believe they can cry like the damned. It's something to see, something I missed when I was young and courting, and older and hard at work. Growing old, being single have their strong points.

"Won't no woman catch me again, anyway," I said.

"Amen," said Tom.

Out in Jake's kitchen the rackety old phone on the wall rang three times. We heard Faye answer, heard her voice change from curious to cold polite the way a woman does when she's riled and showing it. When she came to the parlor door, she looked at me as if I'd sprouted horns and a tail. "It's for you, Luther," she said, her nose all pinched and righteous. "It's Lou Simms."

Tom gave a whoop. "Look out, Luther! Your turn's coming!" He slapped his thigh.

Faye looked at him, bristling. "You stop it right now, Tom Eakin," she said, as if he was five years old instead of seventy, and she his mother. Some women are like that. They go to their graves sure they were put here to save men from disgracing themselves.

Poor Jake, I thought as I picked up the phone. "Hello, Lou," I said. I could feel Faye's eyes on me from behind, could see her sure puffed up like a hen, indignant that a fallen woman could call into her kitchen, summon one of us to the telephone, and her helpless to stop it.

Jake had been right about one thing. Lou didn't talk much and, when she did, it was in a low voice, harmonious, like a good fiddle. I don't think I ever noticed her voice before that night. Turned out, she needed pall bearers, someone to help load the coffin on the truck and get Charley to the Barnes' burying ground. One of his sons had come out for the funeral. The other, filled up with Holy Word, had stayed in town.

"We'll come," I told her. "Don't you worry."

Then, for no reason at all, I started remembering. Like I said, we'd all grown up together, gone to school together, and as kids we'd all teased Lou for following Charley around like he was Chief Injun. There had been one hot day toward the end of summer when us boys had been sent to check fence in the scrub and up on the slope of the mountain. We came down tired, hot, dusty and, when we got to the stock tank, we stripped naked and went in, and never mind who come along to see us. Well, Lou did, riding that little gray mustang she had like she'd grown on him.

She wasn't any prettier then, as I recall, all eyes and pigtails, and solemn faced like she was thinking things she couldn't say. And we started to shout and tease, the way boys do, nasty things, or so we thought, like "Look out, Charley! Here comes Lou to ass-ay you!" And we flipped ourselves on our backs in the water so as to give her a look at us, boys and proud of it. And she sat there a while, hunched up on the pony's back, her mouth tight shut, her cheeks red as coals,

166

and then it was like something broke in her. She set that pony on us in the water, rode straight out a-splashing and a-whipping her reins from side to side, not caring who she hurt or rode over. Just mad and shouting: "Don't *dare!* Don't you *dare!*" at us as if we'd done something awful, touched something sacred and made it profane, and maybe we had just out of dumb cussedness.

Funny thing is, we never talked about it later, not even among ourselves. One of those reins caught Charley across the cheek and left a welt, and I had a sore leg for a month from where that pony's hoof caught me, but we never told no one. We were shamed by that little stick of a girl, and deserved it, too.

Standing there in Faye's kitchen, I could see the whole scene as if it was in front of me. I could see Lou that minute, bony and thin shanked, her mouth closed in on itself. Hadn't she ever been young? I wondered. Skittery? Giggling with the rest of the girls? Or had she always been the way I was seeing her — secretive, hunched around her feelings, letting no one see except for that one time when she rode us down?

"I'm sorry about Charley," I told her. "We all are."

"Thank you," she said. Then she was silent.

I could hear the wire crackling. A storm somewhere, I thought, and her down there alone with Charley's corpse. "You want some of us to come down and set with you a while?"

I heard Faye sniff behind me at the same time I heard Lou laugh, short and dry and not without understanding. "Thanks," she said again. "I'm all right. I'm used to it."

"You need anything, you call, hear?" I said. "Me or Jake, we'll come down."

Faye sniffed again. "I know you mean well," she said, when I had hung up. "And you know I believe in helping my neighbor. But you ain't volunteering Jake to go set with Lou Simms."

I said: "Why is it we call her 'Lou Simms' like she's a stranger?"

She gave me a look. "Because she is. We all grew up together, but she's set herself apart. She's lived down there in sin all this time and nary a word to any of us. Like we was the sinners."

"Maybe we are," I said. I wasn't about to back down from those mean little eyes of hers. That was Jake's problem.

She folded her arms tight. "You forget, all of us got married legal," she said.

"There's other ways of sinnin'," I said and wondered, even as I did, why I was taking Lou's part. Maybe it had been something in her voice. Or maybe it was that memory of her, no bigger than a grasshopper but full of wrath and a kind of shining courage.

Tom was wondering the same thing. "What'd she say to you?" he asked. "Ten minutes ago you were pokin' fun at her."

"She didn't say much. Just asked would we help with the coffin. Would we be there."

"Well, we will," Jake said. "And let that be an end to it. Hell, it's Charley's funeral."

Faye said: "I'm not going." Then she looked at us, daring us to say different.

"Come tomorrow, you'll change your mind," Jake said, and I'd have bet on it. She'd no more let Jake walk alone into that house of sin than she'd let him out of her sight on market day for fear he'd drink too much or be lured into the bawdy house by some female.

I was laughing when I put on my hat. The older I get, the funnier human nature gets. I'd meant it about there being other ways of sinning. Being mean spirited is just as bad as blind generosity sometimes. Faye is mean spirited. Just a-holding on to everything for fear she'll be left without.

I patted her shoulder. "You come, Faye. We'll need protection."

"Don't you poke fun at me, Luther!" she snapped. "I don't understand you tonight."

"Me neither," I said. I went out and sat in my truck a spell before I started home.

Don't know what started me remembering. Maybe it was talking about Charley. Maybe it was remembering Lou on that gray mustang. Whatever it was, it seemed I couldn't stop. All the way up Horse Creek I kept seeing things like they had been. Scenes just as clear as motion pictures went through my mind. I kept remembering about being young, about growing up out here when the land was wide open, when time was still slow, and we were sure we had the best of it.

I remembered Lou's mother, a plain woman, a widow who hung onto her homestead by taking boarders and running a few head of cattle. Lou helped, and a cowboy named Billy who was too old to work for one of the big outfits. No one ever knew his other name. No one ever asked, or asked what the relationship was between him and the widow. There wasn't time for talk or visiting in that house. Nor for laughter, neither. Maybe that accounts for the way Lou turned out. It's like she grew up fast but stayed hungry for the things she couldn't have. Like childhood. Like Charley.

I remembered a dance we had once when Charley was already courting my sister, Annie. Someone had got Lou out of her old pants and shirt and into a dress for the evening. And she had her hair tied back with a green ribbon. When she come in, she stood there by herself, her shoulders bunched up and her eyes watchful, like a filly ready to scatter. Charley was swinging Annie around the floor so her skirts twirled out and her hair flew, and they were laughing the way a man and woman do when they're sure of each other and happy.

But Annie was always looking out for others. It was her way. When the set was done, she whispered to Charley, and he said: "Aw!" loud enough so we all heard. She insisted, though, and he went to Lou and took her out on the floor, gawky legs and all, and swung her around like she didn't weigh more than milkweed down. Probably didn't. There never was much food in the Simms' house.

When the music stopped and he set her down, those eyes of hers were so big they near spilled over her cheeks, and she smiled up at Charley, hardly more than a jerk of her mouth but, I tell you, I remember that look. Like she'd seen paradise just for a minute. And Charley, well, he said his thank you and went back to Annie, and Lou got asked to dance by the rest of us. Seemed like that to her, we weren't even there. That she was still dancing with Charley, no matter who was holding her.

"Wish she wouldn't keep lookin' at me," he said later, when we'd gone outside. "She just looks like she's a mute or something."

"Maybe she's scairt," I said.

"Scairt? Her? Hell, she rode us down." He rubbed his cheek where the welt had been. The mark was still there. You had to look close, under his beard, but it was there.

"Well, maybe she ain't got words," I said.

"Just as well. Then I'd have to listen." He turned and went back inside to Annie.

They were married the next year in mid-summer — the corn high, the cattle fattening, the rains coming often and hard enough to keep the grass green. Annie made a pretty bride. She wore Grandma's old veil and a dress out of the catalogue. White and frilly it was, and feminine, like she was.

Right before the company was expected, Lou rode up carrying a wet gunny sack. "I brought flowers," she said. "A wedding needs flowers."

Now, she's one of those rare women who have a knack for gardening. Make anything grow, she could, from the time she was old enough to dig. She had peach and apple trees she'd raised from seeds, and her vegetables were always tastier than anybody else's. She had herbs, too, and knew what they were used for, and along her corral fence, under the windmill, she'd planted lilies. I don't know where she got them but, when they bloomed, they were like nothing I'd ever seen. Big and white and deep, and purple inside with black stamens that shone when the sun hit them. And that's what she brought in the sack. Bunches of them to put 'round the parlor.

During the ceremony they began to smell so sweet we all got light-headed, like we were dreaming. And off in a corner was Lou in that bad-fitting best dress of hers, her hands in fists and her mouth tight, watching while the preacher made Annie and Charley man and wife. Annie hugged her after. Said thanks for the flowers and come visit real soon, and Lou nodded, the littlest bit, and said: "Maybe," and started for the door.

"Stay a while," I told her. "There's food and Grandma's wine."

She shook her head. "Got to get back to milk. Billy's off somewhere, and Ma can't handle that old cow."

"Those flowers were fine," I said. "Right for a wedding."

She swung up on the gray and looked down at me, still faced. "Or a funeral." She lifted her hand. "See you."

I stared after her dust the longest time, thinking that her feelings ran so deep that for her Annie's wedding *was* a funeral. Then I told myself she must have been fooling, trying to make a joke without knowing how. No little gawk of a girl would take on so over Charley. Hell, she wasn't but fourteen, and Charley a man already. But I puzzled over it a long time, recalled it that night before Charley's funeral, and wondered at just how patient and faithful a woman with her mind made up can be.

Time I got home I was so full of memories I couldn't sleep. I got a beer and my mouth organ, and settled down in my chair under the vine, and I made music a while, the old songs, "Laredo," and "The Cowboy Waltz," except that dead cowboy made me think about Charley some more, and Lou, who's set up with more dead in that parlor than any of us. I got to thinking how she set up with Annie, even laid her out in the same white dress she'd been married in. Only it never seemed like Annie lying there, more like some old woman, her mouth caved in from hard living.

After the first boy come, Annie never got well again. Something happened, a woman's trouble never mentioned in front of the men but there, like a wound that don't quite heal. She got thin, and her red hair that had been so bright turned dusty, and she had a way of stopping to catch her breath when she laughed, or when she was hauling water. Those nights when us boys got together to play cards or make music, she'd disappear, go off to bed like a shadow. She told me she liked to lie in the dark, listening to the songs she used to dance to.

It's hard on a man having a wife who's sickly. Harder still to watch her shut down on living like those lilies do after one day of blooming. I don't know, looking back, whether I always wasn't a mite angry at Charley when he said a second child was coming, and Annie barely able to get around. A man's got rights, but a woman's got rights, too, and Annie was my sister, and I'd always looked out for her.

I was married by then myself, but Kate was like a piece of elastic. She snapped right back no matter what. I never heard a complaint from her, but then I took care not to give her any reason. Just about everybody tried to help Annie. Kate would drive down in the wagon with soup in a bucket under her feet, and she'd set the house to rights and see to Jim, Charley's and Annie's little boy.

Back then was when folks first started talking about Lou. Sometimes she'd ride in late, after her chores were done, put a meal on the table and not ride home till first light. But she never listened to the talk, or didn't care. She was there, making concoctions out of herbs for Annie, serving up dinner for Charley, putting little Jim to bed on time. She must have thought what it would be like with Annie gone. She must have once in a while pretended when Charley come in from the barn, but she didn't have any female tricks. She was just herself. Maybe, if she'd prettied herself up, learned how to smile at a man, Charley wouldn't have taken up with Jo-Etta. But that's not the way it happened.

I see now, though I didn't then, that Tom Eakin was right. Charley did change women every so often. He liked women, the pretty ones first, then the faithful like Lou. He liked being with them, loving them, being made much of by them. He was a tom cat, though I

172

never, till just now, thought that. When Annie had her health and was perky and prettier than anyone else, he was satisfied. But when she couldn't keep up with him, well, he hung around a while, long enough to give her a second child, and then he went off to town and found Jo-Etta.

Once again Lou didn't have a chance. She was with Annie during the birth. She was with Annie, holding her hand, when she died. She washed her, and laid her out, and set with her and, after it was all over, she found a wet nurse for the baby and kept order in that house and in her own with the strength of four women. Charley never noticed. Six months later he married Jo-Etta, and Lou went on home.

I rode down one evening just to thank her for being good to Annie. I couldn't get it out of my mind that Annie had died without anyone there but Lou. The baby had come before its time, and those two girls had brought it to life alone. Only Annie had paid.

Lou was out in her garden. She'd run an old hose from the tank to the plot for water, and the smell of it, of that water, was plain in the dry air.

"I want to thank you," I said. "For being good to Annie."

She nodded at me and went back to picking snap beans. I noticed how careful her fingers were among the plants. Quick, sure, light, leaving the leaves and vines unhurt. "I did what I had to," she said after a minute, her voice muffled.

"You were there. She could've been alone."

She nodded again. "I did it for myself," she said. "Not for her."

I thought about that. "Sometimes, doin' for ourselves, we do for others," I said. I couldn't think how else to say it, but it seems to me that sometimes, helping ourselves, we spread the good around.

She got up, dusted her hands together, and looked at me. "I never wished her dead. You know that."

I did, too. There wasn't any evil in her, only the need to give what she had to one person. Charley. I didn't understand it, but I could accept it, which is more'n most folks did. I put my hands on her

173

shoulders. They felt like broomsticks poking up under her skin, under that man's blue shirt she always wore. "Damn it all," I said. "Why can't you pick someone else? There's plenty men'd have you."

"Because he's mine," she said. She jerked away from me like I had intentions, which I sure hadn't. She went to the fence, took down the bars of the gate. "Come, get a drink before you leave."

Now, it's been my observation that things happen when the time is right. Like the Bible says: "To everything its season," and there's truth in that. Folks can't force things, can't make plans and ever be sure because, if the time isn't right, those plans come to nothing. Lou maybe knew that, even when she was a young 'un, and just settled into herself to wait it out. Because when Jo-Etta run off with that dentist of hers, there was Charley, riding by Lou's more than he'd ever done in his life. He'd stop to talk over the fence, or he'd set on the porch with her till long after dark. Maybe he needed the peace and quiet. A man gets tired running after a while. Even the wild ones want to settle. Or maybe it was pleasant being accepted for what he was by a woman who'd never made him out to be more, who just loved him, come hell or high water.

I never asked why they didn't get married legal. It wasn't my business. They both seemed happy, and who was I to say? Even Kate took a practical view, though she was one of the few women who did. "Let them be," she said. "Folks do what they need, and no words'll change them."

She was right. She was a smart woman who never minded when us boys got together at Charley's. Never minded it when we were served coffee and pie by a fallen woman. "Leave her be," she'd say. "She's had enough trouble in her life."

And now, here I was getting ready to put an end to a part of my own life. I was going to lay to rest the man who, though I'd never admitted it, had killed my sister but who'd been my best friend.

I fell asleep in my chair thinking about that and, when I woke, it was first light and the mockingbirds were making fun of the world in the oak tree, and down over the field the jays were at it, full of argument. And Howler, my old hound, was coming back from where he'd been with a grin on his face and his eyes all yellow and shining.

I showered and shaved, and got out my old black suit I hadn't worn in years. The moths had been at it, but I figured no one would notice or, if they did, they'd figure what a shame I had no woman to do for me. I fed the dog and the couple of hens that had escaped the coyotes, and I filled a basket full of peaches from my tree because folks are always hungry after a burying.

When I stopped at Jake's, I found him dressed up like me and Faye in her good black dress, holding onto a basket of food like a buzzard was about to swoop down and snatch it from her. "Change your mind?" I asked her.

"My parents and Charley's come out here together," she said. "This is the least I can do." She didn't look at me. Kept her eyes down prim and proper.

"That's nice," I said. I meant it. One excuse is as good as another.

Jake drove us in his old Ford, and all the way Faye clucked and twittered in the back seat, brainless as a hen.

Jim, Annie's and Charley's son, was on the porch when we got there.

"Where's *she?*" Faye said to us.

Jake turned around. "You hush, woman," he said. "And you behave. Or I'll turn 'round and take you home and tell them all the reason why. This is a funeral not Judgment Day, and you're not the voice of the Lord."

"I was just wonderin'," she said.

"Well, don't." He opened the car door. "I've always admired a peaceful woman."

Jim, red headed like Annie, shook our hands. He remembered how Lou had come in and cared for him. Like me, he didn't dwell on legalities.

175

"You go in, Luther," he said. "She's grieving, but she won't show it."

I took off my hat and stepped into the kitchen. Now, I've always said you can tell a woman's ways from her kitchen, and I've loved that room of Lou's for twenty years. It has a speaking quality, a happiness I never found anywhere else, not even in my own place. It's got shelves full of preserves and vegetables, the colors just shining out of the jars, and in summer it's cool, shaded by the vine Lou planted that goes right up the side of the house and over the window. And her yellow cat, Texas, is there, sleeping his nights off on the window sill or sprucing himself up for another.

I don't know but that a woman doesn't put her mark on things in a house the way a man puts his mark on the land he works. Whatever, that kitchen is Lou, quiet but full up with things in order, stored away for when they'll be needed. Only some things wouldn't be needed any more. Charley was gone.

She was by the coffin, stiff, like she hadn't moved in days, and I felt for her more than for Charley, laying there at peace. She'd spent a lot of her life storing things up, waiting around, and now she was left looking little and purposeless. I put my hands on her shoulders like I had once before, and felt her, skin and bones, a bird I could pick up in my hands. She didn't shake me off this time, just stayed there looking up at me with those gray eyes of hers. "I'm sure sorry," I said. It was a dumb thing to say, but what else was there?

"I know," she said.

"Anything I can do?" I asked, thinking, if she gave me some chore, I could take my mind off things.

She shook her head. "Help me get through it. Then I can go wait my turn. I'm good at that."

"You sure are." I smiled a bit, thinking back. "You're the waitin'est woman I ever knew."

"I set up last night thinking I could have done different. It was me wouldn't get married legal. I was afraid he'd want out soon as he

176

was tied. But now it's his funeral, and even one of his own sons won't come. Maybe I did wrong. Cut him off from people."

"Some men you can't pen up," I said. "You do and they're gone like a fence-busting bull. But you sure must've been lonely. I know what the women been sayin' all these years, and I wish I could apologize."

She shrugged, gaunt as a scarecrow in her old black dress. "I never cared for women," she said. "And I've never been lonely. I had the land. And I had Charley. No sense being greedy. Even last night I had company. Those poor-wills down the wash just *sang*. Lots of nights we'd hear them, Charley and me. 'Just like folks,' he'd say. 'They talk just like folks.' " She folded her hands tight like she was praying. "To me it was all beautiful. It was right. But it's him I'm worried about. Did I do right by him? Make him happy?"

I looked at Charley, proper in his coffin, hands at his sides. Damned if there wasn't a hint of a smile on his face that even death couldn't take away. He'd gone out loving, and he was proud, the way an old stud horse is proud, stomping and kicking and telling the world. I squeezed her shoulders. I thought a man could come to love her, little like she was, and faithful. And beautiful, too, all eyes and love and worry in them the way we think a woman should be, the way we like to believe they are, even the bossy ones like Faye. "You sure did make him happy," I said. "You did him proud."

She leaned up against me, light as a sparrow, and cried. I held her, thinking how a woman leaves a mark on a man as well as on her house. Thinking about how, over the years, this little woman had left a mark on me.

Faye stuck her head in the door just then and, from the look she gave me, I supposed she'd have a lot to say, come evening. I guessed I wouldn't say much in return. There's some moments in life, so purely sweet, a man wants to keep them for himself.

RUNS-WITH-THE-WIND

I know it's September, when the Indians come to gather acorns. It's women come, mostly, and young girls. I see them down there in the oak trees with their baskets, and they laugh and talk, woman-talk I'd guess, away from their men. Gathering acorns is something they've been doing since before my people came, and we always left them alone to do it. We never had any trouble with the Apaches, even during the wars. Matter of fact, we always gave them a few beeves, figuring they were hungry. "Injuns or white, starvation's no fun," my dad always said, and he'd let them camp and cook down by the wash in those same oak trees.

There were a few years back then, when they didn't come, during the hard fighting when they were hiding out or on the reservation. And it always seemed to me as if those years had something missing, as if the season couldn't be without those bright skirts moving in the oaks and the sound of women laughing.

I was just turned nineteen, and I was helping my dad, breaking horses for a few of the big outfits in the valley. And what spare time I had, I was back in the Peloncillos, chasing a pair of the prettiest steel blue mules a man ever saw. They ran wild in a herd of mustangs, and they were eye-catchers — big, solid, blue like the underparts of a jay's wing. I'd set my heart on those mules, and tried catching them with every trick I knew, but they were still running free that fall before Geronimo surrendered.

After the crops were in, I took a week and went to make another try. I didn't have any fear of Apaches like most folks did then, though my ma said someday I'd meet one off somewhere and that would be the end of me. I met one in the mountains all right, but it wasn't what anyone had expected I'd find, least of all me.

I'd run those mules and that herd pretty constantly for three-four days, and then I staked out a water hole they liked. It was at the mouth of a little cañon that narrowed as it ran back into the mountain. I'd made a brush corral at the narrowest spot, with a hidden gate I could swing tight shut. I figured I could jump them at the spring and drive them on back into that pen where I'd have plenty of time to sort out the mules and any mustangs that showed promise.

So I was there, camped out in the rocks, my horse hobbled in the junipers, the big roan I had that could outrun anything, and I'd been sitting there just watching, listening, thinking that was near the prettiest spot on earth with the cottonwoods changing color and the water running clear, when I saw something move out of the corner of my eye. Bright colored it was, so I knew it wasn't a deer, and I eased around and saw an Indian girl by the water. She was checking around the way an animal does before it drinks, before it bends down and leaves itself open for attack. Then she knelt and drank, putting her mouth to the water and sucking.

I circled around and came down by her, quiet as a leaf. She never knew I was there till I spoke.

Now, I never could learn Apache. It just isn't in me. But I learned Spanish before I learned English, and studied it the time I went to school, and those Apaches, most of them, could speak that language. *"Buenos dias,"* I said, soft as I could, and she jumped up like a doe, and then froze.

Well, the fact was, she wasn't an Indian, though she was dressed like one and had two tattoos on her cheeks like they do. But she had gray eyes, the clearest, lightest gray I ever saw, with black pupils and black around the edges like a rain cloud. And her hair wasn't black. It was reddish, and curly, too, though she'd pulled it back off her face.

Back then everybody had a story or two about white women captured by Indians. Some were used as slaves. Others married into

179

the tribe and forgot their white families. Some had even been bought back and sent home. Some of those went eagerly, but there were always a few who pined away and died, missing their Indian families. But this girl wasn't a slave. Her clothes were good, though they were mended in places, and she didn't carry herself like someone used to beatings and hard use. In fact, the way she looked at me was plumb arrogant.

I figured she had a knife somewhere and would use it if I gave her the chance. But she was white, and that put me in a quandary. I couldn't walk away and leave a white woman out there. I had to try at least to bring her out. Besides, the look in her eyes was so wild and so pitiful, both at once, that I was curious. I've seen wild animals caught in traps that never give up, and I've always respected that courage, that need for freedom. Sometimes I've even opened a trap and let the critter go, if it wasn't too bad hurt, and then gone home and said the trap was empty.

So we stood there, me wondering how to keep her, and she planning to fight or run the moment she got the chance. "You be easy," I said to her, dropping my voice down deep like I was talking to a green colt.

I didn't know how much she understood, but, again, I figured it was the sound that mattered, not the words. "You be easy. I'm not going to hurt you." Those gray eyes flickered at me just a shade, and from that I figured she at least got the gist of what I was saying. "My name's Rule," I said. "I live over yonder, and I'm out here chasing some wild mules." I went on talking, spinning out my words so she wouldn't spook. "You're white," I said finally. "You're no Apache. Do you have a name?"

She didn't answer. Just drew back into herself.

So I went on. Seems like I never talked so much before or since, but I couldn't help myself. She was such a pretty little thing, slender, like a doe. I explained about those mules, and how I'd been chasing them for years, and how slick they were in their blue hides. I said how I planned to train them to ride and pull a buggy, too, all the while taking a chance because Apaches liked mule meat better than beef, or so folks said. I hoped she wouldn't come back with a couple of braves and do what I couldn't.

When I ran out of talk, I started on the Bible. That startled her. She shook her head and frowned like she almost understood or remembered some of it. I was in Jeremiah, just going along, when I noticed she was swaying a bit with the rhythm. I wouldn't have noticed, except I was watching her so close, looking at those eyes like spring water with the sun on it.

"What's your name?" I asked suddenly. *"¿Como se llama?"*

And she said: "Runs-With-the-Wind," and then snapped her mouth tight shut and glared at me as if I'd tricked her.

Well, I had, and I was mighty pleased with myself. That was my mistake. She could run. No one ever had a better name. Straight as an arrow and as fast, and without a sound, she took off up the cañon. I went after her yelling: "Wait!" and then decided to save my breath. She went right up the side like a bird. I swear, she didn't seem to touch the ground, and me pounding along in back of her like a big-footed bull.

I'd never have caught her if she hadn't fallen. Her foot went out from under her, and she went down and lay there, looking at me with that same look of hate and courage. I'd never been with a woman, but I'd seen and heard enough so I knew what I wanted from her. She knew it, too. I saw it in her eyes and in the way her throat moved up and down like she couldn't swallow. She smelled sweet. Like dry grass and the herbs my ma hung from the kitchen rafters. And her face was soft. I can still remember how it felt, smooth to the touch, with small bones underneath.

Maybe it was those little bones that did me in. Or maybe it was those eyes of hers, gone hopeless. Anyway, I couldn't do it. I sat back. "Be easy," I told her. "Let me see your foot."

There wasn't but a bruise, spreading out around her ankle. I held it in my hands a minute, thinking I was a fool not to take what was right there. But in the end I put her up behind me on the roan, and we went a little ways south toward the mountains and her people. They were her people by then. Home is where you're used to. Where you're loved. And someone loved her. I'm sure of that.

She wouldn't let me take her all the way but jumped off by a big old juniper and looked up at me with her eyes so bright I was nearly blinded. And she took my hand a minute and held it to her face, to those bones I could've snapped in my fingers. Then she smiled and ran off — fast — just like her name.

The yellow grass in that valley just swallowed her up. I watched a long time, and never could see the direction she took, except I knew it was toward those mountains between us and Mexico — those mountains that were standing up purple against the sky and burning their picture into my mind.

Now, the funny thing is that I hung around camp a day or two, hoping maybe she'd come back or that the herd would come in to water. I tried to stay on the alert, but a man has to sleep sometimes, and the last night, just before first light, I dozed off. I don't know what woke me. Maybe it was my roan, snorting back in the trees, or maybe the jays squawking and giving their alarm. Better than watch dogs, jays are, if you know to listen for them.

Anyhow, I took my shotgun and eased down into the draw. A man can't be too careful if he's alone, even now, and the Indian wars over for half a century. So I went out slow, hardly breathing for fear I'd miss whatever was out there.

Up ahead I heard a commotion — hoofs pounding, and horses snorting mad. The gate I'd built across the cañon was shut tight, and in the pen were the mustangs and those two mules, their coats just as slick as if they'd been doused in Ma's wash tub. I hunted around, looking for tracks, but never found a one. Those Apaches never left sign, but I knew it was them who'd brought in that herd, with maybe a little help from that gal. She was grateful, and she showed it best as she knew how.

Well, I took those mules home and trained them, and they did me proud, working cattle, pulling wagons and even a buggy when I finally went courting. I never told anybody the whole story, though, figuring it was nobody's business, and she was safe and where she wanted to be. Fifty years ago that happened. But every fall, when those women come with their bright skirts and their baskets, I look out and wonder if she's there. Runs-With-the-Wind, who I let go.

THE STARTLING LIGHT OF DAY

"Now I am become death, the destroyer of worlds."
Dr. J. Robert Oppenheimer, New Mexico, 1945

It was almost dark when Jake and Malva Wisdom turned onto the ranch road. Only the great rock skirts of the barrier mountains to the east still burned in the afterglow. Farther to the north the peak of Sierra Blanca gleamed red, like a beacon.

Jake shut the rusted gate behind them and clambered into the truck. "I don't remember leaving that gate unhooked," he said, as he shifted gears for the climb.

Malva didn't answer. A trip to town tired her these days. Waiting in the doctor's office made it worse. She, who had never given a thought to her body, who had simply expected it to function like a fine machine, now had to contend with it, wrestle with it, contort it into a thousand strange shapes to do the simplest task. Why, how the polio virus had taken her and left her legs useless made no sense to her. She writhed with the unfairness of it, with her dependence on her family, on strangers.

She, who had helped Jake on the ranch with the energy of any boy, who had ridden the toughest horses, driven the wildest cows from their hiding places, was now confined to the house, the porch, the yard. Sometimes, when she was alone, she screamed from sheer frustration, screamed and, outraged, pounded her fists on the arms of her chair. She could hardly bear to look at herself, her body sagging, the long hair that had been her pride and Jake's pleasure streaked with gray. Jake, too, had changed, slowly, imperceptibly.

He was worn thin as a buggy whip, and the laugh she'd always loved was gone.

And why not? First the drought had lingered, burning the pasture to straw, and then, when it finally had turned around, she'd been stricken, lying too ill to move or even care whether she lived or not. The final blow had come when Frank and Dan, their handsome, tow-headed sons, were called up by the draft, and never mind that their father struggled alone doing three men's work while their mother lay in a dark room, weeping what strength she had left into a soaked pillow. Both sons were in the Pacific now, fighting a war that would have seemed, to her, far away, reduced by the immensity of mountains, sky, grasslands leaning in the wind, except for their involvement — and Jake's wearing himself down simply to stay in place.

He'd hired, and fired, a succession of hands. No one and nothing pleased him. He had turned demanding, bitter, impossible to work for. Malva blamed herself for the change in him and pitied the men on the lashing end of his tongue, but there was little she could do for them except smile and, when she had the chance, try to explain, salving their pride. The last, Jesús, really only a boy and desperate for work, had left the day before, sent off without pay.

"I'm damned if I'll pay you!" Jake's voice had carried across the yard and into the house. "You were supposed to mend that fence. Now, there's two good steers out there where Washington tells me I'm not allowed to go. Get your things and get out, and don't come back!"

"But, *señor,* they broke through another place. Where the grass was tall. Not where I fixed." The kid had pleaded, but he wasn't groveling.

Listening, Malva had felt compassion for both men, but especially for the young one, wrongly accused. She'd seen him head off toward the sagging fence line, tools in hand, and she had no reason to doubt that he'd done what he'd been told. She had wheeled herself to the

185

screen door and waited. When Jake had gone, she called through the screen. Jesús had come readily enough, though his black eyes burned with anger.

"*¿Señora?*"

She had handed him some money, bills wrinkled with age and the pressure of her hand. "Here," she had said. "It's all I have. He didn't mean it, you know. It's just. . . ." She had gestured vaguely, then had let her hands fall into her lap. "It's all so hard."

With her he had held his anger in check. She'd been good to him, this woman with the useless legs and the face of a sorrowing saint. And why shouldn't she look like that, tied to that devil of a husband? Taking the money, he had bowed slightly, an old-fashioned courtesy. Then he had straightened and looked at her. "It was fixed, that fence," he had said.

"I know."

"Then why?"

She had spread her hands again, tired, wishing he would go. "I'm sorry," she had said. "I am. Really. But don't stand here with me. It'll just make him mad. *Vaya con Dios, Jesús.*"

He had bowed again and stuffed the money in his pocket. "*Gracias, señora.*"

She had seen the fury in him, had felt it, but simply had nodded and had let the door bang shut. Then she had sat and had watched him go, his feet having raised puffs of dust that had whirled and drifted into the heated air.

Now the old truck lurched into a stony arroyo, hesitated, and lurched again as if in response to Jake's curse. Malva held onto the door with one hand, attempting to ease the jouncing. With the other she reached across to Jake and timidly touched his thigh.

It did little to sooth him. "Damn' truck won't last a year," he said. "Can't get parts, can't get help, can't make out with nothing." He spat out his window, then leaned forward over the wheel, as if willing the vehicle on.

"It'll be all right," she said, but she sounded insubstantial, a flurry of moth wings across the space between them.

"Quit being a damn' fool!"

His bitterness startled them both. She withdrew her hand and sat silently, drawing her body around the pain in her heart, holding herself together by strength of will.

He said, so low she barely heard: "I'm sorry, Mallie."

She nodded, more to herself than to him, and said nothing.

"When the kids come home, they'll be lucky if there's anything left! All that work, and nothing to show for it!" He pounded the wheel with a fist.

"If they come home," she said, and steeled herself for his anger.

It came in a burst. "Shut up! Damn it, just shut up! Where's your faith? Your guts. You ought to be ashamed."

But she wasn't ashamed. She was afraid. She lived with terror night and day, keeping it hidden except for moments like this one. What would happen to them all? To her and Jake, to the sons fighting a war that seemed to be hovering overhead, a menace she couldn't avoid, even in her sleep?

The broad valley that swept down to Mexico, that she'd grown up in, ridden over, loved with a passion unlike any other, was restricted now, fenced off, patrolled by soldiers carrying guns. And to the north the mountains were empty, abandoned, ranchers paid off, asked to leave. There were rumors, shrouded in mystery. Secret weapons, chemicals, who knew what? Unsubstantiated rumors, but based on reality, for the soldiers were there, and the miles of fences. She felt as if even her beloved land had betrayed her, harboring death in place of life. And when you could no longer trust the land, in what could you believe? In God? She ground her teeth. No God would have left her helpless when Jake needed her most. A God that could do that could also take Frank and Dan, leave them maimed, sightless, even dead.

"No," she said slowly. "I'm not ashamed. I'm just facing the truth."

He was breathing heavily, the way he did nowadays when angry. He'd never struck her, but she knew he might if she kept on. Instead he said: "You wouldn't know the truth if it rose up and bit you. All you've been doing is feeling sorry for yourself, so just shut up. I told you once." His voice was hard as obsidian.

A few stars were coming out, early precursors of the brilliance to come, and a chunk of moon rode the arc of sky, flooding the grasslands, the foothills with pale fire.

Why argue? Why fight wars? she thought, looking out, inhaling the sweetness of summer that came through the open window. *Why do we always destroy beauty instead of cherishing it?*

She couldn't answer herself. Answering required an effort she was too tired to summon. She was relieved when the house came in sight, a rambling structure of logs and adobe, rooms added helter-skelter as they'd been needed. The house was her haven, her cocoon, familiar territory, and it bore the stamp of her, as she had been and as she was — the kitchen neat, the pantry well stocked despite her handicap, the great living room warm and inviting. Soon she could lie down, stretch out on the bed where now she slept alone, and ease her aching muscles even if the ache in her heart remained.

"I'll go get us some light. Then I'll come back for you." Jake hadn't forgiven her. His voice was distant, as if what had passed between them was her fault, as if he dreaded having to touch her, lift her, carry her, admitting helplessness, his and hers. What did it matter whose fault it was? Better to forget and go on. She didn't answer but pulled herself straight and opened the door of the truck in readiness. Seconds later, immediately after she saw the glow of a lamp in the front room, she heard Jake's shout. "What the hell!"

She heard his anger at her and at circumstance plain in his voice, and then she heard the shots, two of them, splitting the night's silence. Then nothing. Only the rustle of the cottonwoods and the wind whistling in the wire fence. "Jake!" she called, then clamped her jaws shut, fearful of who would answer, who would come to the open door. *Let it be Jake.* She prayed without knowing to the God she had scorned earlier. *I'll never make him angry again. I'll get over this. Just let it be Jake.*

The words were cut off as she saw the man's silhouette against the screen. A stranger. Faceless in the dark, but broad-shouldered and lean. She whimpered, the death cry of a trapped rabbit, and then even that sound ceased as the man opened the door, crossed the porch, and walked toward her.

He said: *"¿Señora?"* like a question, and she peered through the night, trying to see his face.

"¿Quién es?" she answered in Spanish automatically.

He stepped closer. A hat brim shaded his eyes, and he'd pulled his neck scarf over his mouth and nose. But she knew him. As surely as she sat there, she knew him.

"Jesús?" She ventured his name, for surely he meant no harm.

"Don't talk!" He reached for her, and she drew back into the useless shelter of the cab. He said: "I won't hurt you."

Forcing herself, she asked: "What did you do to Jake?"

He lifted her chair from the truck bed and set it up under the biggest cottonwood, the tree she had planted, watered, watched grow into a giant. When he spoke, his back was turned. "He shot first."

She sat quite still. Only her hands moved, clenched into fists. "Is he hurt?" She couldn't bring herself to say more, to think beyond pain.

He turned and lifted her as easily as she would lift a chick from beneath a hen's wing, and he refused to meet her eyes, to respond.

Then she knew, and the world rose and fell around her, a betrayal of a different kind. "Why don't you kill me, too?" she whispered, her head against his shoulder. "Why don't you?"

"You are a good woman," he said, "and I don't kill women. That man, that bad *hombre,* tried to kill me, and all I wanted was my money.

He put her down, covered her knees with the blanket, and recrossed the yard to the truck. She watched him, unable to formulate more questions. She felt a great nothingness, as if all that was left was herself in her chair beneath a tree, and that self didn't matter at all. He put a water jug beside her, then stood looking down. She could see the glint in his eyes above the scarf. He said: "Lupe will be here in the morning."

He was leaving her to the dark, to the blankness. She stared at him, numbed by her lack of control over even the smallest thing. She wished Lupe were here now to help her make sense of this nightmare — Lupe, whom she had followed as a child, helping to gather the healing herbs, Lupe, who had been midwife for both her sons, Lupe, whose wisdom and kindness she had relied on for as long as she could remember. But here, in the darkness, Lupe and the light of day seemed a century away. What she had was self, a loneliness as huge as the hand of the sky that cupped her. She sobbed once, and then was still, looking up at the boy she had tried to help and who, whether by accident or design, had reduced her to a helpless reed, a bent stalk, a cage of bones, rattling like seeds in a dry gourd.

"I'm sorry," he said.

She remembered saying those same, useless words the day before, and she shook her head, overwhelmed by the smallness of speech. "It's not enough," she said. "You killed him. You think saying you're sorry can make it go away?" Under his hat his eyes were as sorrowful as her own, and as bitter, and in that moment she understood that he would carry the memory of what he had done, the horror of it, with him forever, that he would never forgive himself, never be free. She covered her face with her hands. "Go away," she said. "Go away and leave me alone. Please," and was relieved that he did what he was told, crossing the yard and getting into the old truck.

Why, he was taking it! He was a thief in addition to being a murderer! Without the truck how could she survive? How run the ranch? And then she remembered that, without legs, the truck was of no use to her, and she raised her fists in the air in a useless gesture.

"Damn you!" she called after him. "God damn you to hell!"

The rattle of the truck diminished. She thought she caught a glimpse of headlights, heading north up the abandoned cattle trail, and she thought that it was the wrong direction, that he would be caught in the forbidden valley by soldiers who had no idea of the enormity of his crime, and she laughed, harshly, at the trickery of fate, the minute choices taken by the living.

Jake, for example. If he'd not lost his temper, if, for once, he'd kept quiet or even paid the kid his wages. . . . But no. He'd let his tongue, his actions carry him away. And so he'd spun his own fate.

Her choice was simple — to get through the night. There was no alternative that she knew. She set her chin. She was forty-five years old, and nothing had licked her until polio had come creeping along her legs like a snake and had snatched her will. She'd been born tough out of tough parents who had settled here, labored together, survived to see her married to Jake, their land joined with his. She'd been eighteen, longlegged, as wild as he. Ah, but she'd tamed him, just as she'd tamed her first colt, a young mustang, when she was five. She had him taking grass from her hand, lowering his head to nuzzle her before they'd discovered her. And to the day he died, no one else had been able to touch him.

"Oh, Jake," she murmured, remembering those first, stolen kisses, eager but fumbling. They'd both been innocent, driven by the same hot sweetness, by that passion that belongs to the young and that comes only once.

Where had it gone? She didn't know, only that it had, and in its place had come unity of purpose, years of hard work and the raising of two sons to carry on what had begun nearly a century before. Ranching was a way of life, had been her only way until her illness. After that she'd had no purpose, nothing except fear and defeat.

From out of the past, Jake's voice rumbled. "For God's sake, Mallie! Life doesn't stop, so quit crying."

She leaned back and closed her eyes, letting her mind drift out on the slow tide of memory. In the tree above her the mockingbird sang an experimental trill, the notes falling into the night air like drops of water from a fountain. *Was it the same bird that had sung all night for years?* she wondered. *He whose symphonies she'd listened to on moonlit nights when she couldn't sleep? Whose mastery and repertoire had grown so that it seemed he never repeated a phrase but went on and on improvising, in thrall to his own creation? And tonight would he, in tune with the life around him, sing a funeral dirge?* She thought she couldn't bear it if he did. "Sing happy," she said as if he could understand. "Just sing happy."

As if on cue he burst into a ripple of notes, a wild music, like a dance, so she swayed with it, saw herself light footed and in Jake's arms, her skirts swinging, her face close to his, and his eyes afire with loving.

Always Jake. Except there was no more Jake. He was in the house, and he was dead. *Was there blood? Had he forgiven her, called out her name before he went?* She couldn't forgive herself for stirring him to anger out of her own pettiness. *Why, oh why, had she persisted in melancholy, in bitterness? Why hadn't she been a helpmeet instead of a millstone? She'd been wallowing in self-pity. Oh, she disgusted herself! She'd thrust the problems of the world onto her own man and retreated into that small world of misery. And there was no going back. Only the future existed, and it mocked her, laughed like the wild bird overhead, throwing its heart to the sky.*

She let the tears flow, heard herself sobbing but lacked the will to stop. *Maybe it was a good thing, this wild grieving. Perhaps, once it was out, she could begin again. Perhaps.* So she let herself weep until she was exhausted, and her head drooped on her chest, and she slept.

The laughter of coyotes startled her. *God, the night was interminable!* She struggled to see her watch, and failed. The sky was no help, moonless now, swept by a billion nameless stars. She looked for the few that she knew — the Dipper, the North Star, the Milky

192

Way, found them and was relieved by their presence. In some slow, insidious way the world she knew and trusted had changed. Only the stars were constant, and the sun and moon, and the guardian mountains that had stood in place for longer than anyone could know.

How long till morning? Till Lupe, coming to work would find her, make sense of things as she always did, ease the pain of her body with her powerful hands, the touch of a born curandera?

"Too long." She answered herself, and her voice seemed alien in the summer night. Quietly, then, she sat waiting for dawn, feeling that everything she loved in the world had been taken from her, that she was a stranger even to herself.

So she was awake when the great light cracked the sky, when the heart she had thought turned to stone leaped in her breast and stopped her breath. In the fierce clarity of the explosion, the mountains were visible, each cañon and rift showing dark against flame, and they seemed to draw back into themselves, defying destruction.

It was the end of the world! The jaws of hell opening, red-hot, roiling, devouring everything in sight! She closed her eyes against the scorching light and felt the earth tremble under her.

"Please," she whimpered, and again heard her voice like a bird whistle, ludicrous in the sound of the tempest sweeping over every living thing. "I'm not ready." There was so much yet to do — Jake's body to be buried, the boys called home. There was love she hadn't used yet, hidden under layers of self-pity. She needed to love, had almost forgotten how. There was the land, and she its guardian, helpless or not.

When she looked again, the holocaust had become a pillar of fire that sucked in and consumed all that it touched. Above her, the mockingbird was silent. Like her, the earth seemed to be holding its breath, steeling itself against the agony of a wound that burned straight to its core. Images, notions never crystallized in thought, raced through the blankness behind her eyes. For a moment it seemed as if she herself was the land, the curves and angles of her body outstretched, writing and helpless. *Who had done such a thing, and why? Who, in a single gesture, had the power to turn what she loved, and was, to ash?* She thought the white sands of the valley must be stained red with her blood, that the small creatures, the voles, the mice, and lizards, must be crouched and still, as terrified as she.

And suddenly she thought of Jesús who had driven the stolen truck northward through forbidden territory into certain destruction. After all, there was justice — not the justice of God but the skewed one of men, humans who died as they had lived, who turned violence on themselves and others. The justice of earth was different. Even at its cruelest there was a reason, a balance, misunderstood by human minds but nonetheless rational.

It was easy to let go, to die mewling and helpless, cursing fate. To go on was a harder choice, but choice it was.

Gradually the fire's throat consumed itself, was replaced by a luminous dawn, a fragile light like that in the convolutions of a sea shell, and the land, as if resurrected, lifted to meet the sun, replacing fury with the sweetness of inherent ritual. And the ritual seemed blessed.

Timidly, then joyously, a lark began to sing in the pasture grass, then flew upward, white tail feathers flashing. He was followed by others, small music boxes singing from fence posts and the seed heads of weeds. In the rustling cottonwood the mockingbird spread his wings and fluttered above her, before returning to his perch where he began his salute to the morning.

Without warning, she began to laugh, and the sound shocked her, for laughter seemed out of place in the aftermath of destruction. And yet . . . and yet . . . she could not repress her own relief. She was alive, and life was precious, no matter what the handicap, how great the misery. Life contained solace in these moments of unity with all things, as if the heart of earth was one heart, and a part of it hers, alive and beating in her breast.

She and the land — the mountains whose skirts swept to the valley floor, the valley, itself, green and undulant — had survived and, if her body was weak, her mind was not, nor her heart, that echo of earth time attuned to the seasons, the passage of days. Somehow she must keep going. Somehow she would manage to preserve this place that was part of her blood, her bones, the place that she loved beyond all else, even perhaps more than she had loved Jake. Together they had been stewards, serving and protecting the ground that gave them life. To stop now only because he was gone would be a crime against all that she believed.

The boys would return. She knew that as surely as she knew that she was alive and had hope, as surely as she knew that what she had witnessed was both an end and a beginning.

Joy rose in her, tumultuous as a thundercloud lifting over the mountains. She wished she could dance to the thunder of her heart, to the mad piping of mockingbird and lark. Failing that, she turned to the east and reached out her arms in worship of the coming day.

SAND DOLLAR

For as long as I can remember Noah has wanted to see the ocean. That's understandable, considering he's spent his life here where the widest stretch of water is a stock tank bulldozed into the ground, and the washes fill up only in the rainy season and then only if we're lucky. When I was little and hanging around the corrals or begging to ride on roundup, Noah talked about the ocean. He talked about a lot of things, partly because he liked me as an audience. I never did anything but admire and take to heart what he said, and most of what I know about horses and cattle and this country I learned, listening to him. Then, too, I had him up on a plateau with God and the saints, and sometimes I think I still do. He trained me along with the horses. We worked together, doctoring them when they got sick, consoling each other when they died.

He'd had so many horses and dogs in his life he got across to me the fact that life is cyclical, that seasons come and go, and dogs and horses, and people, too, and that there's not much anyone can do about it. We'd bury the dogs, haul the horses away, and we'd mourn them a bit, and then one day Noah would bring me a pup from a litter he knew about, and once he convinced my dad that a certain colt was right for me, and I forgot my sorrow over death in the excitement of learning about a new life.

When Noah first came to work for us, he had a pack of redbone hounds he'd trained to work cattle. I'll never forget the way those dogs would search out cows and calves and move them along without a word from anyone and without a speck of hound nonsense, either. I remember asking him how he'd trained the need to chase deer or rabbits out of those dogs, and his answer. "Tied 'em to a tree the first time they didn't tend to business and whupped 'em. They learned." And when he saw my shock, he explained. "Like your dad has to give you a spanking now and then so's you won't act foolish."

It sounded hard to me, but actually those hounds had long forgotten the treatment. They loved Noah better than anyone alive, even me, though I sneaked them scraps from my dinner every night. Like I did, they loved Noah because he was honest and respected them, and they'd crowd around him dancing, begging for a pat, a word, and their tails would whip the air, and their feet stir up dust so it looked like a dust devil was starting.

They just never disobeyed, and after a time I understood the wisdom of what Noah had said. Out here, an animal that's badly trained can kill itself or its master. And as far as I know, Noah never trained a bad horse or a fool dog. And I like to think he didn't do so badly with me, either. I was like the child he never had. He poured what he knew into me with more fervor than a dedicated parent. He didn't spoil me. He was as strict with me as with one of his hounds. He never hesitated to tell me when I was wrong and why, or to shame me gently but firmly enough so I'd remember.

We had some dry years back then. The tank dwindled to a puddle, and the cattle crowded around so thick we couldn't see the ground. When the dry spell finally broke with a two-day storm and the wash was running with a roar, I went down to see it. So much rain had fallen that the water had overflowed the rocky banks and was flooding the trees. The main channel was a six-foot wall of water that carried with it branches, stumps, even small animals.

I took one look and went to find Noah. I told him the wash was just like a tidal wave. The fact that neither of us had ever seen a tidal wave or the ocean, either, didn't bother me. I had a good imagination. When Noah told his stories about the great albino wolf or the jaguar that drowned the Jones boys' lion dog, I saw the things happening.

So when Noah said: "You ever see a tidal wave?" I nearly

answered, yes. I had, in my mind, just like I'd seen the white wolf and all the hounds chasing after. "You haven't seen the ocean, either, have you?" he asked, catching me before I could create a full-fledged lie.

I shook my head. I could picture it, though, wide as the valley and blue like the mountains with the summer cloud shadows on them. "No," I said. "Have you?"

He hunkered down in the shade at the side of the house and tipped back his hat, and I, familiar with the signs, hunkered down in girlish imitation and got ready to listen. "I never saw it," he said. "But I come close." He went on: "From the time I was younger than you, I had a hankering to see the ocean. It was something to think about. Different. I always thought maybe it was like the desert, only it was water, hundreds of miles of it that you couldn't see across."

I said I thought that's just what it was like. I closed my eyes and filled up the whole valley with waves. I washed away the mountains and made a great and moving sea.

"The fact is, though," he said, "you don't know, and neither do I. Seein' is different. You got to see something to understand it. You got to touch it and smell it and walk around it a while. And, when I was a boy, that's what I had it in mind to do. My grandmother came here from Ireland, and she'd lived near the sea and then come across it, and she told me what it was like. Afternoons she'd set out on the porch and have her tea. That's what they did where she come from, so she always did it here. And she'd tell me stories like I tell you." He smiled at me and nodded his head, and I felt easy about things, about listening to stories the way he had done. "Anyway," he said, "when I grew up and went to work, I kept thinking about how I wanted to see the ocean. Some folks are born and die without ever seeing anything but their own backyard, but I think a person should travel, see what other folks are like. So, when I was about nineteen, I took a job on the cattle cars goin' to Los Angeles." He sighed.

Noah has a whole range of sighs. The small ones express regret

198

or disillusionment. The big ones usually mean something profound is coming. This sigh was small. I scrunched up on the sand and waited.

"It was hot work on those cars. And dusty. And you know how cattle bawl when they're penned. They bawled all the way through Yuma and down into California, but I didn't care. I was going to the sea and gettin' paid for it. And, when we got there, I handed the cattle over and went out in the street. I asked the first fella I saw how to get to the ocean. And what do you think?" His eyes, bright blue, probed me.

"What?" I asked.

"He just looked at me, and laughed. That fancy dude laughed and turned away, and me, I got so mad I said: 'The hell with it,' and come back home, and I never have seen the ocean."

I sat there with my arms around my knees, watching a pinacate beetle bury its head in the sand. I had the urge to squash it but didn't. I'd learned that much from Noah. You let creatures alone to go about their business. "Don't it make you mad still?" I asked.

He gave a big sigh from the bottom of his belly. I held my breath and waited. "Jenny, there's all kinds of folks in this world. Some good, some bad, some downright mean who don't give a hoot for their fellow man. After a while a man gets so he accepts the world for what it is. I'm not mad. Not now. I just want room to think in peace."

"When I get big," I said, "I'll take you to the ocean."

"Maybe you will. I'll count on it," he said.

I always remembered my promise, even when I grew up and went away to college and Noah, and the ranch, and the mountains and pastures of childhood blurred together in a gentle dream. Sometimes I'd find myself looking at someone, trying to see through them to what they really were, what they wanted, just so I wouldn't turn out like the stranger who had laughed at Noah. But I enjoyed the university and the city, though it took me a while to understand that

199

city folks thought ranching was glamorous and that my childhood had been filled with handsome cowboys and swift rides across open range on a wild horse. When I tried to explain that no one in his right mind wanted a wild horse under him, that roundups were hard, stinking, dirty work, that few cowboys were handsome and that most of them limped on smashed feet or walked bent over from broken vertebrae, I was met with such disbelief that I learned not to mention any of it.

When I tried to tell Noah what city people were like, he sniffed. "Dudes won't learn. When you coming home to stay?"

He was growing old. He didn't ride much any more. He'd broken too many bones, hamburgered his fingers at the forge or generator so often he had trouble moving them. But he stayed on at the ranch where, as he said, he had room to think in peace. My parents would no more have turned him off than they would a relative. He belonged and, when I went home, it was to him as much as anyone.

But I stayed on in the city after graduation. I had fallen in love with a man who wrote poetry and played the guitar, who was tall, bearded, civilized, and who saw in my dreaming something profound. "Like a mountain. Like the desert in the sun," he would say and disappear into himself, listening for voices.

I'd never been in love. I guess I thought it would never happen to me. I never pictured myself married and keeping house the way my mother did, or being dependent on another for my joy. I never asked for love; it simply came; and it changed me into a woman I didn't know, a woman who no longer took for granted the beauty in her life. Beauty hung by a thread. And happiness. At the other side of joy was the terror of being less than whole, and so I loved, holding desperately to that man who was the dark half of myself.

After a year he left me. We were young, and he was a wanderer. I like to think that someday, when he's wandered enough, sampled women enough, found the voices he searched for, that he'll come back, but I don't know. I haven't set my heart on it. That's something else I learned from Noah — never to count on anyone but yourself.

I wandered, too, after he left me, so I wouldn't have time to remember moments of stillness, hands and eyes and bodies touching. But one morning I woke up, hollowed out by loneliness, needing a talisman, something to cling to, to believe in, and I remembered Noah and his dreams, and how I'd never seen the ocean. So I went down to Baja where there was no one, only birds, lizards, and whales that rose to the surface of the incredible blue silk that was the ocean, and blew and bellowed, and smacked their tails until the very earth reverberated.

I walked the beach for a week doing what Noah had told me — seeing, hearing, touching, taking note of how the sun set, throwing its fire so high that everything quivered, burned before darkness fell. And how the tide went out and exposed yet another world of snails, barnacles, crabs, and little silver fish that flashed like bird's wings in their narrow pools. And I thought that the sea *is* like a desert. It exists, self-contained, uncaring of the life that survives above and within it. *We* do the caring, I thought. People care, or should. Earth, sky, water *are*.

I watched the water change color the way mountains and desert rocks will do. I listened to the wind coming from far away. It sang about things lonelier than I, and I lay down in the sand and let it heal me, let the heat burn through and cleanse me. Then I sat up and looked in surprise at the shell I found under my hand. It was round and pale with a design like a cross in its center, and so delicate I couldn't believe it had survived the sea. I put my tongue to its surface and tasted salt. I weighed it in my palm. Its weight was nothing. I sat in the brilliant afterglow and looked around me as I'd never looked before.

I found more of those small relics scattered on the sand, picked up a starfish, filled my pockets with shells, pink and striped and mottled, and walked back jingling and light on my feet like I hadn't been for a long time. I heard my young voice saying: "I'll take you to the ocean . . . ocean," repeating like the waves, far out now and small, and I thought about Noah who always had answers.

I packed up and drove through the desert, past the cactus and the rock peaks that turned red in the dawn. My mother was in the kitchen when I got home, cooking the usual eggs, bacon, toast, flapjacks, and the sun was splitting the mountains into cañons and turning the junipers gold.

"You look like you've been racing the devil," she said as I dumped my pack and my box of shells near the door.

"I have," I said. "I won."

"About time." She's not a talkative woman. Restful — my dad and Noah call her, and she is. Restful, and a believer in food as a cure-all. "Wash up and eat," she said. "Then take some down to Noah. He's not been well."

Noah not well? I couldn't remember a time when he'd been ill. Smashed up, maybe, but never ill. "What is it?"

"Old age mostly," she said. "And we can't get him to a doctor. You know how he is about doctors." I knew. Indian cures were what he believed in — prickly pear and yucca root and all the rest. But he'd never had a cure for old age, nor had any Indian I'd ever heard of. "Now you eat," she said. "He's not dying, and you look like you need feeding. You're mighty stringy. Noah can wait ten minutes."

"I can't." I grabbed the loaded plate and the box of shells and ran through the back pasture to Noah's blue trailer. He was lying on the couch. I couldn't remember ever seeing him lying down, and I stood, peering through the screen door, fighting off panic so strong it hurt. "Noah," I called. "It's me. You O.K.?"

"Gettin' old is all," he said. "Come on in."

"I brought your breakfast," I said. I wanted to cry. Skin and bones is what he was, and those blue eyes, like the sea. "Oh, Noah," I said. I sat down on the lumpy couch. "I'm home."

He looked at me, keen as a hawk. "Some fella been foolin' with you?"

"How did you know?"

"It's on your face. You're not a flighty young 'un any more."

"I wish I was," I said. "I wish I could have it back."

"Times change," he said. "And people. You can't ever get it back. You just keep goin' to the end, and growin', if you're lucky. You home to stay?"

I nodded.

"About time." He twinkled at me to soften the scolding. "You never were cut out for the city, only you're too stubborn to figure it out quick."

"Do you remember," I asked, "how you and I talked about the ocean?"

"I sure do," he said. "Did you go?"

"Yes." I sat back to tell him about it, the colors, the waves, the gulls hovering over the way the hawks do, and about the immensity of it, not so different from the desert, after all.

"That's about how I had it figured," he said, when I finished.

"And I brought you something." I pulled out the shells in all their brilliance, and the sand dollars, for that's what they were, those lovely cool round things.

"Well, look at that." He turned one over and over in his big hard hands. "That's something, isn't it? That really is." He held it up like I knew he'd do, and put it to his tongue and tasted, and to his nose and smelled the far-off scent of salt. "Something like this," he said, "it makes you think people aren't near as important as they like to make out."

I nodded. People come and go — even poets with blue eyes and infinite words for things, and childhood, and old men, and spotted hounds with feet like flowers. Earth, sea, and sky remain, and the hope within the human heart that keeps us going, keeps us learning until the end. I sighed, as deeply as he had ever done, and he looked

203

at me. There was an eagerness in him, a purpose.

"Now you're home," he said, "maybe you'll tell me more about that ocean. And those whales. They must be a sight. I'm gettin' old, but a man's never done with learning."

CHARLEY TUNA AND THE JUNKYARD DOGS

Charley Tuna was riled. For the second weekend in a row someone had tried to break into his trailer, and the dog he himself had stolen from Tavvy Ortiz had disappeared, probably stolen back. Charley had a junkyard at the edge of town. He was out there now, looking for bits and pieces to make an extra lock for his back door and talking to himself, a steady stream of words and curses. He kicked a fender out of his way and bent over a bin where he tossed hasps, bolts, screws, the small useful things he could never find when he needed them.

"Damnation," he said. "What in hell do I have that anybody'd want, snuffling 'round my door like a pack of coyotes?"

He didn't have much for sure. His dead wife's, Mary's, old sewing machine, the one he'd given her as a wedding present. A thirty-year-old radio he picked up the ball games on, and the news, and the late-night talk shows when he couldn't sleep and lay there getting a kick out of the nuts who phoned in questions. A bed, a couch, his shotgun, a box of old photographs. He stopped at that and stared over the tin roofs of Stinking Flats to the eastern mountains.

Stinking Flats had a long and violent history. Trouble seemed to come out of the ground it sat on, like the gold that had caused it to spring up overnight back in the 1880s, and the sulphur spring that gave the town its name. Before the gold, it had been a desert — alkali, cactus, bad water that even the Indians avoided. But with the gold came people, and with them so much trouble decent folks couldn't go out on the street without fearing for their lives. And decent women! The few there had been went armed like the men, even to church socials. It got so bad that the town council had sent for the law, and it had come in the person of Clyde Lovell, deputy marshal, now a Great American Myth.

Charley knew more about Clyde Lovell than anybody still alive. Clyde had been sweet on Charley's grandma, Honoria, had even returned to Stinking Flats after Buns Lafferty, his first wife, risen from whorehouse to respectability, had died. Clyde had courted Honoria, disregarding the fact that she was married. Then he'd taken off for the gold rush in Alaska and got himself killed. His worldly goods were shipped back to Honoria, the woman he'd loved. Or so it was said. Honoria hadn't talked much at all. It embarrassed her, she said, at her age, though she blushed at the mention of Clyde's name until the day she died.

In a trunk under Charley's bed was enough memorabilia of the mythical marshal to stock a museum: love letters, tintypes, Clyde's straight razor, his gun belt and a gun — the famous Colt .45 with which he had shot the cowboy rustlers dead in the dirt of Front Street in Stinking Flats.

"Haw!" said Charley.

He sat down on the trailer steps, tipped back his hat, and thought some more. Over the years he'd refused all offers to tell what he knew about Clyde except to his friend, Tug McNeal. Tug was dead honest, had grown up on a ranch near town, and had come back here to live after he'd finished college. He knew the country, the people, the history of Stinking Flats and the valley it sat in, enough so that he'd written a book based on Charley's recollections and his own family's diaries. The book sold well; the profits kept Charley in groceries and Tug on the ranch where he'd been born.

Lately, though, two dudes, pale-faced writer fellows in city clothes who talked a lot without saying much had been hanging around and pestering the daylights out of him. They popped up out of the junk like jackrabbits, loaded with cameras and notebooks. They shouted out questions about Buns and Honoria, about Charley himself, about Clyde, and what they called "the definitive story of the shoot-out." Charley was riled, all right. He had reason. His door busted, his dog gone, and the two dudes probably staked out behind the auto parts or the propane refrigerators, waiting for him to leave.

"The pair of 'em's got hips like a loose-assed whore," Charley said, taking a good look into the pile of metal. He laid the hasp at his feet, hammered it straight. Then he attached it to the door frame, feeling as he did that they were out there, watching him.

When he finished, he figured he'd go down to the Singletree and look for Tug. Maybe between them they could come up with a plan. Besides, Tug was a top hand at dog stealing, and Charley had a notion to get his dog back. He'd stolen it in the first place because it was scrawny and had come up to him, wagging its tail and looking sorrowful behind Tavvy's chicken-wire fence. Tavvy's woman fed it on tortillas and beans. He'd fed it dry food and a couple cans of good stuff, and it had fattened up considerable. Muley, he called it. Turned out it had a bray just like one and used it often. Hell! He needed that dog to keep the other thieves away!

"Linin' their pockets," he muttered. "Just hopin' to get rich off me." He jammed down his hat, padlocked the door, and headed for the Singletree.

Tug was sitting in his favorite seat, back to the wall facing the door, and looking more dangerous than any man should. Surprisingly, the dudes were in a dark corner, heads together, watching Tug surreptitiously.

Tug nodded at Charley.

"I'm sure dry," Charley said. It was the end of the month, and he had seventy five cents in his pocket.

Tug's eyes danced. "A glass of your best tap water," he said to the waitress.

"And a draft to wash it down." Charley turned to Tug. "How long them two been in here?"

"Followed me in," Tug said. "Maybe they're going to try and off me."

"What for?"

Tug shrugged. "I'm the competition. The only person besides you who knows anything like the truth about old Clyde. It riles them. Hell, you know what these people are like! They'd cut their own mother's throat to find out something."

Charley snorted into his glass. "Crooks!" he said. "I'm betting they tried to break in my place. And Ortiz must've stole Muley back, too."

"Oh?" Tug raised a black eyebrow.

A prickle ran down Charley's neck. When Tug looked like that, he was dangerous. "I want you to help me get Muley back," he said.

"Why not the bunch? They're all starving."

"I can only feed the one, is why. Besides, Muley picked me out."

Tug put on his hat. "I'll take the rest out to the ranch. Let's go."

At that point the heavier of the two dudes got up. "Excuse me," he said, his mouth in a smile that didn't reach his eyes. "McNeal, isn't it?"

Charley snorted again.

Tug silenced him with a wicked look. "Yes," he said. He drew himself up to his full height and waited.

Kinda like Clyde would've, Charley thought. Again he felt his neck prickle.

"I'm John Hammer, and this is Paul Dauphin. You've probably read some of our work in the Lovell area."

Dauphin, who was shaped like a fig, bobbed his head.

Tug's expression didn't change. "You were in that trouble at the historical society a while back, weren't you?"

Hammer's grin spread over his face like pudding, but Charley was watching his eyes. They were as hard as ball bearings.

"Mistaken identity," he said. "Somebody else took those papers. You know what people are like, especially about Clyde Lovell. We do serious work. We've been researching Lovell for years, and we wondered if we could talk to you." He jerked his head. "And Mister Tuna, too. We're trying to do the real thing, and we'd like some real facts. Recollections. Diaries. That kind of thing."

Dauphin nodded and flashed yellow teeth. "We understand you have a collection of Lovell's relics," he said to Charley.

Relics! Hell, he talked like an old lady! "Maybe I do, and maybe I don't," Charley said. He wished he'd never heard of Clyde Lovell, and that Honoria had never been born. He wished Stinking Flats would sink back into the ground and take these two with it. His solitude was being broken apart and, with it, his peace. "Got to go," he said. "Got some business to attend to."

"We'll see you around," Tug said. "I'm sure Charley here has lots of reminiscences for you."

Out on the sidewalk, beyond the swinging doors, Charley glared at him. "Why'd you go and say that? I ain't talking to those fakers!"

Tug squinted against the sunset, then stood a minute watching the sky change colors over the mountain. He grinned, wicked as a tomcat. "Oh, yes you are," he said. "You're going to give them the straight scoop. Those two stole the county records office blind in addition to the historical society. And they probably tried to bust in your place. This is Stinking Flats. Clyde Lovell country. You know what he did to crooks. Are you going to let them get away with stuff like that?"

Charley rolled the idea around. "It's a . . . ," he groped for the words he wanted. "It's a . . . invasion of my privacy. I don't want anything to do with either of them."

"We're not talking about your privacy. Tell 'em whatever comes into your head. Then they'll likely leave you alone."

Charley hooted. "You mean lie?"

"Whatever you want to call it. Spin them a few yarns. They won't know the difference, and serve them right. Think it over. Now let's go steal us some dogs."

They took all four, Tug reaching over the sagging fence and lifting them into the back of his pickup. "Poor critters," he said, eyeing them. "Haven't been fed in days. Let's take them to McDonald's."

"I ain't ate either," Charley said.

"You, too. You're indispensable."

"Damn' right," Charley said, wondering what Tug meant but deciding to agree. He was hungry.

"While we're at it, we'll figure our story." Tug shifted gears and moved up the alley, the dogs' tails sticking up like flags behind.

"Them dogs'll puke," Charley said, still thinking about his own appetite. "Best let me dole the chow out slow."

Tug swung onto Front Street and floored the gas, narrowly missing John and Paul who were standing on the sidewalk, staring at them. "Cut out thinking about your stomach," Tug yelled over the roar of the engine. "We're going to fake out the fakers!"

By the next evening Charley had swept out his kitchen, washed the week's dishes, wiped the table, and shaved. He even put on a clean shirt, black and western cut, though, because he was heavier than the last time he'd worn it, he had to leave the last button open and shove it all under his belt. He fastened the buckle with care. It was an old one of Navajo silver that had come down to him from his mother. Maybe, he thought, it had belonged to Clyde, too. His fingers lingered on it a moment. Then he took a quick slug of the whiskey Tug had left and sat down on the step beside Muley to wait for his visitors.

It was a cool high desert evening. The mountains softened, turning purple and dun, and the wind blew off the crests, scattering tumbleweeds that piled up against the car and tractor parts, nestled in the basins of sinks, the sagging seats of old chairs. In the draw at the edge of town coyotes howled, and Muley made an answer deep in his throat.

Charley went back inside and poured another shot. He wasn't sure he was ready for this. Not at all. Even though he'd spent the day listening to Tug and agreeing to the plan. Still, it made a damn' good joke, and the two dudes wide eyed as kids. He chuckled. Muley let out a bray.

"Hush up," Charley told him. "It's company."

John and Paul were picking their way down the path. John carried a flashlight aimed dead ahead like a sword. Its beam struck Charley in the face.

"Turn that contraption off and learn to see where you're going!" he yelled. "It ain't dark yet anyhow."

"Sorry, Mister Tuna," Paul said. "We just didn't want to step on anything."

"Clyde Lovell never carried no flashlight," Charley said. "Out here you learn to make do. The rattlers generally keep out of your way." He hid his grin by turning to open the door. "Now you're here, come in," he said.

They stood just inside, looking around, stiff legged like a pair of hounds in a new place. "Comfortable," John said at last.

"Yes," said Paul.

"Suits me just fine," Charley said. He raised the bottle. "Drink?"

"Well . . . ," John began.

"Just a tad," Paul said.

"What's that?" Charley asked Paul.

"What's what?"

"That what you said. A tad?"

Paul waved his hands. "You know. A drop."

"Ain't no such thing." Charley filled the glass to the brim. "You fellas want to learn about the West, you better start speakin' the language. And learn to hold your liquor while you're at it." He was beginning to enjoy himself. He sat down at the round table, his face in the shadow. "Now," he said, "where do you want to start?"

"At the beginning." Paul clicked on a tape recorder.

"Now, there'll be none of that," Charley said, pointing at it. "You want to know, you listen is all. That's the way it's done out here."

"But," said Paul.

"No buts. You can listen, or you can leave. Don't make no difference to Charley Tuna."

"Put the damn' thing away," John said. "Let's get on with it."

"Ain't no hurry, is there?" Charley asked. Then he tipped back his chair, folding his hands across his middle. "Let's see. The beginning. Hell, wasn't no one here in the beginning. Just coyotes and snakes and such. And Injuns. A few. Apaches mostly, just passing through. Then that prospector, Fred Bell, fell into a hole out there and found gold nuggets. Then folks come from everywhere. By the thousands. Lived in tents, lived out on the flats just a diggin' and a stakin' claims and fightin' over 'em. Then come the whores and the gamblers, and the crooks wantin' to line their pockets. My folks were here already. They come from Texas in the 'Seventies. Had a ranch up Fool Creek. Sold cattle to the Army and the reservations, and probably helped the rustlers, too. Lots of folks did. That's how they held onto their own stock."

The story was taking hold of him. Maybe it was the sound of his own voice, maybe it was the memories released by talk. He was seeing the grass the way it had been, the emptiness, how you could look down the valley clear to Mexico and see nothing but the land, the mountains, a line of cottonwoods along the river bottom, and the river running bankful nearly all year. He held up the finger with the missing joint, snubbed off by a rope thirty years before. "I'll tell you something," he said. "Stinking Flats is cursed. It was cursed then, and it is now. Still filled with crooks and folks who come out here and think they're above the law."

"What about Honoria?" John interrupted, uneasy at the mention of crooks. "She's the one we're interested in . . . along with Lovell, of course."

Charley shot a look across the table. "You interested in all the back history or just the scandalous part?"

John tightened his lips. "Well, all of it, of course, but it's Honoria and Clyde we'd like to get the dirt on."

His words riled Charley more than he already was. "You writin' serious stuff or them stories for the scandal papers?" he asked. " 'Cause there ain't no dirt. None at all. It was love, pure and simple." He glanced at them. Paul was scribbling on a tablet balanced on his knee. His words sounded so good he repeated them. "True love, and one that lasted till Clyde met his Maker. Honoria's folks were respectable. Wouldn't let her have nothing to do with no gunman, even a marshal. Married her off, they did, but that love kept a-burning. Even after Clyde made off with Buns Lafferty." He tipped his chair forward and hit the floor. "You ever see a picture of *her?*"

John gripped his hands together. "You mean you have one?" His voice cracked in excitement. Muley lifted his head from the mat and growled.

"Sure do. Got old Clyde's gun, too."

They rose from their chairs like Siamese twins. "His gun?" they chorused.

"Now, you set," Charley said, "and I'll show you things no one's seen for more than fifty years."

"Oh, my God," said Paul. "Do you know what that gun is worth?"

"Shut up," John said through tight lips. "Just shut up."

In the back room Charley pulled out his trunk. He and Tug had salted it that afternoon, replacing Clyde's .45 with an old pistol that had belonged to Tug's father. They'd put in an old hunting knife, too, and a green velvet skirt from somewhere. And they'd left Charley's tintypes stored in a tin biscuit box. "Let them steal the pistol," was Tug's advice. "Better yet, sell it to them. Soon as they try to sell it as Clyde's, they'll get laughed out of the business."

Charley returned to the kitchen and reverently laid the gun, wrapped in a piece of quilt, on the table. "Now, this here is the true, honest-to-God gun that Clyde shot them rustlers with," he whispered, trying not to laugh. "Ain't nobody but me touched it since Honoria was laid to rest." He pulled away the quilt with what he hoped was proper reverence.

213

"That's it!" John whispered.

"It really is!" Paul reached across the table. "Can I hold it?"

"It's loaded," Charley cautioned. "I don't keep empty guns around."

Paul's hands retreated. "You mean it shoots?"

"Bet your ass," said Charley.

"How much do you want for it?" John looked straight at him with those ball-bearing eyes. "I want to start a museum, and this would be the prime exhibit. Clyde Lovell's pistol. People would come from all over the world to see it."

Charley shook his head. "I can't sell that pistol. It's a family . . . a family whatucallit?"

"Heirloom," said Paul.

"That's right. And when I die, Tug McNeal gets it. It's in my will."

John slapped the table so hard that Muley jumped. "Now look here! This is nonsense! This gun is history. It belongs to the world, and you have no right to hide it here. In this place." He looked around in disgust. "Or give it to that McNeal, either. I'll give you a hundred dollars. Cash."

"Haw," said Charley.

"Two hundred."

"As you say, this gun is history." Charley picked it up and held it with care. "How much is history worth?"

"Five hundred. That's my best offer."

"Seven hundred. Cash, no check. I get the cash, you get the gun."

"Deal," said John.

"And I'll throw in this picture, too," Charley said, leering. "You can see why they called her 'Buns.' " He flipped a postcard at them. It lay there under the lamp, showing a female, her back to the camera. She was naked except for her stockings and a garter belt.

"Oh, good lord." Paul sounded cross. "Is that what the fuss was about?"

"I'd say there was plenty there to fuss over." Charley chuckled at his own wit. "Honoria was a lady. She was different." He thumbed through the photographs. "I got her in here somewhere. I doubt she had to do with Clyde more than a couple times after he come back, though, her bein' married and all."

"What?" they shouted.

"Times was different then," he said, letting his voice trail off. Lord, it was hell not laughing! He got up and went to the door where Muley was scratching. "Dogs sure can pester," he observed.

"Are you saying . . . ?" John's voice squeaked like an old recording.

"Well, it wasn't talked about," Charley said, "times bein' what they were. But my ma sure didn't get her blue eyes from her daddy."

Paul stared at him as if he'd risen from the grave. "There is a resemblance! I can see it. I really can. Look at him, John. Look close."

"Naw," said Charley. "I take after the other side. The Tunneys. That's my real name. Kids started calling me Tuna in school, and it stuck. Funny thing about kids. . . ."

"Let's stick to the point," John said.

"Ain't no point. History is all wound around."

Outside there was a crash. Muley howled, then began to bark. "¡Cabrón!" yelled a male voice.

" 'Scuse me a minute," Charley said. He slipped the pistol into his hand. "Got some business to take care of. Folks been bustin' in on me lately." He stepped out into the dark.

"He's going to shoot somebody!" Paul whispered. "It's in the blood! Let's get out of here." He jumped up and headed for the door.

"Not that way! He'll shoot us. Out the back. And grab that stuff. We'll get the gun tomorrow."

"Tavvy . . . ?" Charley roared. "That you?"

A stream of curses came from behind the tractors.

Charley pulled the trigger, heard the slug ricochet off metal. "Don't come stealin' my dog, or I'll blow your idjit brain apart." He pulled the trigger again for emphasis. "You starved him. I fed him. Now he's mine, you hear?"

215

There was silence broken suddenly by the sound of running feet. Muley stuck his nose hard into Charley's crotch. "Keep outta my business," he said to the dog, but he dropped his hand and stroked the big head.

They stood a while, listening to the night sounds — crickets, wind in the screens, a poor-will calling from the wash, and far off the music from the Singletree. Probably the same sounds old Clyde had listened to on an ordinary night nearly a hundred years before. Charley could almost feel it — the history, the danger, the quiet of valley and mountains, and the woman's skirts swishing toward him through dry grass. He could almost see her white arms, shining in the dark, her head thrown back, laughing. He shook his head. A fella could scare himself out of his wits if he got to thinking.

"Come on, Muley," he said. He went inside and poured another drink, catching sight of himself in the little piece of mirror over the sink. Funny how his eyes looked in the shadows. Blue. Hard. Gunfighter's eyes that could see to shoot in the dark, that backed down from nothing at all. Eyes that had never appeared in his family before or since. He raised his glass to his reflection. "Here's to you, Grandpa," he said, and drank.

THE BIRD, THE ASHES, AND THE FLAME

"The dead don't die. They look on and help."

D. H. Lawrence to J. Middleton Murray

Mabel Dodge Luhan came to Taos in 1917. A thrice-married millionaire, a semi-mystic, patron of the arts and power seeker, she read D. H. Lawrence's work and invited him to New Mexico, hoping, as she later wrote, "to seduce his spirit and make it work for me." Lawrence — and his wife, Frieda von Richthofen — found the situation intolerable, eventually moving to a ranch high in the mountains and then leaving for Mexico and Europe.

D. H. Lawrence died in Venice in 1930. In 1933 Frieda sent Antonio Ravagli, the Italian with whom she was living, to cremate the body and bring the ashes to America. In Taos, Mabel attempted to steal the urn, seeking to possess in death what hadn't been possible during Lawrence's life. Ultimately, Ravagli resolved the crisis by building a shrine in Lawrence's honor and cementing the ashes within.

"You vampire! How dare you do this!" Frieda screams, and her green eyes glint like the edges of knives. She is all the elements in one, at her best a thunderstorm raging over the mountains.

"I dare. Oh, I dare. Because he was never yours. He never belonged to you." Where Frieda is earth and fire, Mabel Luhan is ice, the crystalline edges of a glacier on its way to the sea.

Frieda's chin juts out. She is dangerous when she wears that expression, volatile, fighting for what she loves, what she believes,

217

what her blood tells her, and the marrow of her bones. "Lorenzo belongs to the world."

Fools, both of them brawling over ashes, *my* ashes, the pathetic residue of my body released from the struggle, the constant aching for unity. The struggle is theirs alone, two harpies worrying a bone, a victim who is not the issue. What is at stake here is power, essence of female domination over what, earlier, they had no control at all.

"Fools!" I want to tell them. "Go home to your husbands, to those ordinary men you deserve. Scatter my bones to the four directions. Let them fly on the wind, sink to the magnificent earth, dance on the water. Let me go. Let me be!"

Even in death they tear at me as if I am, indeed, the "lovely phoenix" of Frieda's intuition.

"You lovely phoenix," she hissed at me that night, like the fire hissing in the wood. "You're all of it. Bird. Ashes. Flame." And she beat me with her fists in a passion, not understanding but knowing, nonetheless. And to my shame I agreed with her, puny male creature that I was, full of belief in the vision, the word.

We'll see who wins this battle. Mabel of the iron will, selfish to the last, or Frieda, earth mother, whose bosom sustained me, whose loins nourished and fought me, who brought out the best — and the worst — in me in what seemed to be the centuries of our lives. Oh, God, I was lost in her bounty, loving it, hating it because it wasn't mine but hers, because she *knew,* while I, tentatively, on the edge of a scream, only *felt.*

What was it that I felt? The white-hot center of the world, the fierceness, the oneness, the beauty pouring out and out, faster than I could grasp and understand it. The dark seas of Italy, the desert stretching its violent heart across an endless horizon, those mountains clutching their secrets like some eternal heaven. Now, free of the wanting, the loveliness is sweet like the taste of autumn grapes, the shock of cold water in the heat of day, those rare moments when life is brilliance bursting in the loins, in the darkness behind closed eyes.

218

"What will you do? Pray to him?" Mabel is playing the great lady, cold, haughty. She addresses Frieda is if she is a peasant — my Frieda with the blood of warriors hot in her veins. "He never loved you. He was greatness and you, ah, you fought him. I wish these were your ashes. I wish you were dead."

Hauteur never daunted Frieda. She has enough of her own. "He hated you from that first week. You with your ugly body and no soul. That's what he said, and he was right. What will you do with these?" Her lip curls and she waves her hand in a gesture meant to erase her adversary. "Gloat? Pretend he's alive? Stir his ashes like a fortune teller? Ach!.You make me sick, you and your greed. You make me ashamed."

"What would you know about shame?"

"More than you."

Frieda summons a great dignity. She rings with it like a bell, and I love her for it, would reach out for her if I could, absorbing that mighty radiance into my own flesh. But I have none. I, Lorenzo, creature of flesh and senses, have none! Strange, strange to be so disembodied while these two wills collide over the poor remnants of what they remember as hotly physical.

"Frieda, Frieda, my Queen Bee, take me away!" I shout but she doesn't hear. She rarely heard in life and, when she did, she argued out of that stubborn, Teutonic mind of hers that admitted no equal. She was my opposite, a foil, a perverse reflection in a jagged mirror. "Take me away! To that high country I so loved and had to flee because of this monster who is trying to steal my secrets, my heart even in death."

"I willed him here. I gave him Taos. I gave him America. That's more than you ever did." Mabel will go to her own grave clutching her poor self in her hands. She is all she has, and she is nothing. Nothing! She's an empty pot, pathetic, despicable.

Yes, she willed me here out of the purity of her evil. Yes, she gave me Taos, and Mexico, too. But they are greater than she, their goodness, their wisdom unaffected by Mabel's will or any other but their own. Having nothing, she gave nothing, while Frieda gave everything, gave in, gave up family, children, homeland to follow me, the raggle-taggle gypsy on my endless journey in search of perfection.

"Take me!" I howl again for what good it does, and yet, for one moment, Frieda seems to respond. She cocks her head; her silver hair forms a halo around her face. She smiles, slyly, the ever-present cigarette dangling from the corner of her mouth. And then she swoops down, takes the urn, nestles it securely against her breast.

"I," she says clearly, her words falling like stones into a stream, "I was his wife. I *am* his wife. And you . . . you were a disturbance. That's all. A barrier in the road. A joke. We will go home now."

She pushes Mabel aside, sails from the room like the Queen Bee she is, all golden in the light of afternoon as if covered with pollen, bathed in the triumph of love. And Mabel is left pounding her fists on her thigh, sobbing without tears. She has none, cannot summon them from the dry well of her body, and the discovery of her lack horrifies her, makes her sob harder.

"Lawrence! Lawrence!" Her keening splits the air but leaves me untouched. What does any of it signify, even the poor words that were all I had?

I am flying now, into the dazzling air, above the desert that courses with the colors of the world — umber, violet, the faded pink of Italian hill towns, the blue of Indian turquoise, the flame of *chamiso* in autumn.

In the West the sun splits the plain and burns. It consumes itself, gnaws on the earth, burning, burning. In the end there are no words, no gestures, no passion but the flame and the soaring. And I soar, dipping invisible wings in soundless farewell.

PARADISE

Looking back it was the worst Christmas, ever. In the first place Jimmie James, whose daddy owns the Double J horse ranch and who I was intending to get engaged to over the holidays, had a horse fall with him, and he ended up in the hospital with his leg in traction and his jaws wired together, so he couldn't talk if he wanted to, at least not so anyone could understand, and you can imagine how I felt about *that,* with everyone wondering when he was going to pop the question, and me just going along smiling like I knew but didn't want to say. Then my daddy, who owns the Cadillac dealership and sits on the town council and the school board and all, he told us we're going to Grandma Klinghofer's for Christmas.

"Grandma's getting old," he said, "and it's time to get this thing settled."

He meant the squabble that's been going on forever between the Klinghofer brothers over that land, though what difference it makes what happens to it is more than I know. I mean, it's just an old ranch squatting in grass and sand like a thousand other places, except that my Uncle Leban got religion one night and gave his share that was promised to him by his daddy to the Paradise Valley Tabernacle Assembly, and all of a sudden there's a bunch of strange folks living in tents and trailers, praising the Lord, and there's Uncle Leban driving around the valley in his pickup that says **Jesus is Coming** on it in big red letters, and my Uncle Ed, who owns the general store, and my Uncle Paul, who they thought was the village idiot before Uncle Leban got religion, trying to get the land back into the family and away from the "Jesus freaks."

That's what my daddy calls them. Calls Uncle Leban that, too,

221

whenever he gets to thinking about it, which is most days around dinner time, though it doesn't stop him from eating, just gives him indigestion after. Well, what girl in her right mind wants to spend Christmas with people like that, even if they *are* relatives?

"Why can't I stay here with Aunt Rona?" I asked him. There were Christmas parties and dances I just didn't want to miss, even if Jimmie *was* stuck in that hospital. I had new makeup from Merle Norman, had my face done in the store in the mall last week, and the girl there said I looked just like Madonna. She really did. "You ought to go to Hollywood," she said to me. And when she was done, well the resemblance was *remarkable*. I couldn't *wait* to get dressed up and go out dancing, and then the horse fell and smashed up Jimmie James.

"This is important," Daddy said. "There'll be lots of Christmases, but that place may be yours someday. Time you get back, that boyfriend of yours'll be up and walking. Besides, I'll buy you that black outfit you've been wanting."

Well, that got me right where I live. I'd been hinting for weeks about that dress in Hoover's store window — black lace and sequins with a cinched-in waist. So I gave in. Then Chris, my sister, who inherited the fat Klinghofer genes just like my daddy and my Uncle Paul, said: "Me, too. I want a new outfit, too."

I knew the one she wanted. A kind of blue toga thing that she thought hid her belly, except that it couldn't. It only made it worse. "You'll look like a hog in a gunny sack," I told her, but she gave me a dirty look and stopped listening. She never does listen. She's got this picture of herself in her head that's unreal. Only she'll never get a man, looking like she does, and I guess it's just as well. Two Madonnas in one family would be too much. We'd get so confused over clothes and men and all, we wouldn't know what was happening.

So two days before Christmas we got in the car, the new pink Seville that Daddy let me pick out, and drove with all the presents in the trunk and Chris and me in the back seat with a bag of candy bars and the popcorn balls we'd made to put on Grandma's tree. Only Chris kept eating them, even though I told her not to fill up on trash.

You'd think Mama would tell her, but she doesn't. Chris is her favorite. She hardly ever says "Boo" to Chris. "Baby fat" is what she calls Chris's middle, but it's worse than that. Why, she can pinch four inches at least, and I think it's disgusting, all white and smooth like a fish. Chris is afraid to diet for fear of loosing her boobs, but what good are boobs if you're all in one piece like a sofa cushion? That's what I keep saying to her, and she just tosses her head and all that hair she won't get cut off, and keeps on doing just what she wants. Sometimes I wonder how two such different people were born into the same family, but then I look at my daddy and his brothers and stop wondering.

It's a long drive to Paradise, and there's nothing to see but cactus and sand and some mountains, sticking out like busts of people half stuck in dirt.

"You keep eating, pretty soon you'll look like that," I said to Chris, and my mama said: "Leila, you *hush!*" to me, so I hardly talked at all after that, just sat there and thought about Jimmie James and the fun I was missing, and how I've never seen even one good-looking man in all of Paradise.

Maybe that's just as well because, if I met somebody, I'd have to admit I'm kin to Uncle Paul who spends his days riding a bike up and down the highway and waving to folks he doesn't even know, his beard so long and so white he looks like Santa Claus in bib overalls and a big straw hat. Or to Uncle Leban who's scrawny as a grasshopper and does the same thing except it's in the Jesus Wagon, and I'd sooner *die* than tell anyone they're my uncles, those ridiculous old men with round blue eyes poking out like headlights.

When we got there, it was nearly dark, and Grandma came out on the porch and jumped up and down. She's little, and waving her arms and legs and hugging my daddy, she looked like a tick squashed up against his middle. I wondered how she managed to have all those fat babies, if they were fat when they came, and I bet they were, especially Uncle Paul who's been that way since I can remember. Then he came out and blocked out all the light from inside, and I mean every *bit* of it, and she said: "What's the matter with you? Go switch on the porch light, so's I can see my baby girls."

"Better let them in," he said. "It's going to snow. I think it's going to snow."

Sometimes I think he isn't dumb, just silly. "Snow," I said. "It can't snow."

"Who says?" His blue eyes were twinkling and rolling over that beard of his. "Who says? Christmas is for miracles."

"I don't want to *hear* miracles," Grandma said, turning and shooing him like he was a chicken. "The only miracle I want is to have those folks off my land. All of 'em dirty, none of 'em with sense. Why," she looked at my daddy, "why they had a preacher come all the way from Kansas, and first thing the dang fool gets himself snake bit. Did he go to the hospital? 'Course not. He trusted to the Lord . . . that's what he said . . . and the Lord showed him what was what. He swelled up and died. The Lord don't put up with fools. Fakes, neither. Now, come in the house so I can see my babies."

That's Chris and me. Grandma never had any girls — just whales and grasshoppers — so we're special. At least there's that about Paradise. She won't let us do a thing, and she fusses. My, she fusses over us all day and gives us dollar bills when she thinks nobody's looking, and pieces of jewelry she's had since who knows when, and it's nice because Mama isn't a fusser. She believes we should learn to keep house and cook and things, and she doesn't talk about it, just expects our rooms redd up and the bathroom clean and, if it isn't, she walks around, looking hurt all day, till we can't stand it and give in. Mama's good at looking hurt. I swear that's how she manages Daddy because he can't stand to see a woman cry. Maybe that's how she got married, just stood there looking like she was going to fall apart for love and the pain of it. And maybe, if Jimmie James doesn't say something soon, that's what I'm going to do, and hope my eye makeup doesn't run. I'll have to practice it, if I can keep Chris out of the bathroom. She'd tell if she knew. Sisters are such a drag.

Uncle Ed and Aunt Marsha had gone to the school where Aunt Marsha teaches third grade for a Christmas carol program there. Uncle Leban wasn't around, either. He was at a revival.

"Shoutin' and hollerin' and carryin' on," Grandma said. "Wouldn't surprise me if 'twas like those two used to be on television that looked like corpses. All painted outside and black as tar inside. Now, go wash up and come eat."

There's a feel about Grandma's kitchen that's so comfortable, even though it's not pretty or the least bit modern. The floor is old bricks worn smooth as glass, and the stove is one of those green enamel monsters with the oven off to one side and funny little knobs for the gas. But the table is big enough to feed half of Paradise, and there are plants everywhere Grandma can fit a pot. And a shelf over the stove with herbs in little decorated tin cans and jars, and the cut-glass salt and pepper shakers with little red tops. Her kitchen drives my mama crazy. "She ought to throw it all out and start over," Mama says. "Those herbs have been there since the Indians surrendered." She and Grandma are polite to each other, but you can tell they aren't friends, both thinking they know best about everything and everybody, but being good about it to keep the peace, what there is of it with the men mad most of the time.

They were mad at supper that night, mostly over Uncle Leban, and Grandma joined in. "Senile!" she kept saying. "That I should live to see my own son senile."

Uncle Paul tried to keep things light by telling jokes, and he tells the *worst* jokes, and he tells them twice, sometimes more, until somebody laughs, and then he says: "You get it? You get it?" all the while laughing. He's a chore, my Uncle Paul, but he's better than

Uncle Leban, shouting prophecies and wickedness. Well, it *is* better. I know, because didn't he jump on me like a duck on a June bug? I can hardly stand thinking about it and that awful old man.

After dinner I decided to leave them all and go try my new makeup as there wasn't much else to do. Chris came with me, and I did her face, too, putting dark shadows in her cheeks so you couldn't see how fat they were, and teasing her hair so it didn't just hang the way it usually does and, when I was finished, she looked so different, almost pretty, and I was so pleased, like I'd painted a picture that was all mine.

"Now, you wait," I told her, "and I'll do me, and then we'll go in and show Grandma like we used to do when we were little." So she sat on the edge of the tub and watched me while I lined my eyes and used three shades of eye shadow, and painted a black beauty mark at the corner of my upper lip.

"That's a kissing mark," I said. "It draws men's attention to your mouth."

"Who's here to kiss?" she asked.

"The point is, you have to practice. So, when there is somebody, you know how and don't act foolish."

"I don't," she said. "Act foolish, I mean."

Well, that stopped me right in my tracks! The way she said it and all, because it was true. She's never silly or giddy or anybody but Chris all the time, and what do you say to somebody like that, how do you tell them that they've got to be somebody else just to be interesting. Like this month I'm Madonna, but who knows who I'll be next?

"Honey . . . ," I started to say, and then I couldn't think of how to tell her what she should have been born knowing. "Let's go show Grandma," I said instead. "She likes pretty things and makeup and all."

We went out into the kitchen where they were sitting just the way we left them except, Daddy and Uncle Paul had out the bourbon bottle and were laughing.

I said: "Look at us, Grandma!" And she turned around and saw us and said: "Well, my goodness. My babies are grown up."

That was all she had a chance to get out because then the back door opened and in came Uncle Leban. He was smiling. "Hey," he said. "So you got here." Then he saw Chris and me, and his face changed and his eyes swiveled till I thought he was going to have one of those fits, the kind where you fall down, yelling and biting your tongue. "Leila?" he said. "Chris?" like we were strangers.

I said: "Hi, Uncle Leban," and smiled as nice as I know how because I had no fight with him. I just thought he was nuts, but then he came up real close and looked at me like I was a bug, and he said: " 'Instead of sweet smell there shall be stink, instead of well-set hair, baldness, burning instead of beauty.' "

It was like he was cursing us, and all we'd done was pretty ourselves.

"You mean old man," Chris said real loud, or maybe it wasn't loud but sounded that way, the room being so quiet.

"Chris!" Mama said. "You apologize to your uncle right now."

"I won't," Chris said, and she turned around and left, and I ran after her, feeling tears running down clear to my beauty mark.

Behind me I heard Grandma's voice shrill as a cicada. "Blast you, Leban! They're just girls. They sure don't teach sense or manners in that church of yours."

"Old son of a bitch," Chris said.

I got into bed and pulled the covers over my head, but not before I warned her. "Don't you let Mama hear you cuss like that," I said. "She'll wash out your mouth."

Chris made a noise. "Well he is one," she said, "and I don't care."

As it turned out, Grandma issued her orders then and there. No fighting on Christmas. And to Leban: "If you quote any more Scripture in my kitchen than 'Silent Night,' I'll put you out. This here's your family." He said he was going to the widow Gallego's for Christmas, and Grandma said: "I wish you'd marry her. She wouldn't put up with those hippies for a minute." Grandma calls everybody not like folks she's used to "hippies," even if they're not.

For Christmas I got my black outfit from Hoover's in a pink box with a lacy gold ribbon, and Chris got her blue top that shimmered like silk and looked so good on me I wished I could wear it, too, which was ridiculous because Chris could *never* fit into anything of mine. We got all dressed up for dinner and had a good time, and afterwards Chris and I played some of our tapes and danced out on the sun porch and even got Mama and Daddy dancing and out of breath. Grandma kept time with her foot but wouldn't join in. "I'll wait till New Year's," she said, "and someone my age."

Everybody in the neighborhood comes to Grandma's for the annual New Year's party. They come to her house because it's the biggest around and has a glassed-in room with a tile floor and a rubber plant that climbs up the wall and hangs from hooks stuck in the ceiling. She and Uncle Ed prune it every year, Uncle Paul being too big to trust on a ladder, and they cut off a whole truckload of branches that grow back before you know it. But with the leaves and the smooth floor it's a good place to dance, and everybody does, even the broken-up cowboys who go two-stepping around, pumping their arms and grinning and having a good time even if they don't know any new steps and think the Grateful Dead is a religious tract.

We spent the next five days getting ready, cleaning that old house, waxing and mopping, and hanging strips of crêpe paper from the rubber plant. Aunt Marsha came in one afternoon to help and said to us: "Wait'll you girls see who I bring to the party."

"Him!" Grandma said, and Marsha said, "Oh, Ma," and rolled her eyes at Chris and me.

"Who's she mean?" I asked.

"They didn't allow school teachers like that when *I* was a girl, let me tell you," Grandma said. "You'll find out quick enough."

Meantime my daddy went over to the court house and found out that Uncle Leban's land had never been deeded, just kind of promised to him by my grandpa, which meant that Grandma had the right to put the "hippies" off any time she pleased, and was she *pleased!*

"Thank the Lord," she said. "And I do mean it. I'll run my spring calves over there. It's the best grass on the place. I never did understand your father, handing it over to a fool."

"Better watch they don't have a barbecue before they leave," my daddy said.

She looked at him. "*I'm* no fool, Alford," she said, which is true. She manages that place good as a man.

New Year's Eve we didn't eat supper, just set the big kitchen table and went to get dressed.

"Do my face again," Chris said, and I did, and fixed her hair, too, high up on her head with a few curls hanging down for softness. I put her out of the bathroom while I soaked in lots of bubbles and then sat at Grandma's little dressing table and did what the Merle Norman lady showed me. Then I put on the earrings Grandma gave me for Christmas — blue stones set in seed pearls — and didn't they bring out the blue in my eyes! When I was done, I didn't look like myself. I was somebody else, tall and elegant, and sad faced, like I had a tragic romance in my past. I practiced looking like that a while till my mama knocked at the door and said: "There's others here, too, you know," sounding sarcastic, which she's good at.

So I went out to the kitchen. Folks had started arriving; Grandma's friends who'd been young in the valley when she was and widowed about the same time. They brought cakes and pies and casseroles, and platters of ham and potato salad, deviled eggs, and pots of chili.

Merle was there who taught me to ride when I was knee-high to a horse, and Harvey who's broke his back so many times he walks bent over, and Grandma's "beau" as she calls him, Dan Tippet, who has one leg that won't bend any way except what fits in a stirrup, and the *wickedest* eyes. It's a wonder Uncle Leban hasn't said anything about the pair of *them,* but Dan being a tough old thing and

Grandma being his mother, maybe he's scared to. Uncle Paul was out there in a clean pair of overalls and a red plaid shirt, and he was telling jokes as fast as he could find a new face. All in all, it was pretty boring.

I went out to the sun porch and put some music on, slow country stuff I figured the older crowd would like, and I turned down the lights to make it look romantic, and it did, leafy and shadowy, like what's called "a trysting place," except nobody was interested in such a thing. They all stayed by the table where the food was, and the refrigerator where they'd put beer and pop, and they were gossiping like they hadn't seen each other for years instead of a few days. I went up to the biggest group and said: "Anyone want to dance?" and Merle turned around and saw me.

"Why it's little Leila all grown up," he said. "I'll dance with you, honey." He took me by the hand like I was five years old, and led me out to the porch. That's how come I missed Aunt Marsha and Uncle Ed and Slick. I heard them come in, heard shouting and laughter and knew something interesting was finally happening, only I was two-stepping in a square and stuck in it, and time I got back to the kitchen Slick had Chris up against the refrigerator and was talking up a storm.

He was wearing a yellow and black plaid shirt and the *tightest* jeans I ever saw, and he had on real expensive lizard boots. But it was that man's eyes that fascinated me, like a snake's. They were dark, hypnotic and, when he looked at you, they lingered like he couldn't believe what he saw and had to stare. He was looking at Chris like that, and she was smiling like she was delighted with herself. Well, I knew right off, this wasn't the man for her. She wouldn't know how to handle a man that good looking or conceited, and I just knew he had to be conceited in pants that tight. He'd walk right over a girl like Chris and leave her crying.

"Who's that?" I asked Deedee who helps Uncle Ed in the store.

She giggled. "That's Slick. He teaches fourth grade, can you believe it? If he'd taught my fourth grade, I'd never made it to the fifth." And she opened her mouth and bawled like a cow. She made such a noise everybody turned to look, even Slick, who took me in head to foot as if to say: "Well, where did *you* come from?" and then turned back to Chris like I wasn't even there.

It made me so mad! Nobody's cut me like that since I can't remember when, and after that it got worse because he and Chris went out to the porch and started slow dancing while I stood there like those ugly girls in high school, looking so pathetic up against the wall of the gym. And there was Chris, her arms around the best-looking man I'd seen in ages, with three inches of belly fat showing between her top and her slacks.

"Mama," I said, "can't you do something? Get some pins and take her in the powder room. That's really too gross."

"She's having fun. Leave her alone," my mama said.

And I said: "Fun! What about me?"

"You're pretty," Mama said. "No need to fuss." As if being pretty is enough and I shouldn't want anything else. I wanted to cry. I wanted to say: "What good is pretty if nobody cares?" but she was talking to Aunt Marsha and there I stood, my arms and legs feeling as gawky as those wall-flower high school girls, my black lace dress and Madonna face no damn' use at all.

It went on like that, Slick glued to Chris's belly button and every now and then looking at me over the top of her head. I got so disgusted I went in the kitchen and mixed a drink and smoked, and didn't talk to anybody. There really wasn't anything to say.

Finally Grandma brought out the presents. She and her friends spend all year hoarding knick-knacks and wrapping them, and then they put them in a pile and make everybody stand in a circle and pick one. Only if somebody likes *your* present, they can take it, and the games turns into a free-for-all with everybody forgetting their manners.

I saw my chance when Chris went to the powder room. I got in the circle next to Slick. When it got to be my turn to pick a present, he said to me: "Take the one that looks like a bottle."

"There'd be nothing in that bottle *I'd* want," I said.

He gave me that snake look and the chills with it. "I bet I have something outside you'd want," he said.

"I bet you do." I picked up a package and unwrapped it. Inside I found a mirror with a picture of a horse's rear end painted on it. People in Paradise have the *weirdest* sense of humor! "You take the bottle," I told him.

He grinned. The skin tightened over those high cheekbones of his, and I wondered if he wasn't an Indian or Mexican or such. He picked out what was an ashtray. "Trade you," he said.

I'd had all the fooling around I could stand. "I'd rather dance," I said.

He pulled me out of that circle and up against him so fast I couldn't think. "I thought you'd never ask," he said.

"I'm not supposed to. My name's Leila."

He laughed deep down in his throat like a hound growling. "You talk too much. Just dance."

I closed my eyes and did what he said, and did we move together! This time it was me glued to him and loving it. This time it was me spinning light as a leaf and everybody watching, wishing it was them out there on the smooth tile floor. I looked around and didn't see Chris, and figured she was out in the kitchen, eating. "What took you so long?" I asked him.

"You didn't leave, did you?"

"No," I said. "Where would I go anyhow?"

"Then what's it matter?"

"I was so *mad* at you."

He pulled me closer. "You needed it, honey," he said.

That didn't sound right. I didn't need anything that I knew of. "Who do you think you are?" I said.

"I'm Slick. There's enough of me for you and your sister."

"You're so conceited," I said. "I never met a man so conceited."

"Truthful. Want to take a walk?"

"You sure aren't wasting time now," I said, keeping him waiting.

He lifted one of those black eyebrows. "They don't call me Slick for nothing. You coming? Or should I ask your sister?"

That was too much! He needed a lot of taking down before anybody could handle him. "Go ask her," I said. "Make her happy. I'll do fine just like I am." I dropped my arms and made as if to walk away.

"Hey," he said. "I was just teasing."

"I don't play games. I don't have to."

He focused those eyes of his on me, and I felt they were burning holes clear into my brain. "Like I told you, you talk too much. Go get your coat."

Now, the first thing I learned about men like Slick is you let them cool their heels a while. You don't run after them like you need them. So I went into the powder room and fixed my hair and sprayed more perfume, and then I looked out the window at the moon. It was nearly full, and the cactus and trees showed up like it was daylight, only with silver around their edges. For a minute I thought about Jimmie James back in that hospital, drinking his dinner through a straw, and how I should be faithful to him on account of the engagement, except that there wasn't one, and I was in Paradise bored to death, and the sexiest man I'd seen in years was waiting to take a walk with me in the moonlight. And if I didn't go, Chris would, and I just *knew* she couldn't handle him, would likely get into trouble out of foolishness. So I picked up my fur jacket and edged around the people toward the door.

I found Slick surrounded by a bunch of widow women who were gabbing at him like geese, and flirting, too, which was *disgusting,* considering any one of them could have been his mother. I wondered if I'd get like that when I got old, but the notion was so awful I stopped thinking about it as fast as I could and walked in amongst

233

them, smiling like butter wouldn't melt in my mouth, which they hated, but they couldn't do anything except smile back and make old lady comments.

"Ooooh, Leila, you watch out for old Slick here," and "I sure wish I could go courting again." Courting! Lord, what a thing to say! Then Harvel, who drives the school bus and is younger then the rest, said: "You watch out for your Uncle Leban. He's death on young folks."

"Leban!" I said. "Is he here?"

"Sure is. He was telling us about the sinfulness of drink just a minute ago, wasn't he, Slick?"

Slick rolled his eyes. "Yeah. Let's get out of here." He took my arm and led me out the door.

Outside I looked around. It wouldn't have surprised me to see Uncle Leban up a tree with a flashlight. "That awful old man," I said.

"He's a joke. Come on."

We walked down the driveway toward a line of cars. It was cold, and the moon had a ring around it. Looking at it, I thought of Jimmie James again. "Where are we going?" I asked.

"My car's right here." He stopped beside a big red 4X4, one of those monsters men drive in mud pits and up the mountains to prove how tough they are.

"I thought we were walking," I said.

"We were. Right to here. Get in." He opened the door. The inside looked as big and as dark as a tomb. Then he reached out and fluffed my hair. "You're beautiful," he said. "Your hair's all silvery."

My heart started jumping around inside so I couldn't say anything, just look at him. Finally I said: "Well, thank you," only my voice came out funny, and we both laughed. I thought maybe he wasn't so bad after all; everybody seemed to like him, even the old gossips, and they're hard to fool. "How come you acted so hateful in there?" I asked him.

"Because you did. I figured you were just stuck up. Besides, your sister's fun."

"She is?"

"Yes," he said. "She is. Now, are we going to stand here and freeze our butts, or are we getting in?"

I climbed in, him helping, and he got in his side, and neither of us waited. He kissed me, and I kissed back, and I didn't think about anything at all for a long time. There are some men you can kiss and never want to stop, and Slick was one, and all those old ladies must've known it by instinct.

I swear, I could've kissed him till the sun came up and never even *thought* of doing anything else, but men are *always* thinking about sex, and Slick was no different. I have the same problem with Jimmie James, but he's a gentleman and wants to marry me besides, and Slick wasn't thinking about any wedding, just about himself the way men do. I never understood it, but I have to deal with it, same as all women. He had his hands up my dress and down it, too, quick as you please. Truth was, I liked it, but I figured to stop him. "It's almost midnight," I said.

He didn't even slow down. "Happy New Year," he said.

"Now you *stop*." I twisted around in the seat, trying to catch my breath, and I looked out the window right at Uncle Leban. His eyes were popped, and his mouth was open, but nothing was coming out, and I thought for a moment, and still do think, that he was enjoying himself like one of those peeping toms who get a kick out of watching women in showers and things. "Slick!" I said. "It's him!"

He looked up for the littlest bit, and he saw Uncle Leban, too, and his mouth fell open so he looked like the mirror image of my uncle, the two of them staring at each other and me in the middle. Then Slick said: "Oh, hell!" and that snapped something.

Uncle Leban came out of his trance with a roar. "Fornicator! Harlot!" He pulled open the door, and I nearly fell out except that

Slick grabbed my wrist. " 'Come out of there that ye be not partakers of her sins, and that ye receive not her plagues!' "

Slick burst out laughing. *Laughing,* mind you, and me accused of having plague.

"*Do* something. Cut out laughing," I told him.

He laughed harder.

Uncle Leban grabbed my other arm. " 'How much she hath glorified herself and lived deliciously, so much torment and sorrow give her,' " he yelled, and between the two of them, they nearly yanked me in half.

"Uncle Leban," I said, "you stop now." But of course he didn't, and Slick wouldn't let go of me for fear I'd fall right out on top of Leban. "I'll scream," I said, right into that wild face of his. "I will."

And then I did. I opened my mouth and the loudest noise I swear I ever made came out. It echoed over the valley, and it reached the house so people started coming to find the trouble. It wasn't long till they found it.

Uncle Leban was still making the most awful speeches, mostly about fornication, and pulling on me so I couldn't even pull down my skirt. That's how they found me — in between two men and my skirt up to my waist — and it was so terrible I burst into tears.

"The harlot repents!" Uncle Leban yelled.

"Get him away from me!" I meant Uncle Leban, but they thought I meant Slick, and they started yelling at *him* like he'd done something.

"You leave that gal alone." That was Merle.

"What have you done to my little girl?" That was Mama, looking fierce.

"Tell them!" Slick said to me. "I didn't do anything. I'm innocent."

" 'The fruits that thy soul lusted after are gone from thee,' " Uncle Leban said to him.

It was my turn to laugh, and I did, though I was crying, too, and couldn't seem to stop. Some help Slick had been, and now he was asking me for it.

"Leave her be. She's hysterical." Grandma's voice cut through everybody's noise like a knife. She had the most sense.

I pointed at Uncle Leban. "It was him," I said. "He started it. Peeking in the window and calling me bad names."

"It's midnight! It's midnight!" Uncle Paul came down the road, all out of breath and waving his arms. "Happy New Year! Happy New Year!"

He grabbed hold of Harvel and kissed her and went after the next lady who tried to duck but couldn't get around his belly. Then everybody started kissing everybody else, all except Slick and me. My daddy was talking to him.

Mama grabbed me and said: "You go back to the house right now."

I thought if anybody else shoved at me or gave me an order, I'd scream again, louder. I was black and blue, or felt like it. "We weren't doing anything," I said. "It was him. Uncle Leban. You hear me?"

"Don't talk to me in that tone, miss," she said. "You just march!"

Now, when Mama talks like that, you do what she says. Her daddy was a general, and she got the ordering habit from him. I went. I never got to see Slick again or to kiss him Happy New Year. I didn't get to see anybody again. The party broke up on the road, and folks drifted off like tumbleweeds.

Chris was in the kitchen, eating leftovers. "That was dumb," she said. She chonked on a deviled egg and licked her fingers. "What's Jimmie James going to say?"

"Nothing unless you tell," I said. I wondered if she would for some kind of revenge.

"Not me." She picked up a stuffed celery. "But it was still dumb. You should've stayed in here."

I said: "I did it for you."

She rolled her eyes and laughed, and for one awful minute looked just like Uncle Paul. "You're a jerk," she said. "Either that or an awful hypocrite." Then she walked off and left me with the used paper plates and the dirty ash trays, the piles of confetti and the crêpe paper streamers, wilted, all the curl gone out of them.

I could hear Grandma out in the yard, laying down the law to Uncle Leban. "Next week," she said, "you get those hippies out. Then you come back home where I can keep an eye on you. God knows, you need it. You got no more sense than a goat."

Her voice was drowned by the roar of a motor. It was probably Slick, taking off in a cloud of dust, running away from the harlot and what must have looked to him like a looney bin. My dress was torn, and I was sore all over, and I wondered if Madonna had ever had a worse time, and if being beautiful wasn't somehow a curse, and maybe not worth the trouble.

HOME

Martha started the truck and drove away without looking back. She knew if she did, her husband would remember something else he needed from town, or his mother would come out, the shrieking infant in her arms, and their combined needs would slow her, bind her, and she was already late. She hated to be late when she knew Rudd was waiting, and today was special. He had a surprise for her, something he wanted her to see, and a fear was in her that she would arrive and find him gone, that her day would shatter around her while she stood, wondering what to do with the pieces.

She resisted her impulse to speed down the dirt road. A flat tire, a broken axle wouldn't help. Time enough for speed when she hit the Interstate. Tumbleweeds bounced across the road ahead of the pickup and fluttered against barb-wire fences like birds seeking escape.

"Escape," she thought, her mouth curving out of its usual straight line. "To where?"

Beyond the fence the dry winter plains spread to the sky. There was no avoiding them, no place on them to hide. Sometimes she felt like them, brown, furrowed, blowing away. And useless except for the stark beauty that few saw but herself, that no one responded to except in anger or despair. Two years before, after the baby, Lark, was born, her husband, without consulting her, had sold off his cattle, invested the money, and announced that he was through fighting the drought and the cattle prices.

Norman was a sullen man with a quick temper, and she had not argued. She knew better. Sometimes he slapped her when he was angry, when he couldn't find words. So she had retreated into the novelty of motherhood, looking out now and again to see Norm, tending the garden, playing nursemaid to the pheasants, the top-notched quail he raised in cages behind the barn, or stroking the flanks of the two spotted mares, their bellies swollen with life. That he touched the mares with a tenderness he had never showed to her had hurt at first, and then she put it away deep in her mind. Such ideas were best forgotten. You couldn't dwell on them or you became like the tumbleweed, clawing the fences, the plains, blowing away in despair.

"Leave him be," his mother had told her. "He's working something out in his head."

That was the trouble. Norm was always centered upon himself, his problems, and he never seemed to arrive at an answer or tell her if he did. So she left him alone, poured her love into the child, marveling over the strength of the petaled fingers and laughing into the bright eyes. She found her own joys, apart from those of her husband, and sometimes they infused her with radiance like the mesas that burned crimson in the sunsets, or the windmill that flashed in the light of noon. She thought she was happy in the cocoon she had spun around herself. And then she found Rudd.

She wouldn't have found him if she hadn't begun to read to fill up the silence, if she hadn't tired of the farm journals that came in the weekly mail. She began going to the library in town. She became fascinated by books, by the people in them, and she read voraciously, filling her silence with words, reading in the evenings when Norm and his mother sat on the porch, and sometimes long into the night when cricket shrill filled the house and the poor-wills cried from the reeds by the cattle tank.

She thought about the men and women who lived between the covers, the Victorians chained to their houses, the pioneers as isolated on their prairies as she was on her mesa, ringed by sand hills, scrub, the teeth of the far mountains. She thought about bravery, the courage of explorers, generals, women in covered wagons, and wondered how you called it forth, how you knew whether or not it was even there. And she wondered if she herself were brave.

The library was in the high school, an old brick building reached by steps that slanted steeply from the sidewalk. One afternoon, burdened by books, she had tripped, and the books bounced into the dust. The man behind her helped her up and then helped her gather the books, glancing at each title.

"That's a lot of reading," he said, and there was a curiosity in his voice, an eagerness that she, unused to strangers, heard and shied away from. She nodded, a sharp gesture meant to discourage, and she took the books from him, meeting his eyes as she did so.

He was a big man, and capable looking, as if he knew his strength and limitations through experience, not merely through the pages of books. He had Indian-black hair and quick eyes that caught the light, and they were watching her kindly, without threat. "I'm Rudd Safford," he said, and waited.

"Martha Grant." She hated her name. It was so unsuited to her, tall, with capable hands and a steady chin. Sparrows were named Martha, and wrens, and she was too big, her joys too intense.

He said: "Martha." It sounded different in his mouth, like wings. He looked at the top book. "What did you think of this? Did you like it?"

She shrugged. "I guess so."

"Why?" He kept pace with her, held the wooden door wide.

"The people were real," she said after a moment. "They felt things like I do."

"There are more like that," he said, "if you're interested."

She was interested. That had been what kept her there talking, adding to her pile of new books, asking questions, her distrust blown away like a dust devil in the sweep of his enthusiasm. She had gone home light hearted, eager for the lives that awaited her between the new covers. And she had met him again, until the weekly trips to town took precedence over all else, until she looked forward to them, caught herself remembering things they had said, thoughts they had shared, lives they had lived together. Gradually her life with the child, with the silent mother and son on the vastness of the plain, became less real than that lived each market day.

When she thought about Rudd, which was often, it was with a pain in her breast that she didn't understand and tried to ignore as she ignored anything that seemed to have no cause; it was with the same yearning she felt when she looked out and saw the sand hills burning in the light or a hummingbird caught in the throat of the trumpet vine. She began to save things up in her head to tell him. How Lark loved the spotted mares. How she had seen an eagle on the corral fence, and it had looked at her, unafraid. How the cranes called when they passed overhead in the spring, sometimes late in the night. He always listened to her with such eagerness, questioned her with such intensity, as if he, too, wanted to see, to be there in the old house, on the silent earth.

It seemed she could never get through the week fast enough, or get over the road that curved ahead in decent time. She wished she had wings and could circumvent the trip, the bumps, the cattle guards, the Interstate's black, heated trace through the brown land. "Wait," she said out loud. "I'm coming." And she bent her strong body over the wheel as if, by doing so, she could move the pickup faster.

She passed the crumbling hills and the marsh where the geese and cranes took refuge in winter, and still the road beat before her, still the arroyos gouged the earth, and the cattle stood, hopeless, above them. She saw the white arms of the cottonwoods in the *bosque* by the river, and the line of tin-roofed shacks, and behind them, far beyond but close enough to tell her she was nearing town, the mountains, jagged and snow covered.

"Almost," she said, and "come on, you," to the truck. Then she grinned. She was as bad as a lone cowboy, talking to his horse. That was what happened with Norm and his mother and their odd communication that excluded her, wove around her as if she were not

242

there. ". . . Recollect that deer we had when you were young?" And the answer: "Yeah." Or: "Looks like that mare's due." And again the stark reply: "Tonight's likely." Then the silence that wasn't really a silence, that was filled with music had anyone listened. Or maybe they did listen without feeling called upon to remark on it, only sat, cardboard figures in the dying light.

Telephone poles flashed by, and more houses. The ache in her breast throbbed and plunged into her belly. She frowned, looking down at herself as if she stood outside her body, examining it for the source of the pain. "Rudd," she thought, and her foot went down on the gas as she took the turn-off.

The gas station, the Sundance Motel, the Yellow Front, and then the restaurant where he said he'd be if she weren't too late, if he'd waited. "Please," she said. It came out a whimper, the same sound that Lark made when she didn't want to be left.

She parked, jumped down from the cab, and entered the restaurant, hands clenched in her pockets. He sat in a booth, facing the door, a book in his hands. Like her, he was always reading. It was what you did if you were lonely and lived alone as they both did, she regardless of family. Besides, Rudd taught in the high school, a career that fascinated her. He was like no teacher she had ever had, listening to her as if what she said was important.

She stood, looking at him, feeling joy kick in her stomach where minutes before the pain had been. It felt like a living thing, a child impatient to be born. She slipped into the booth, saying nothing.

"Hi," he said. He smiled that gentle smile that always startled when it came over his keen face.

"Sorry I'm late. Lark's cutting a tooth and crying and got every-body upset."

"Want breakfast?"

She'd run out without anything but coffee. She nodded.

"What time do you have to be home?" he asked when he'd ordered.

"Supper time, I guess. And I've got the shopping to do." She leaned her elbows on the brown plastic table. "What is it you wanted to show me?"

"Wait and see," he said, grinning. "It's out of town a ways. Eat up and we'll go."

But she couldn't eat when the plate came — eggs, ham, hash browns. She poked the potatoes with her fork, then pushed the plate across to him. "You eat it," she said. "I'm not hungry."

He didn't look surprised. He never did, but always acted like he knew her feelings. It was comforting. With Rudd she didn't have to pretend to be smart or flirt to get attention. She sipped her coffee. That, at least, she could swallow. "I liked that book," she said. *The Song of the Lark.*"

"Why?" He always asked that, as if he were interested in what she thought, or maybe because he was a teacher and that was what teachers asked.

"Because it showed you can do what you want, be what you want, even if you're nobody. Even if you're born out here and only have dreams." She watched him over the brim of her cup, hoping he wouldn't laugh.

"What would you be if you could be anything?"

The question stopped her. She had never imagined being anything but what she was. "I don't know," she said. She searched herself carefully, thinking of women in the movies, in magazines, women who, for the most part, bore no real resemblance to her with her routine of chores, caring, silence, with her sudden moments of seeing. "I'd just like to be me," she said and ducked her head, feeling she had spoken nonsense.

He didn't smile. "Who is me?" he asked. "Do you know?"

Feelings welled up, choked in her throat. She had no words, and shook her head.

He reached across the table and took her hand. "Easy," he said in a voice that started the pain again. It had been a long time since any man had touched her. Her fingers warmed beneath his, curled against

244

his palm. She wanted to touch his face.

She thought about the pheasants in their cages, the dog on his chain, the mares cross-tied in the barn when the farrier came. She thought of Norm, of herself moving from chore to chore, never touching, never sharing, and the old woman who kept them apart by insuring their silence. "They got me tied down, I guess," she said.

"You're a flesh and blood woman," he said, his voice deeper than she'd ever heard it, and almost tangible so she felt she could lean against it. "And you've got a mind. That husband of yours ever tell you that?"

She shook her head, a quick little jerk meant to shield Norm as much as admit the truth.

"And you're pretty, too," he said.

Her lip quivered. "Don't fool with me," she said.

"I'm not. I'm telling you things about yourself you need to know."

"What's the use of it?" she demanded, the pain in her breast rising until it threatened to burst out like a flood. "What's the use of knowing things unless you can use them?"

"So you'll know you're alive," he said. "You and your moments, and that heart of yours." He stood up. "Come on. We've got some driving to do."

She hurried after him. "Where're we going?"

"Dos Caballos. You ever been there?"

"No. No reason. There's not much there, is there?"

"Oh yes," he said. "There is. We'll take my car."

He led her outside, opened the door for her. She had never gotten used to the way he did things like opening doors, helping her with her coat. It made her seem special. Like the pretty woman he said she was. Cat-like, she curled up on the seat.

The road went west toward the mountains. She could see them, black with patches of snow that made them seem dark, inhospitable. Then they entered a valley, a vast, golden thing, treeless, rippling toward the horizon. She leaned toward the window staring, her heart beating fast. She wanted to touch it, the rising and falling earth, to hold its velvety pelt in her hands. She opened the window, let the wind push against her face. She laughed.

"What are you thinking?" He had been watching her from the corner of his eye.

"I feel like the earth," she said, forgetting her shyness in the happiness of being able to share a moment. "Like that." She pointed.

"How does that feel?" He turned his attention full upon her, his eyes filled with the yellow light of the field.

"Big," she said. She curled her fingers in her lap. "Big. And waiting."

"For what?"

"To be put to use. To be scooped up. Planted. Look." She pointed again. "Doesn't it seem like you could reach out and pick it up in your hands?"

"Demeter," he said. He reached and tucked a strand of her flying hair behind her ear.

"Who's that? Demeter?" She turned to him, curious.

He told her, and she let his words fall into her lap, into the bowl of her cupped hands. "We'll get you a book on mythology when we get back," he said.

And she said: "Oh, yes, please," and she didn't know whether to keep looking at him, his hawk face, his burning eyes, or to turn back to herself, to the fields rising, falling, calling out. She wanted to run with the wind, keep running until she reached the end, the place of belonging, but she couldn't imagine such a place, only the impulse that took her there.

"I'd like to scream sometimes," she said.

"Go ahead. Do what you want." He was watching the road again.

"You mean that?"

"Sure," he said. "I don't care. If it helps, do it."

She giggled. "It's enough to know I can. Wouldn't they die at home if I did?"

"Might be good for them," he said. "It might wake them up to the fact that you're alive."

She pictured it. Herself on the porch, bellowing, and Norm and his mother, placid as cows, staring at her in alarm. "No use," she said, and sighed.

"Thoughts have their uses." He turned to her again. "Now you know something you didn't know before."

"A whole lot of things. None of them worth a damn."

"They will be," he said. It sounded like a promise.

The road narrowed between two hills, and then the little town spread out before them. An Indian woman in a bright skirt watched them from the door of a laundromat. At the gas station a group of young Mexicans turned to stare as they passed. Everything glittered in the December light: the branches of elms, the old adobe walls, the vacant lots strewn with bottles, decorated with dry weeds. To the west the mountains rose like hawks in the sky.

"Like it?" he asked.

She did. It didn't intrude, didn't dominate the great valley, but tucked itself in upon a flank. "Yes," she said.

He turned up a road that curled off into the scrub. Jays rose, beating blue wings; juniper bent under the weight of mistletoe, paler green, voracious. He pulled onto the shoulder and sat looking out as if satisfied. "Come on, let's take a look," he said finally.

She got out, followed him across dry earth, across a strand of barb wire. She didn't see the house until she was almost upon it, it was so much the color of earth, so hidden by brush. The windows were broken; the door lay splintered on the porch. She stepped over the threshold into a small room with a tiled floor. Many of the tiles were missing, swept into corners with bottles, plates, an old tin pot, its handle gone. The windows looked out over the valley that seemed to enter the room and swell around them.

He came up behind her, put his hands on her shoulders. "Well?" he said.

247

Under his hands her bones re-shaped themselves, rounded into his palms as if into gloves. Her body stretched out, rippling like the fields. She thought, if she looked down, she would see grass and earth where belly and thigh should be.

"Whose is this?" she asked in a whisper, cautious, feeling her way toward knowledge.

"Mine," he said. She heard laughter in his voice and turned to look up at him.

He would bring a woman here. Someone shaped like her and filled with longing. He would live here, and she would be left, hungry and screaming. The pain in her breast grew, burst into her loins, her mouth. She moved against him, blinded.

"Don't leave me," she said, terror, desire mingling in her, turning her helpless so that, when he bent and kissed her, she let herself be taken up into his mouth. She cried out in a voice not her own, willing the plow, the planting, the gathering up of one and the other until there was no difference between them. They lay still a long time, as if each had come, by separate and united routes, to the place of peace. She sighed once.

"What?" he asked, holding her. "All right?"

"Yes," she said. "Stay."

"You stay," he answered. "With me. Here."

She took his words, examined them as if they were stones or the hard kernels of corn that she held before planting. "If I don't get home, they'll wonder," she said, tentative, searching.

He said: "I don't mean now. I mean the rest of our lives."

It was what she had hoped he would say, willed him to say as much as she had willed him into her body, but hearing it cast a shadow over her, a fear. What was she, after all, but shadow, vague and filled with dreams? "The baby," she said, pulling words out of her ghostliness. "I can't leave the baby. Not with them."

"Bring her. She'll be ours. We'll raise her." He lifted his head, took her chin in his hand, and turned her face toward his. "I'll fight for you if I have to," he said.

"No one to fight except me," she said.

She pulled away from his hand and stared at him, noting with relief that his eyes no longer burned with the terrible fire of the fields but were dark, tender, filled with the same wonder that was rising in her and that she would examine later, turning it over and over as she would a piece of richly-woven cloth.

"You'll fight yourself," he said.

And that, she knew, was the truth. She, the shadow, would wrestle with the demon earth, the parched soil, the yearning for rain. She thought of herself, treading unseen through her house, accepted as were the furnishings, as a wind that swept through, swept clean. And she looked down at their bodies, side by side, joined by a law she didn't understand, couldn't reach except through her knowledge of earth and how it was with the things of earth.

The hair on his groin was dark brown and grew in small whorls like moss, like the innocent curling of a child's hair, and the sight of it moved her, cracked her heart, as if she, with her strong hands and quicksilver moments were all that stood between him and chaos, the nighttime of despair. And in that discovery was something awful, as if she no longer had a will but was governed by need, and that need was not even hers but his and every woman's who had ever loved. She moved to cover him, to defend and protect, and in doing so she sloughed off the gray invisibility that had held her, now turned supple as the green corn, sure as the cranes that flew, singing, on their journey home.

ARE YOU COMING BACK, PHIN MONTANA?

The trains don't stop at Lick Log Station any more. They come across the *playa,* moving through the heat waves like a mirage, like colored beads strung on a black string, and the engine slows down for the grade but doesn't stop. For years I've watched them come and hoped that, one day, Phin Montana would jump off, carrying his duffel bag and that old high-cantled saddle, those blue eyes of his shining through the dust like the first time. I was nineteen and minding the lunch counter, and I was feeling the magic of the engine, shaking the ground, listening to the whistle blow, and holding onto myself with both arms to keep still.

That whistle was the world calling to me. "Come see," it said. "Come see." I never did. The world came to me, all those names and places. *The Santa Fe, The Way of the Chiefs* with the huge Spanish cross painted on its cars, *The Burlington, The Way of the Zephyrs, The Cotton Belt, The Corn Belt, The Route of the Phoebe Snow.* Those names made pictures in my head. I dreamed at night of Spaniards and Indians, cities and fields of corn as big as the *playa,* of strange mountains with brilliant snow on their peaks. I dreamed oceans and ships, and how one day I, too, would sit inside a passenger car, wearing a hat with a feather and a sleek black dress.

Well, I'm grown now, and the trains don't stop, and Ned Kuykendal is sitting in the cab of his semi out in the parking lot, waiting for me, only I'm having trouble putting the padlock on the door. It's like I'm locking up the past, condemning Phin Montana to Limbo, and there's a part of me that still wants to hold onto a dream, to the lightness of youth when living was simple, when I did what I did

250

without conscience or regret.

That first day I could tell Phin hadn't paid his fare. He came out of a box car before the engine stopped, but he didn't act scared or even like he was in a hurry. He just stood there, looking around, wiping his face on his sleeve, and taking note of his surroundings. Then he walked toward the cafe, light on his feet and ready for anything, like a horse in bear country.

"You could break a leg, jumping off like that," I told him when he was standing in front of me, all yellow haired and showing those white teeth in a grin.

"Better than busting broncs," he said. "You got anything cold to drink?"

"Ice tea. Water. Pop in the cooler." I pointed to the big machine up against the wall.

"Water's fine." He wiped his face again. "This is sure one dry part of the country."

"The rains are late." I put down a glass and a pitcher in front of him.

He drained the glass and refilled it, then he grinned again, suddenly, like sunrise, the lines around his eyes showing up clear, the stubble on his cheeks as yellow as his hair. "I'll toss you double or nothing for a bottle of that pop," he said.

That wasn't what I'd expected. People came in, got served, and paid. Sometimes they left tips, but nobody freeloaded. I said: "My mama would skin me."

He shook his head like I was foolish. "How old are you?"

"Nineteen." I wished I was older and knew more about men like this one — footloose, reckless, and so good looking he made my throat ache.

"Hell," he said. "I was on my own at fifteen. Tell your mama that. Tell her you'll hop one of those trains out there if she lays a hand on you. What's your name?"

Again his question surprised me. "Reason," I said.

"Reason? Reason? That's no name."

"It's the only one I've got. Reason Sunderland. What's yours?" It took courage to ask him, and him leaning over the counter, looking straight into my eyes.

"Phin Montana."

It was my turn to laugh. "That's not a name. That's a state."

"And a darned sight prettier than anything in this one. Except for you. You going to give me a pop or not? I'm flat broke."

Pretty! He thought I was pretty! Me in my old shirt and blue jeans with my hair pulled back in a braid. Reason Sunderland who hadn't ever been spoken to or courted by a fellow, and for good reason. There weren't any boys my age out there, just cowboys grown old before their time, and the few tourists who got off the train to look around and say they'd been some place, and never noticed the girl who served them. "I guess," I said. "Then you'd better leave."

He raised the lid to the cooler and looked in, taking his time, mulling over the flavors. "Any work needs doing around here?" he asked, finally choosing one and popping off the top.

There was always work at Lick Log, and not enough hands or money to get it done. We lived behind the cafe in an old wooden house that had been there since the tracks were laid. When it rained, the roof leaked like a colander. When it didn't, alkali dust blew through the cracks. There was always a wind. And windows and doors rattling, and the fences humming like telegraph wires. Sometimes I wanted to scream at that wind. I still do, though I'm more or less used to it.

And now there's Ned saying how it blows up on the high plains where his ranch is, where we're headed, where I've never been and am scared to go. Ned, Phin, and the wind blowing, and the echoes of train whistles, carrying across the white flats for miles and miles . . . and me with my hands shaking so I can't get the padlock shut. What am I doing, cutting off part of my life, the only part up till now?

252

I said: "My daddy just brought in a bunch of Mexican steers. He's down at the corrals. You could ask him."

He walked to the window and looked out. I knew what he was seeing, thinking. He said: "What in hell do they eat? There's nothing out there but scrub and tumbleweeds."

I came out from behind the counter and stood beside him. To the east the *playa* shimmered and dazzled in the heat. To the north the land rose gradually into foothills and bare-topped mountains. I said: "There's good grass and water. He's got pasture up there."

"He better." He drained the bottle and squinted, looking out again. The corrals, what remained of the old shipping pens, were on the other side of the tracks beyond the wooden water tower where the name, Lick Log, had long since been worn away by weather. A haze of dust rose over them. "Geez," he said. "If this isn't the end of the world, it's next to it. You *like* it here?"

How could I explain my dreams, the nights spent in all those places I'd never seen but knew so well? How talk about the books I read, putting myself into the story, or how the land and the *playa* lured me? "It's all right." I went back behind the counter. It seemed safer there somehow. "Leave your things till you talk to Daddy. I'll watch them."

He waved and went out, walking in that light-footed way I came to know so well. Of course my daddy hired him. Not for money — he didn't have any — but for room, board, and a ticket out after the fall shipping when there might be cash enough. And, of course, Phin stayed. He was broke, and young, and he had his eye on me.

"The first time I saw you," he said later, and more than once, "the very first time, and you all wide eyed and spooked, I said to myself: 'Now, there's a real woman.' "

I believed him. I believed because of how he touched my face like I was glass and might break. How he kissed me and made the ground shake under my feet like a train was coming and with it the excite-

253

ment, the mystery that became more of a mystery in spite of the seeing, the doing.

That year the summer rains were late. They moved up through Mexico slowly, heartlessly, the way nature is, or the way we think of its being. Night after night we watched the storms far to the south and cursed, and hoped, and waited.

"At least somebody's getting it," Phin said. "At least we know it's out there."

"And not doing us a damn' bit of good," my daddy answered. "Not one damn' bit, and my pasture blowing away."

But when the drought broke, it broke hard. The washes ran. The *playa*'s dry lakes filled and reflected the sky and the thunderclouds that formed behind the mountains early every morning.

I started taking Shotgun, my line-back dun mustang, down into that place of sawgrass and tulles and strange birds. In the winter the cranes were there, and sometimes they danced, a strange whirling dance that I watched with the same thrill I got from the trains. And I watched their practice flights in late spring, saw how they rose in formation and climbed through the air on determined wings, how they wheeled and circled according to some plan no one understood but themselves. I wished I could go with them. I wished I could look down and see the earth spread out for miles — *playa*, desert, mountains, the threads of stream beds running through like a tapestry.

One night, just at sunset, with the sky turning rose red and a full moon showing over the eastern mountains, Phin followed me. "What's down here anyhow?" he asked, catching up, which was easy to do. Shotgun had short legs, and Raisin, the slab-sided roan he was riding, really covered ground. "I see you headed down here every night. You meeting somebody?"

"Don't be silly," I retorted. "I come to watch the birds. But you have to be quiet or you won't see anything."

I hoped the herons were in their favorite spot where the tulles stood up high and made a moving cover. The huge birds fascinated me with their wings the color of blue steel and bigger than both my arms stretched out. I took his hand and led him along a path between the ponds. I was in my own territory, so I could hold his hand without feeling ashamed of myself, like I was making an advance.

He came along, taking note of everything in that way I admired. Here was one who wouldn't be lost or wandering in circles. Here was a man used to the country, who always, every minute, knew where he was and why. He knew why he was there that night. I didn't. Then.

I dropped down quietly behind the grasses and pointed. The herons stood, tall as fence posts and as still, their strange eyes bright as stones in their little heads. We watched while they hunted the frogs that came out with the rain, while they darted and fed, and the pond water turned the red of the sky and rippled and danced as if it were alive. Suddenly, without warning, the herons flew, running a few steps, flapping powerful wings, and taking off so close overhead we could have touched them, and there was awe inside me like a pain because I couldn't put any of it into words.

Phin broke the silence. "Well, well," he said, looking at me.

"You see?" I said, meaning the place, the power, the glory of it.

He put out his hands and cupped my face. "You *are* a pretty thing," he said.

I was disappointed. He didn't see. Or didn't want to. And then something happened with the feel of his hard fingers on my cheeks, the warmth of his breath on my lips. I discovered I'd been lonely, for years and years, without knowing it, filling up the emptiness with dreams and the coming and going of trains, and the birds that came and went without warning. And suddenly I knew those things weren't enough, that people need other people, that a woman needs a man and the touch of another body.

What happened next was as natural as breathing, with the grass sighing over us, and the moon rising, turning the water to gold, and under me the ground shaking with the power of discovery. I guess I knew it was wrong, or wrong the way people I knew looked at things, no matter how right it felt to me, because I never said anything but hid it away like the secret it was.

Phin said: "If your daddy finds out, we'll catch hell. He'll send me packing and no pay."

"Well, he won't find out from me," I told him, and in agreement we set out for home, the horses picking their way through the shadows made by the moon.

In the end, though, it was me who gave us away, sneaking across the yard to the bunkhouse after I thought my parents were asleep. Every night that summer and through a golden fall I'd gone there, like a moth lured by a scent, a wildness, and Phin the honey I couldn't do without. That's all I had before my daddy burst in on us, dragging me out of Phin's arms and throwing me at the door where I caught myself on the frame and tried to make excuses.

"We weren't . . . ," I started, but he cut me off, his face creased with anger.

"Shut up and go on back to the house before I horsewhip you both! You and this no-good saddlebum I gave a bed to."

He went for Phin, but Phin ducked away, putting the table between them. He said: "Mister Sunderland . . . !"

But daddy cut him, too. "I don't want to hear!" He grabbed Phin's clothes and threw them at him. "You son of a bitch, you pack up right now, and then start walking. The next stop's ten miles from here, and you'd better be on the morning freight or I'll shoot you for a mad dog."

I said: "Please."

He turned on me. "I don't please, and you standing there like trash. Now go on back to the house."

I looked at Phin for help, but he was doing what he'd been told, stuffing his gear into the bag and not looking at me. I could have been one of those moths, beating on the screen, for all the notice he took. I ran across the yard.

When my mama saw me, all she said was: "Did he hurt you?"

I didn't know what she meant, but her words started me laughing and crying at the same time, remembering, wanting, and knowing what it was going to be like at Lick Log without Phin. "Hurt me?" I got out between gasps. "Hurt me how? Phin never hurt a fly."

My mama was a hard woman. Life had made her that way. "You'll get over it," she said and left me to cry. I missed even a last glimpse of Phin, walking west along the tracks to nowhere. It would have been better if I had the chance to say good bye, to ask him, did he think he'd be back and would he write now and then? It would have helped to know something, anything at all, to have had a word, a touch, a kiss to set me free. Maybe then I would have gotten over it, but there was Glory. She was born eight months later, the image of her daddy, blue eyes and all.

"You shamed us," Mama said when she found out. "You and that tramp and your bastard have shamed us all." And she never treated her grandchild like she was anything but a cardboard cut-out that belonged to somebody else.

That was fine with me. Glory was mine and nobody else's, and I had the raising of her, the pleasure of her company long after Mama and Daddy were gone and while I waited and hoped that Phin Montana would come back and claim his own. Daddy's horse fell with him up in the hills one day, fell and rolled and left him there to die. When the horse came in limping, I backtracked and brought the body home across my saddle. I did it like in a dream, me, far away out on the *playa,* watching — watching while we laid him to rest in the little cemetery beside the tracks where the old-time whores were buried, and the railroad men with strange names, scratched on stones and crooked wooden crosses.

"I'll be next," Mama said, and I didn't contradict but let her go on talking as if to herself. "I'll be next, and it'll be just you here. You and her, and serve you right."

She was bitter, but she was tough, too. When the trains stopped using Lick Log for water and passengers, she didn't die with the place but turned her sights on the highway just behind the hill.

"I'll put up a sign," she said. "Folks'll come to eat on their way through."

And they did, a few tourists, ranchers, truckers who, with their big rigs, were replacing the railroad. They all came to eat Mama's pies and chili, drink her coffee, to say hello and take a breather before or after crossing that forbidding stretch of white alkali.

Glory grew and asked questions. "Where's my daddy? Why don't I have a daddy?"

I said: "He's gone, honey."

"Like Gramps?"

"Yes. Like Gramps."

My mother looked angry. "Why don't you tell her the truth?"

"Not yet," I said. "Not yet and maybe never." What good would the truth do, and her shamed because of it?

"Why do you watch those old trains all the time, Mama?"

"Because they're pretty. Aren't they pretty, all strung out in a line?"

A quick shake of her yellow head. A quick answer. "Dirty, noisy old things! I hate them!"

When my mother died, only a few people came to see her buried in that patch of weeds and wooden markers. Then we were alone, Glory and me, and the ghost of Phin Montana.

"Why do we have to stay here? Why can't we move to town?" Glory thought of a hundred ways to talk about her longing for something other than the *playa,* the sky, the cafe where strangers came and went. And I thought of a hundred answers for why I couldn't leave, some of them true. Mainly I believed that someday Phin would come back, and how would he find me if I'd gone?

Glory ran away for the first time when she was twelve. She didn't get far, only about a mile down the Interstate. It was pure luck that

I went to her room and found her gone, chased after her, praying I'd taken the right direction. Sure enough, there she was in her old jeans and T-shirt and carrying the pink plastic suitcase I'd given her for Christmas.

I pulled up and opened the door. "Get in this truck right now!" I said, and my voice sounded wobbly instead of mad. I'd been scared and trying not to think too hard, but seeing her there, my daughter, with her chin stuck out and her feet planted in the weeds, and those blue eyes that were Phin Montana's, I wanted to cry.

What did she know about the things that went on in the world, that little kid? What could she know? I hadn't ever told her. So I started in. I showed her the pictures of missing kids that were on the milk cartons and hanging in the post office. "They ran away and never came home again," I told her. "There's bad people in this world, people who take kids, and you'd best learn that right now."

She looked me straight in the eye. "They won't get me. I'm smart," she said. It could have been him talking.

I didn't tell her about the woman who had disappeared somewhere on the *playa*. A young woman, studying birds, who'd never been found. She worried me, that woman. I kept thinking I'd find her caught in the tulles, that her eyes would be open under the water and they'd be looking at me. Then I'd see myself in them like they were mirrors. I knew I wouldn't like what I saw — a woman past her prime, a woman who'd never been beautiful, with sadness scrawled across her face.

Life wasn't all bad, though. The cafe did good business, and I had my regulars, guys who drove the semis and the cattle trucks, a couple of real estate developers, real sharks who thought a woman on her own was easy money and who made the rounds a couple times a year, and the highway patrol who stopped in for lunch and coffee breaks and who kind of looked out for Glory and me, living on our own and making do. That's how I got to know Ned Kuykendal. He came in a few times, and we talked. Business was slow, and he liked

259

my pie and said the chili was better than he could make.

"You cook?" I asked, trying to picture his six feet bent over a stove.

"A man has to eat," he said, and I guessed from that he wasn't married, though I couldn't imagine why not. He was good looking, with a twinkle in his dark eyes, and broad shouldered and slim around the middle like a good horseman. When I didn't answer, he went on talking like he hadn't had anybody listen to him for a long time and was grateful for company. "My brother and I own a cattle ranch up on the high plains. We had a few bad years so I'm on the road, and he's running the place. We'll be caught up in a while. The rains were good, and I'm glad. I miss the place."

"The high plains," I said. The words caught my fancy like the names of the trains. "What's it like there?"

He tilted back his chair, and those dark eyes of his got darker like they were seeing far away. "God's country," he said finally. "Grass, wind, and sky."

"Doesn't sound much different from here."

He let his chair down. "It is, all right. You can't say till you've seen it."

"I probably never will," I said. "I've been here all my life."

He shot me a look. "Do you good to leave once in a while . . . if you don't mind my saying so."

He sounded like Glory. "It might, but I'm not." I turned back to work, through talking. What was there to say?

He took to stopping often after that, and a few times he helped me fix things I couldn't manage, like my sign that blew down in a bad wind. I was out in the parking lot, wrestling with it, hair in my eyes, and the sand blowing, and the sign nearly banging me flat when he pulled in.

"Let me do that."

"Damn' wind!" I tried to talk around the nails between my teeth.

"And give me those nails before you choke."

I spit them out. "I could do it if it wasn't for the wind," I shouted.

He took the nails and the hammer I was holding between my knees. "I bet you could," he said. "But right now you ought to go in and heat up that chili pot. I've been thinking about your cooking the last hundred miles."

That riled me. It felt like I wasn't a person, just a pair of hands that cooked, but I went in and turned on the gas and set him a place, scolding myself all the while. There he was doing me a favor, and all I could do was get mad. "Damn' wind!" I said again, blaming the weather.

The door slammed behind him. He came in just in time to hear me. "It'll die down soon enough. Then you'll wish it hadn't."

"Sometimes it gets me."

He nodded. "It'll do that. My wife left me on account of it. Said she wasn't built right to listen to it."

That shocked me out of bad temper — that and the regret in his voice. I said: "I'm sorry."

"It was a long time ago," he said. "Better this way. She wasn't cut out for living on a ranch. But hell, what did we know? We were kids."

I thought of Phin and me. And Glory. "Not much," I said. "There ought to be a law against kids." Then I laughed, more at myself than anything, and he laughed with me, tossing his black hair off his face. I said: "I mean, their getting married before they know what living's like."

"You did, didn't you?" He looked at me.

"Sort of. Dumb me." But I wasn't going to tell about Phin. It didn't seem right somehow. "Go wash up," I said. "And thanks for the help."

"Anytime."

He headed for the restroom, and I watched him go, feeling like something had been said that had moved us from where we'd been comfortable into the open, a place where, if I wasn't careful, I'd see myself in that truthful mirror.

* * * * *

Glory disappeared again when she was fourteen. The day it happened, I never stopped for a minute, and she took advantage. By the time I noticed she wasn't around, it was late afternoon, and I couldn't tell how long she'd been gone. I came flying into the cafe where the phone was and nearly tripped over Ralph Huff's handmade boots. Ralph was a developer, making his yearly rounds and hoping he'd find me down and out.

"What's your hurry?" he asked. He always talked to me like I was so far below him I didn't count.

I didn't stop to answer. Johnny Garcia, the highway patrol, was sitting at the counter, drinking coffee.

"Thank God!" I said. "I need help."

He called the sheriff who got there in half an hour. He wanted a description and asked where I thought Glory was headed.

"Probably Albuquerque, maybe Tucson," I told him. "Last time I picked her up on the Interstate, but this time she sneaked out. I was busy all day and never saw her." I started to cry, blaming myself, and all the time could feel Ralph's fat face watching, taking it all in.

The sheriff patted my shoulder. "Now don't worry," he said, though he sounded worried himself. "We'll get out the alarm. We'll find her."

But they didn't. It was Ned Kuykendal who called from a rest stop south of Albuquerque. "I've got Glory with me," he said before I could tell him. "I'm bringing her home. Let the sheriff know before I get picked up for rustling minors."

They pulled in at first light — Ned, Glory, and a truckload of bawling steers.

I hugged her before I got mad and let fly. "You're lucky!" I yelled at her over the noise of those cattle. "Fourteen years old and hitching rides like a whore! You're lucky you aren't out there on the desert with your damn' fool head bashed in!"

She was crying, too, and Ned took my arm. "Leave her be," he said. "She's dead beat, and I could use breakfast."

"Leave her be?" My voice was so high it cracked. "What about me . . . not knowing? Scared to death?" I shook off his arm. "You go in your room," I said, not thinking how much I sounded like my daddy. "I'll see you later. And don't think you'll get off easy this time."

She went, rubbing her nose on her sleeve.

"And get a handkerchief!" I yelled after her.

Ned was shaking his head. "You'll get nowhere fast, going at her like that."

"What do you know about it? She's mine! She's all I've got."

He gave me a glance straight from under those eyebrows of his. "I know more'n you think," he said. He took my arm again. "Now, come on. I'll make *you* breakfast. How long's it been since somebody did for you?"

"Never." I spoke before I thought. Then the tears came, hard as hail, and I hunched over, holding myself before I fell all apart.

Most men would've run. Ned didn't. He put an arm around me and said: "Easy now," like he was talking to a green colt. "Be easy."

I don't know, maybe it was his voice, or the feel of him, but I turned around and bawled into his shoulder like a baby, like I'd wanted to since Phin Montana up and left. I was a well without a bottom.

He got me up the walk and into the restroom where he ran cold water on a towel. He handed it to me. "I promised you breakfast," he said. "You come when you're ready."

Then I was alone with the ache in my throat. I hated it. I missed the strength of him, all muscle and bone and kindness. It was the kindness that shook me. *Why?* I wondered. What did he want, or was he only one of those do-gooders trying to save himself? Who needed that? Not me. Not Reason Sunderland. I'd been on my own too long, and be damned to Ned Kuykendal and his charity. I stuck out my chin and went out to find him looking at home over the grill where

263

ham and eggs were cooking.

"What do you want, anyhow?" I demanded, and he turned and looked at me like I'd gone crazy.

"Breakfast," he said. "Lots of it."

"Get out from there! That's my job."

He wasn't taking any orders. He waved the spatula and pointed at a chair. "Now, you set," he said. "You've been through hell, probably didn't sleep all night, worrying." Then he turned back to the eggs.

I said: "Why are you doing this?"

He didn't answer straight away, just watched the grill a minute. Finally he said: "People got to help each other. Hell, you're out here on your own, doing your best, but every once in a while you need help, so I'm here and glad of it. And every once in a while on the road I start thinking about you, and that kid of yours, and I wonder if you need something, and I stop by and we talk, and it's comfortable. Like having a home."

"You think about Lick Log as home?" I asked, trying to figure that one.

"A home needs a woman in it," he said. "There isn't anybody where I come from. Just Jake and me, and it gets lonesome." Then he reached and got two plates, flipped the eggs and ham onto them, and set them down on the counter.

"I've done without a man," I said, thinking I sounded like I was boasting, and tough, and hoping it wouldn't rile him.

"Yeah," he said. "You have, and I can't answer for you, but that kid needs a daddy. She needs kids her age and fun. What fun you got around here?"

"Fun?" I said. "Life isn't fun. It's just you do the best you can. You get on with it. She's got to learn that same as the rest of us."

He sat down beside me and picked up his fork. But before he ate, he looked at me. "That's bullshit," he said. Then he bent his head and went to it, leaving me with my mouth open. After a while he said: "Sorry. I shouldn't have said that."

I'd been thinking, looking at those yellow eggs and the green rim of the plate, and what rose in my mind was how, over the years, the magic had gone and with it that ability to see. I remembered how I'd watched the dancing cranes, the herons flying, and how the sound of it all gave me goose bumps, made me bigger than I was, and powerful. I remembered the trains and how I'd learned to read and dream by putting their names together — *Santa Fe, Aroostook, The Way of the Zephyrs.* How the world had once spread out across the *playa,* over the mountains to the sea, and how the thought of its size had dazzled me. I remembered Phin, though all of a sudden it was hard to see his face. All I could catch were those blue eyes like a mirage, shimmering over the sand hills.

"Don't be sorry," I told Ned. "It may be you're right. It may be I have to think things out and do different. But it's hard."

He swiveled on his stool so his face was on a line with mine. "If you need me," he said, "holler."

"I will."

"Don't take too long about it." The twinkle was gone from his eyes, replaced by something else, tiny, dancing golden lights like bees. "You're too much woman to stick yourself out here."

Was that what it was all about? Was he after me for whatever reason a man went after a woman — because I could cook? Because I was a stopping place on the road, a place he wished was home? I stood and took the plates. "You'd better get those steers wherever they're going before they die of thirst," I said. He looked like I'd punched him. "I'm sorry," I said. "Now it's me apologizing. It's just . . . just . . . I don't know what to do about what I'm feeling and thinking. You understand?"

"Sure." He reached out and took my chin in his hand, a gentle touch that nearly started me off bawling again. "I'll be around," he said.

He closed the door quietly, and it was like the light had gone out, like it was dark, and I was lost in a place I didn't recognize, groping for solid ground.

Glory looked up at me from her pillow, her eyes red and swollen. "You going to do that again?" I shook her. "Are you?"

"I don't know."

"What do you mean by that?" I shouted. "You'll end up dead, I keep telling you. Is that what you want?"

She sat up and hollered so loud the window rattled. "No! It isn't! I want to be alive, but out here I might as well be dead, and who cares? You? You're not alive, either. You're like some robot, walking around. Why? You tell *me*, Mama. You tell me why!"

I was quiet. What could I tell her? The truth after years of a lie? That I was waiting for a man who'd become a ghost, who I couldn't even picture in my head any more, a man she believed was dead? My mama had been right. You tell a lie and it traps you like a spider's web. Soon you're in the middle and no way out except what will hurt worse than you do already. "I don't know, honey," I said. "But if you promise to be good, I'll try to think of something. Is it a deal?"

She didn't believe me. Who could blame her? But finally she gave a little nod. "All right," she said. "Just don't take forever."

After I closed up, I went for a walk down by the pools, among the reeds. Something like my old excitement came back to me when a flock of ducks started up, their wings making a whirring sound. The sky in the west was gold and pink with a few clouds like butterflies crossing it, and the small ponds took and held the colors and shivered in the wind, so it seemed the whole world was in motion. I hunkered down at the edge of the water, not trying to think so much as trying to let go — of the past, of my own self, of the shell I'd built between me and the world, including my own daughter, and all because of a man I hadn't laid eyes on in years. *You damn' fool!* The voice was so loud I jumped. Then I realized it was in my own head.

"Why?" I asked it, and didn't wait for an answer. I knew. I'd been forcing my dreams on a kid who had a right to her own. I was all

266

she had, and, plainly, I wasn't enough. She'd called me a robot, and she wasn't wrong. Because of one summer's foolishness, I'd robbed her of childhood and myself of a chance at life.

I thought about how good it had been in Ned's arms, and about the little fires I'd seen in his eyes. I thought about how gentle his hands were, and the strength in his shoulders. Then I shook my head. "No!" I said out loud. "Whatever I do, it'll be for Glory and me, not for another man."

It seems to me now that, once you choose the right path, the way becomes clear, obstacles vanish, and you move straight ahead like a platoon marching. Not two days later Ralph Huff pulled into the parking lot. I'd hated him the minute I'd first seen him years before, that fat face, that fatter belly, and driving a truck that would cost me half a year's profit. He came in and sat down.

I said: "Coffee?"

"Something cold." He wiped his face on a clean handkerchief. "Ice tea."

Then he looked around — at the clean counter, the tables with their checkered cloths, the ceiling fans swishing overhead. "Still a nice place," he said.

"It's all right."

He drained the glass and held it out for a refill. "You ready to sell yet? Or you gonna wait till that gal gets in real trouble?"

He never quit. Hate rose up in my throat, tasting like alkali water. He wanted my life, my memories, the falling-down bunkhouse where my past was buried. "I hadn't thought," I said, putting the pitcher down with a thump.

He flipped a card out of his pocket. "Well, if you do, here's my name and number. Leave a message if I'm not in. I'll get back to you."

"What're you going to do with it?" I asked.

He shrugged. "A person could do a lot," was all he said.

My mouth was dry. "How much?"

267

"That depends." He stood up and put his black hat firmly on his head. "Can I take a look around?"

I nodded. "Just be careful. Those old houses aren't in good shape."

He didn't answer. I watched him cross toward the tracks and the old water tower, saw him climb the fence into the cemetery where the Chinaman, Sam Chen, the unnamed Mexicans, the women with aliases lay buried alongside my parents, the cemetery where I always thought I'd be in twenty years, or fifty, or however long it took to die. Quick as a flash I went after him. He was reading the names on the boulders that served as headstones.

"That's my mama and daddy," I said. "If you want this place, you have to leave them in peace."

He turned pale eyes on me. "I don't go digging up graveyards."

"Then make me an offer." I could hardly believe it was me talking.

"Twenty thousand, lock, stock and barrel."

It wasn't enough. Dreams are worth more. I shook my head and turned away, but he caught my arm.

"Thirty" he said.

I laughed. I was fighting now, and it felt good. "You must think I'm crazy, mister. That cafe all by itself brings in that much."

"Net or gross?"

"Gross."

"State your price." He was sweating under his Stetson.

"Fifty thousand," I said, feeling like a poker player with a full house. "Cash."

"Forty."

"No," I said. "That's my price. It's not enough, but that's it."

He sighed. It sounded like air going out of a balloon. "All right. We'll close in two weeks."

I felt deflated myself. "I can't get out of here that fast," I said.

"Take your time. We'll just close the deal."

We shook hands.

After he'd gone, I stood there, watching the dust devils whirl across

268

the flats, feeling the ground shake as the evening train came around the mountain and headed straight west. I'd done it. Sold out, and I wasn't sure how I felt or what to do next. Travel, maybe — me and Glory. Visit the cities, eat in fancy places, buy the clothes she'd always wanted. Maybe I could find her a good school, get her off to college.

And what would I do then? I wasn't made to be idle, to lie around watching the TV like some women. So many questions! And only a short time to answer them, before we went out on our own into a world neither of us really understood. What on earth had I done?

We closed the deal, and Ralph Huff came out and put up a **SOLD** sign. A week later I put up a sign of my own. **CLOSED**, it said. I tacked it up over the words **LICK LOG** that had been painted so many years before. Then Glory and I set about packing.

I hadn't realized how much stuff there was lying around in drawers, in closets, in old suitcases and boxes under the beds. None of us, not Mama or Daddy or me, had ever thrown anything away on the theory that it might be useful someday.

Glory said: "We could have a flea market, all by ourselves." She was looking through a box of her grandma's dresses, laughing every now and then and holding the clothes up to herself in the mirror. Since learning about the sale, she'd become a different kid. She was talkative and, as she'd told me long before, smart. Now she said: "Grandma didn't like me."

"Grandma didn't much care for anybody," I told her. "Don't take it personally."

"Why?" She turned, holding up a flowered print dress that had been one of Mama's favorites.

"Because she never wanted to be out here, either. They were headed for California when their car broke down right outside. They stayed, and she blamed my daddy for it. Blamed him for me when I came along."

"What about *my* daddy? She hate him, too?"

"Him most of all."

Glory smoothed the flowered material down over her hips. "I wonder if she'd have hated Ned," she said.

I put down the box I was holding. "Now why on earth would she hate him?"

Glory grinned and gave a little hop. "Because he's sweet on you, Mama," she said. "Didn't you know?"

For a minute I didn't know whether to laugh or take her seriously. Finally I said: "Where'd you get that notion?"

Her grin broke into a giggle. "He couldn't stop talking about you when he brought me back. All the way back he kept saying: 'Now, you stop worrying your mama. She's a fine woman, and she's doing her best for you.' "

"Daydreams!" I said, trying to sound like my heart wasn't pounding in my chest. "You best forget about what he said."

"Why?" she was frowning. "Why should I? Don't you like Ned or something? Don't you want a real home and a family?"

"Why, honey . . . ," I started then stopped.

"Well, don't you?"

"I don't know," I said. "I haven't thought."

"I bet you never even told him about leaving here. I bet he'll come looking for you, and you'll be gone, and then what?"

I stood up, feeling like I'd had enough. "Then he'll go find somebody else," I told her. "Now you decide what you want to keep out of here, and we'll take the rest to the dump."

She said: "I always wanted a real family. I think you're weird." Then she started to cry.

My temper snapped. "I thought you wanted to go to the city. That's all you ever talked about from the time you could open your mouth. Now you want a family. Now you want to go out and be on a ranch some place you never saw, and wouldn't like if you did. And you expect me to believe Ned Kuykendal's sweet on me because of some notion of yours. I'm not the weird one around here, Glory. Now, you finish up what you're doing, and no more talk. You hear?"

She didn't answer. She'd gone sullen again and wouldn't look at me.

Kids! I thought. *You give them what they want, and then they change their minds and turn on you.* I went out and wandered around the old streets that were overgrown in weeds. I listened to the wind singing its same old tune in the wire fences, and the quail out in the brush, barking like little dogs. I listened for the old voices, trying to call them up out of the dust, but all I heard was Ralph Huff saying how he was going to turn Lick Log into a Real Live Ghost Town. Well, there were ghosts enough, even if I couldn't hear them.

I said: "Phin! Phin Montana!" It sounded foolish, even to me after all those years. Then I heard the sound of a semi gearing down, the squeal of brakes as it took the exit and came up the hill.

"Now who?" I said. "Guess he can't read." But I started to run as if my body knew something I didn't — or hadn't admitted — my legs stretching out like a horse on the home stretch, my heart hammering in my chest.

Ned switched off the engine, got out, and stood watching me. "Where's the fire?" he asked.

"No fire. I just heard your truck and wondered who it was."

"Catch your breath," he said, "then tell me what in hell that closed sign means."

"I sold out."

"Where you headed?"

"I don't know. Maybe Albuquerque. Maybe El Paso."

He leaned up against the cab, and he was mad. He said: "You were just heading out. Without telling anybody. Is that it?"

"Yes," I said. I looked at my feet, afraid of what I saw in his face.

"God damn it!" He grabbed my arms. "You're the most stubborn damn' fool woman I ever met. What'd you think I'd do, coming in and nobody here?"

271

"How'd I know you'd come?" I whispered. "And, anyway, I didn't think, I just went and did."

He shook his head. "Well, it's time you quit wandering around in a daze. How'm I going to court you if you're gone?"

I looked up then and saw those dancing lights in his eyes, saw the anger fading, being replaced with something else, a gentleness, a fire. I said: "Court me? You want to court me?"

"I've *been* courting you . . . the part that isn't out there in a dream. If you weren't such a damn' fool, you'd have figured that out long ago. What do I have to do? Kneel down?"

He let go of my arms, and for a minute I thought he actually would kneel down in the dust. "Quit!" I said. "Don't make fun! What if somebody saw?"

"The hell with them," he said. He put his hands on my shoulders, shook me just a little. "I never have got you out of my head since the first time I saw you, and I'm tired driving down the road just hoping. Comes a time when hope isn't enough. I want you to come home with me. I want to know you're where I can find you. You understand?"

I tried to call up Phin Montana's face, but I couldn't. Ned's kept getting in the way. I'd been lonely when I met Phin, but now it was more than that. My heart was empty. My hands wanted to work, to touch, to give to somebody. My body needed laughter, warmth, a shoulder to lean on. You get tired being alone, and nobody to share with, to do for. You get worn down, old before time, and useless.

There's all kinds of love in this world, and I don't know what's best. Maybe everybody has to decide that for themselves, but it's the choice that counts. Phin and I had never had a choice, just let ourselves get swept along like leaves on the water; and, whatever we did, I wasn't sure I could call it love. So, standing there in the dust with the tumbleweeds blowing past my legs, I made my choice. I'd have this man who'd been kind to me, who'd worried about me and Glory, done the best he could for us both. I had the hunch he always would.

I said: "You want me?"

And he said: "Only if you're willing."

"Kiss me," I said. "Please."

He didn't wait. He cupped my face in those big hands of his and bent down, and what happened then was that my body filled with thunder like the sound of the trains, with wings beating, with that long cry that comes out of a cloud of flying swans, and I held onto him and thought how I never wanted to let go. I thought how dumb I'd always been and probably would be again, given the chance.

So now I'm here, and I'm putting the lock on the door. I'm saying good bye to Lick Log, to the playa, to the people who lived and loved and hated here — to Phin and Reason, those kids who took what was there and never thought about choice or the making of a life. One last time I say his name — "Phin Montana" — and the words get taken by the wind and fly across the *playa*. One last time I watch the train coming up the grade. No one gets off. I hadn't expected it, but the cars still carry those magic names, the ones that formed me, shaped me, gave me an old life and a new — *The Way of the Zephyrs, The Santa Fe, The Route of the Phoebe Snow. . . .*

About the Author

Born and raised near Pittsburgh, Pennsylvania, Jane Candia Coleman majored in creative writing at the University of Pittsburgh but stopped writing after graduation in 1960 because she knew she "hadn't lived enough, thought enough, to write anything of interest." Her life changed dramatically when she abandoned the East for the West in 1986, and her creativity came truly into its own. *The Voices of Doves* (1988) was written soon after she moved to Tucson. It was followed by a book of poetry, *No Roof But Sky* (1990), and by a truly remarkable short story collection that amply repays reading and rereading, *Stories From Mesa Country* (1991). Her short story, "Lou" in *Louis L'Amour Western Magazine* (3/94), won the Golden Spur Award from the Western Writers of America, and she has also won three Western Heritage Awards from the National Cowboy Hall of Fame. *Doc Holliday's Woman* (1995) is her first novel and one of vivid and extraordinary power. It can be said that a story by Jane Candia Coleman embodies the essence of what is finest in the Western story, intimations of hope, vulnerability, and courage, while she plummets to the depths of her characters, conjuring moods and imagery with the consummate artistry of an accomplished poet. *Moving On: Stories of the West* is her first Five Star Western.